DEATH IN FREEDOM
AN OMEGA THRILLER

BLAKE BANNER

RIGHTHOUSE

ISBN-13: 978-1-63696-346-4

ISBN-10: 1-63696-346-3

Cover design by: Damonza

Printed in the United States of America

www.righthouse.com

www.instagram.com/righthousebooks

www.facebook.com/righthousebooks

twitter.com/righthousebooks

THE OMEGA SERIES
Dawn of the Hunter (Book 1)
Double Edged Blade (Book 2)
The Storm (Book 3)
The Hand of War (Book 4)
A Harvest of Blood (Book 5)
To Rule in Hell (Book 6)
Kill: One (Book 7)
Powder Burn (Book 8)
Kill: Two (Book 9)
Unleashed (Book 10)
The Omicron Kill (Book 11)
9mm Justice (Book 12)
Kill: Four (Book 13)
Death In Freedom (Book 14)
Endgame (Book 15)

ONE

SHE DIDN'T DIE, BUT SHE DIDN'T LIVE EITHER.

Marni lingered in a coma, somewhere between life and death. At first, the hours dragged past through empty hospital corridors: bright lights on black glass, doctors and nurses, and listless cleaners making their rounds, while I waited for her to die. But morning broke, pink and yawning among cold birdsong, and Marni was not dead.

So then the days began to drag by, in a relentless procession to and from the hospital, walking the same ancient, sandstone streets, seeing the same morning faces, nodding as they became familiar, meeting day after day with doctors who always told me the same thing: we had to wait and see, she might live and she might die.

And gradually the days became a week, two, three, and one morning at the end of the fourth week, I awoke in her bed and realized that the crisis and horror of that night, when she had been shot, had surreptitiously become a way of life. She might continue for months, or even years, in a near permanent vegetative state. She might open her eyes at any moment, or she might die that very day.

Either way, it was time to take her back to where she was born, to where we had spent our childhoods together, reading comics, playing board games on rainy days and battling countless enemies in the New England forests when the sun shone. So I arranged an air taxi and a private nurse and a doctor to attend to her during the flight, and I took her back to Weston. She had three paths she could take: live, die or linger. Whichever one she took, she would take it at home, with me by her side.

I put her in the room next to mine, arranged twenty-four hour care seven days a week, a doctor to visit her regularly and a physiotherapist to keep her muscles moving and the blood flowing. And so we settled into a new life.

When Kenny, the butler I had inherited from my father along with his house, had begged me to return home and settle, this, I am pretty sure, was not what he'd had in mind. But when I'd said this to him and Rosalia, my cook, standing in the kitchen drinking coffee with them, she had flung her arms around me and wept.

"We know you and Marni all our life. You like our own children," she'd said. Then she'd stared into my face, her cheeks shiny and wet. "She gonna be OK, *hijo mío*, you gonna see! She gonna be OK."

Shortly after that, Jim Redbeard had come to see me. In a world where the majority believe that the smartest thing you can do in life is mortgage yourself to a bank, take on the responsibility of kids so you can't afford to pay that bank what you owe them, and then teach those kids to do the same stupid thing you did—Jim Redbeard was the craziest person I knew. Which made him pretty sane by any other standards. He looked like a Viking and behaved like a Viking, with a vast appetite for food, wine, women and life. His creed was 'do as thou wilt shall be all of the law,' and he lived by it.

He had been a professor of philosophy at UCLA and was an expert in Norse mythology. He described himself as an anarcho-capitalist and had made a fortune writing self-help best sellers. Now he devoted his life, as I had, to bringing down Omega. And between us, we had almost managed it, but the price had been high. The price had been Marni.

During his visit, I had avoided the subject of Omega, but on his last night, sitting in front of the fire in my study, drinking old Irish whiskey, he had said to me:

"Lacklan, you have paid the ultimate price, but the job isn't done. If you give up now, they will have won."

"I have no intention of giving up, Jim. I told you I am going to hunt each one of them down and kill them.[1]"

"When?"

"When Marni dies... I am not leaving her side till then."

He'd sighed and sat back, crossing one vast leg over the other. "That could be years, Lacklan. Hell, she could outlive you."

"I am not leaving her side."

"So they win." He waited. I didn't say anything. "They win, and she goes unavenged. Are you sure that's what you want? You destroyed Omega here in the States, you destroyed them in Europe and Latin America, and you crip-

---

1. See *Kill: Four*

pled them in Africa. But in China and Russia they are strong, Lacklan, and they could grow back to become more powerful than ever.[2] And if they do, I don't need to tell you that they will come after you, *and* Marni. They will punish you."

I had stared into the flames, hearing the crackle of the wood, feeling the warmth on my face. I knew he was right, but it was a truth I did not want to face.

"If I go and, while I am gone she dies..."

He sighed. "You're like a surgeon, cutting out metastasized tumors. You've cut them all out, but you've left one, for fear that while you are removing it, your patient will die." He had leaned forward then, with his elbows on his knees and the orange flames dancing in his glass, wavering on his face. "If you don't destroy them, she will certainly die their victim. If you finish the job, she has *some* chance of living."

Then he had drained his glass and stood. "I am returning to L.A. tomorrow morning, Lacklan. Tomorrow is Wednesday. I'll expect you there on Saturday at the latest, to discuss our plan and our strategy. We have to finish the job. There is no other way."

And he had gone up to his room.

I had spent most of the next day with her, talking to her, though the doctors had told me she couldn't hear me. I explained to her why I had to do what I had to do, why I had to go, even though she couldn't understand. I had sat by the open window, smelling the coming fall on the cool breeze, watching her and remembering our childhood together, and

---

2. See *Kill: One; Kill: Two; The Omicron Kill and Kill: Four* respectively.

our teens, our first adolescent kiss. We had always known we were supposed to be together. But the gods had not agreed.

Finally, I had packed a bag, climbed into my Zombie 222 and headed for Los Angeles.

It was a forty hour drive and I did the whole thing like an automaton, driving by the numbers, barely aware of my environment or what was going on around me. I kept my eye on the mirror and on the sky, to make sure I was not being followed, and I slept twice for four hours. Otherwise, the journey passed in a kind of blur.

At ten o'clock on Friday night, I pulled up outside his house on Paseo de la Playa, at Malaga Cove, and killed the engine. As I climbed out of the car, Jim came down the garden path to greet me. Behind him, warm light was spilling from his open door into the dark garden, silhouetting the palms and the yuccas that fronted his house. In the background, there was the heavy sigh of the ocean at the foot of the cliff.

He took my hand and slapped me on the shoulder. "I'm glad you came."

I slung my bag over my shoulder and closed the trunk.

"I didn't have much choice."

"You could use a drink."

"Yeah, I could at that." I walked past him, up the path to the door. "Is Njal here?"

"No." He followed after me. "He doesn't believe you should be here." I stopped in the hall and turned to face him as he closed the door. He held my eye and added, "He thinks you're spent."

"I'm not spent."

"Leave your bag on the couch. Mioko will take it up. Go ahead out to the terrace. I'll bring out the drinks."

I stepped out onto his broad terrace, with the gardens running down to the cliff edge and the luminous, moonlit ocean beyond. I sat at the big, oak table he had there and he followed me out with a bottle of Bushmills and two glasses. He poured two generous measures straight up and sat.

"He didn't like the way you handled things in South Africa.[3]"

"The job was impossible, we had no preparation and we had to improvise. It was suicide. It was a miracle we got out alive. You know it and he knows it."

"He said you became emotional, erratic, unpredictable. He said you lost perspective."

I drained my glass and put it down. "Then what the hell am I doing here?"

He shrugged. "I'm telling you why he's *not* here. I am more pragmatic. You're right. You went into a mission which was all but impossible and you both came back alive. To my mind, *res ipsa loquitor*, the facts speak for themselves. But I respect Njal. He's damn good at what he does and his judgment is sound, so I think you ought to be aware of what he's thinking."

I pulled my cigarettes from my jacket, flipped my old, battered brass Zippo and took my time lighting up. As I let out the smoke, I said, "OK, so I'm aware of what he's thinking. I go to China alone."

He shrugged again, more elaborately. "We need to formulate a plan, see who we're dealing with, what's

---

3. See *Kill: Four*

involved. Besides, Njal's a good friend to you. Don't write him off too soon."

"What's that supposed to mean?"

He sighed and picked up his glass, but instead of drinking, he squinted out at the ocean, where a vast sheet of moonlight lay fractured on the water.

"His refusal to be here was not because of a lack of trust in you. It was more concern. He thinks you need a break. He believes you're burned out and need time with Marni."

"He's right."

"I know." He turned back to face me. "But we can't afford that luxury. We—all of us—need you to go into China and Russia and finish the job, and you have to hold it together till the job is done."

We watched each other a moment. Finally, I gave a small laugh. "You're a ruthless son of a bitch, aren't you?"

"Yes." Then he echoed my laugh. "I believe you're the president of that club, aren't you?" He sipped and set down his glass. "Believe me, Lacklan, if I had your skills, I would do it myself. But I haven't and we both know—all three of us know—that you are the man for the job. Nobody knows Omega as well as you do. Nobody has the experience you have. We have no choice. It has to be done and you have to do it."

I nodded, then heaved a deep sigh. "I know. So what are we dealing with?"

He reached over and took my pack of Camels. He shook one loose, stuck it in his mouth and lit it, then inhaled. He spoke with a trail of smoke issuing from his mouth.

"Omega Five covers not just China, though that is where the heart is, it covers also Russia, Japan, southeast Asia and all the islands. Their cabal..." He paused, studying my face, then repeated, "Their cabal, I don't know if you remember this, is Phi, Chi, Psi, Omega... and Alpha."

I went cold and felt my hair prickle. "Alpha was Ben. I killed Ben."

"He may have been replaced."

I refilled my glass and said, apparently contradicting myself, "I saw him, Jim. In Africa, in the pyramid, when I was placing the bomb. I saw him."

"You thought you did, Lacklan. You said yourself it was an hallucination."

I sighed and rubbed my face. "Maybe Njal is right. Maybe I'm losing it... mentally."

"Or maybe they're just fucking with your head. The texts, the hints..." He shook his head. "You told me you shot him..."

"Twice, in the heart. He was dead, Jim. I know he was."

"Then they're fucking with your head. It's what they do. It's what they specialize in. How many programs of theirs have you come across that were all about mind control? The Richard John Erickson Institute, the Sun Beetles, the lab at Cosalá... Don't let them get to you."

"How could they make me hallucinate that?"

"Hallucinogenic drugs pumped into the air, coupled with the suggestions they had already implanted in your brain... Hell! Even holograms." He spread his hands. I helped myself to another shot of whiskey and thought about it. It made sense, up to a point.

"Why would they want to do that to me? How does that benefit them?"

"You got me there, Lacklan. But if you'll forgive me saying so, I think the question is irrelevant. We need to destroy them and kill them. It doesn't matter why or how they did it. You killed him. He's dead. Now we have to kill the rest of them."

I nodded. "Yeah, you're right. But this operation can't be like the last one, Jim."

"It won't be."

"I aim to come home alive. Marni needs me and I am going to be with her till she dies."

"She may recover, Lacklan."

"No. She won't. But I plan to be with her at the end. So we plan this out thoroughly, in detail. I want a separate identity for each hit. I want a workable extraction and an identity for that extraction. No improvising, no last minute plans, no escaping by the seat of my pants."

He shook his head. "It's your show. You plan it, you design it, you tell me what you need. I'll use what influence I have to make it happen. You want me to talk to Njal, see if I can change his mind?"

"I don't give a damn. But if he wants in, he needs to decide before I start making my plan."

"He'd be useful."

"Sure, and in China we'd both stick out like a couple of neon dildos at a vicar's tea party."

"Only part of your mission would be in China, and you would pose as visiting businessmen, I assume." He paused, tipping his empty glass this way and that. "Part of Njal's concern was that you were responding emotionally to situations where you should have been dispassionate..."

"Like feeling bad about murdering a woman in cold blood? Or giving three innocent hookers the chance to get away? The day I stop doing that kind of thing is when you need to start worrying." I sighed. "Sure, he's useful and I know he's got my back. I think I've proved I have his too. If he wants in, I'll be glad to have him along. If he doesn't, I don't care. I'll do the job either way."

"OK, let's look at the outline of the plan. I'll decide after that whether to ask Njal to join you. You want some food?"

I shook my head. "I need to sleep. But before that, tell me who Phi is."

"Gregor Ustinov. He lives in Moscow. Former director of the KGB, now a private industrialist, billionaire, not surprisingly with ties to the Russian Mafia." I didn't ask, but he pressed on. "Chi, Haruto Kobayashi, head of the Kobayashi corporation, lives outside Tokyo. Psi, Liu Wang—or as they would have it, Wang Liu—one of the new billionaires, remarkably young at thirty-two, has ties to the Chinese Communist Party. Omega, Abba Roth..."

"Abba Roth? That's an Anglo-Jewish name."

"Indeed. In Omega Five, things are a little different. The last shall be the first, Jormungand, the worm Ouroborus."

"Spare me the mysticism, at least till tomorrow. Who is this guy?"

"There is very little information available on him. He lives in Moscow, but travels a lot to China and Mongolia. A dot com billionaire, but has since invested heavily in armaments, nuclear energy and lithium-ion technology." He waited for me to say something. I didn't, so he went on with the list. "Alpha, Benjamin Walker, your brother, dead and buried in the family graveyard. As far as I know, Alpha has not been replaced."

I stood. "OK, Jim, thanks. Let me get some sleep now. We'll talk in the morning."

He raised his glass to me. "You got it. Rest."

I went up to my room, lay down on the bed and passed out.

TWO

I SLEPT EIGHT HOURS, ROSE AT SEVEN AND HAD A long hot, cold, hot shower. Then I went down to the terrace, where Jim was sitting at his oak table being served coffee and hot bread by Maria, his Latina, live in cook-cum-house-keeper. He watched me sit with inquiring eyes as he sipped his coffee. Maria smiled.

"What can I get you, Captain Walker?"

"Black coffee, Maria, and rye toast with butter." I had given up telling her I was not a captain anymore. She poured me a demitasse of strong, black brew and hurried inside to get my toast. I sipped and spoke as I set down the cup. "OK, if Njal will come in on this, I'd like to have him along. You can tell him this operation will be well planned, down to the fine details, no improvising, no hallucinations, no rogue action."

"Good, I'm glad to hear that."

"Step one, we go into China and take out Liu Wang. We can't make it look like an accident."

"Why?"

"Because they'll know, as soon as he winds up dead, whatever the apparent cause, that we're coming after them and they'll go to total lock down."

He frowned. "So what are you suggesting?"

"He has to go on holiday, on a trip, to his country house —whatever—and he has to remain in contact, sending messages, Whatsapps, emails... That will afford us an opportunity to go after Phi, and Omega in Russia."

Maria came out with a basket of toast, which she set beside me, and patted me on the shoulder. Jim broke a croissant and as he buttered it, he said, "Spell it out for me, Lacklan. I'm not following you."

"We take him out, kill him, but we make it seem he's on holiday."

His eyebrows rose on his forehead. "OK, what about Kobayashi in Japan?"

I nodded and started spreading butter on hot rye. "We are going to lure Kobayashi into a visit to Wang in China, or we'll lure Wang into visiting Kobayashi. Either way, it works. We get the two of them together in a private meeting—on a trip, a yacht, a country house, it doesn't matter at this stage —somewhere isolated. That will justify their relative silence and their absence and give us time to hit Ustinov and Roth in Moscow."

"That means getting you from China or Japan to Russia very quickly."

"Can you do it?"

"I'll have to."

"We haven't much choice, but we can nail down the details later. We're going to revise this plan a hundred times before we go in." I bit into the toast and spoke with my mouth full. "In Moscow, we take out Ustinov and we interrogate Roth. I want two things from him: one, access to their computer network…"

Jim nodded. "Good."

"I am going to need Philip Gantrie in on this operation, from the beginning."

"The neutron bomb guy."[1]

"I'll need him to set up the meet between Kobayashi and Wang, to hack their private phones and computers, send out messages on their behalf. And when we have Roth, I'll need Phil to take control of their network."

He frowned. "Take control?"

I studied his face a moment. He looked worried. "Long enough to make sure they haven't spawned a baby Omega somewhere. When we destroy that network and wipe out their funds, I want to know that we are annihilating Omega for good."

He looked relieved. "OK, that's fine. It's a tall order for Gantrie. Are you sure he can do it?"

"No." I shook my head. "But if anybody can, he can. He was recommended to me by my father. Don't forget, my father was Gamma, so Phil must have some knowledge of Omega, and how they work."

He raised an eyebrow. "Can you trust him?"

I shrugged. "He designed the cyber bomb that brought down Omega Europe, you tell me."

"All right. Can you arrange a meeting?"

"I'll talk to him. He's tricky and shy, but I think I can

---

1. See *Kill: Two*

persuade him. Meantime, we are going to need IDs to get into China, IDs to get from China to Russia, IDs to get out of Russia, and two spare IDs in case things go south."

He shook his head. "You can't travel around with all those IDs. If you get stopped..."

"No, they'll have to be left at collection points, banks, attorneys' offices, PO box, left luggage at the airport... You know the drill."

"OK, for now we'll get them made, then we'll think about how we get them to you. What about hardware?"

I thought about it, gazing out at the brilliant turquoise ocean. "How hard is that going to be?"

He made a face and shrugged. "Hard. I can get you a couple of Sigs and a Glock that you can collect at the U.S. embassy in China. Otherwise, it means crossing over the border from Myanmar or Vietnam. If you make the hit in Japan, it's easier."

I shook my head and drained my cup. "We don't need a lot of hardware for the first hit. Couple of hand guns, some tracking devices, bugs. How about Russia?"

He smiled. "You upset those boys when you killed their couriers."

"They upset me. They almost screwed the operation."[2]

He chuckled. "I know. I told them that, but I need to build some bridges. We'll see how it goes. Either way, Russia should be easier than China. What will you need?"

"I don't know yet, but I don't think we'll be blowing up the Kremlin. Probably just handguns and electronic surveillance equipment." I paused. "There is something else,

---

2. See *Kill: Four*

Jim. I want Senator Cyndi McFarlane briefed on the operation."

"Are you out of your mind?"

"Think it through, Jim. OK, we go in, we finally destroy Omega, Omega is no more, then what? You know as well as I do that Omega was only ever a symptom, it was never the original cause. So when we bring Omega down, what are we going to put in its place? The Bilderberg Group? The Illuminati? The Fourth Reich? Islam? The Sinaloa Cartel..." I shook my head. "The problems that brought it into existence are still there."

"OK, I get it. And I agree. But how the hell do you think Cyndi McFarlane can help?"

I sighed, poured myself more coffee and looked back at the vast, placid Pacific. I wished vaguely, irrationally, that I could be like that: placid and still.

"I detest what Omega were trying to do, Jim. Or at least, I detest the way they were going about it: the two tier world with the elite sipping Martini while the obedient, lobotomized masses served them, happy prisoners in their own, unquestioning minds. And you know I would fight to the death to stop that. But that was just their *solution*. What we are fighting is their *solution*."

"I'm not following you, Lacklan."

"What we have consistently ignored, from the start, is the *problem*—the problem they were trying to solve. They were proposing a solution to a problem, and that problem will still be there after they are gone. It will still have to be addressed, and solved. I want Cyndi McFarlane involved because I trust her, and when Omega come down, I want her picking up the pieces."

"How will she do that?"

"You need to talk to her. That's your department. I kill people, you philosophize. We need people in the White House. You need to start exerting influence in the legislature. We need people in place who we can trust, who are willing to tackle the problems Omega is tackling; and we can do that through Cyndi."

"You're beginning to sound like a politician."

"Yeah, I love you too. I just don't want to spend the rest of my life fighting Son of Omega and Grandson of Omega. Omega existed for a reason. You and I, and Njal, we can destroy Omega, but we can't destroy the reason they exist. Senator McFarlane might, if she can muster enough support."

He spread his hands and made a face. "OK, I can't argue with that. But nobody else, Lacklan. The risk is too high. You, me, Njal and Cyndi. That's it. A cabal of four."

I nodded. "A cabal..."

We spent the rest of the morning discussing details, giving the plan some shape and looking at possible ways it could be carried out. We decided provisionally that it made more sense to lure Wang to Japan, partly because two westerners would be less conspicuous in Japan than they would in China, and partly because it would be easier to get black market hardware there if we needed it. Exactly how we would lure Wang to Japan was a moot point which we would need to discuss with Philip Gantrie, the cyber wizard, but our thoughts were running along the lines of covert messages purporting to be from Kobayashi himself.

As far as the hit in Russia was concerned, I favored the idea of drawing Ustinov and Roth together, so I could take them both down at the same time, and we explored several ways that could be done.

By lunchtime, we'd gone about as far as we could and Jim sat back in his chair and looked at his watch.

"We can't proceed any further until we know for sure that Njal is onboard."

I nodded. "We also need to be sure of Phil, and I want to talk to Cyndi."

"Take a flight. Go to Washington and meet with her. Meantime, call Phil, arrange a meeting with him. While you're in D.C., I'll have a talk with Njal, discuss the plan with him. I'm sure he'll agree. But you need to reassure him too."

"I'll take the car. I need to go via Wyoming."

He frowned. "*Wyoming?*"

"Yeah, there is something I have to pick up there. It might be important. If it is, I'll let you know. On the way, I'll call Phil and Cyndi and arrange to meet them. I'll see you back here in a week."

"What's in Wyoming, Lacklan?"

"My old house. There is something there I need to pick up. It may be nothing, but it may be important," I repeated. "If it is, I'll tell you."

He smiled and shook his head. "Have it your way."

We talked some more over lunch and at two o'clock, I climbed back into the Zombie and headed east toward Corona, to pick up the I-15 toward Nevada and Utah. On the way, I called Phil on my hands free. He answered in his characteristic way.

"Amtrak customer services, how may I direct your call?"

"What are you going to do if one day it really is a wrong

number and somebody really does want Amtrak customer services?"

"Can you say something else, please?"

"Hello, Phil, this is Lacklan calling, I would like to talk to you. What did you do, run me through voice recognition?"

"Yes, and stress detection. In answer to your question, I can patch you through to Amtrak if I need to. That is child's play. What do you want to talk about?"

"We're going to finish the job."

"Dear God... Your father never imagined..."

"I need your help."

He was quiet for a long moment. Then he said, "What kind of help?"

"We need to meet."

"I don't like meeting."

"I know, but we haven't much choice, Phil. You want to meet me at my house?"

"In Boston?" He sounded alarmed.

"No, in Boulder, Wyoming."

"Oh..." I heard him swallow. "I guess..."

"I'm on my way now. I figure I'll get there in twelve to fourteen hours. I could meet you there tomorrow."

"Yes, I guess..."

"Come on, Phil. This is serious. I can't do this without your expertise. Just come over and we'll talk. You want me to pick you up somewhere now?"

"No!" Then again, more softly, "No... I'll make my own way. I know where it is. I'll see you there tomorrow PM."

"OK, thanks, Phil. I appreciate it."

He hung up without answering and I called Cyndi.

"Well, if it isn't the Lone Ranger. I just know you're not calling to ask me on a date."

"Y'all ain't wrong, farm girl, and you ain't right neither."

"Did you learn to speak like that in your Boston prep school, or in the British Army?"

"I need to talk to you, Cyndi. We are finishing the job."

She was quiet for a while. I could hear her breathing. Finally, she said, "What does that mean?"

"It means what you think it means. It also means we need to talk face to face, and not in D.C."

"OK, where?"

"I'm on my way home now. I have to stop for a day in Wyoming..."

"My god, you are becoming a cowboy."

"Yes, ma'am. I'll be there a day, then I'll head home. So you could come to Weston, day after tomorrow. Come for dinner. Stay over. We have a lot to talk about."

"Do you know you are very bossy?"

"I'm used to giving orders and being obeyed." I let the smile show in my voice. "But it's more fun with senators than with grunts. Can you make it?"

"I'll clear my schedule. It is really what I think?"

"Yeah, it is really what you think. But I need you to be thinking about what happens after..."

"Yes, I see. It's very sudden."

"Important change usually is."

She sighed. "Yes, that's true. How is Marni?"

"The same."

"I'm sorry. It's taken its toll on you, hasn't it?"

"Yeah, well, you know how it is with life, Cyndi. Sooner or later, it'll kill you."

"That's not funny, Lacklan."

"No."

"I'll see you in Weston in a couple of days. Stay safe."

"You too."

I hung up and ten minutes later, I pulled onto the I-15 headed north and opened up the massive twin engines under the Zombie's hood. In absolute silence, we streaked into the desert at a hundred and thirty miles per hour under the midday sun, with nothing but dry wilderness stretching out before me.

Wyoming.

It must have been no more than a couple of years ago, though it seemed like another life. Marni and I had stayed there together for six months, as man and wife. They had been the happiest six months of my life. Then she had left for Oxford, for Gibbons and her work—her father's work. After that, we had drifted apart. I had married Abi and Marni and I had rarely spoken. But when we had, she had asked me several times the same question—had I done my reading. It had never registered at the time that she was urging me to read her diary: the diary she had given me, the diary she had left in Wyoming, the diary she had told me, just before she was shot, contained all of her father's research. It was that research that had driven Omega to have him killed. It was that research that had driven Marni to go on the run, and caused my father to beg me to find her, protect her, and bring Omega down.

Nobody had ever found that research, and all along it had been in Marni's diary. That raised a lot of questions: why had she not simply come out and told me before? Why had she left it in my hands in the first place? Why had she and Gibbons not accessed and used that research, if it was so damaging to Omega? But she had been shot before she could tell me.

We had been together six months in Wyoming, with the diary, and she had never mentioned it. Then she had left, and left me with the diary. Why?

The diary was still there, in my bedside drawer. And before I did anything else, I planned to find the answers to those questions.

THREE

I DROVE THROUGH THE HOT, SCORCHED DAY AND into the evening, and by the time I reached Fillmore, in Utah, the sky was on fire on my left, and on my right it was engulfed in darkness, seeping in over the Pahvant Mountains.

I didn't pause to rest. I had coffee and sandwiches in the car, which kept me going, and my mind was wide awake.

At ten, I skirted Salt Lake City and started to climb into the Wasatch Range, following the I-80. I figured I was four hours from my house in Boulder, and in my mind I kept going over the damned diary, entry by entry, searching for the clue as to how he had inserted his research in among those pages. I hadn't read the whole thing. I had dipped in here and there, but at the back of my mind, something was troubling me.

At about midnight, it dawned on me that I wasn't sure where I was. A while back, I had passed a turn off for the town of Kemmerer. I should have been on highway 230, but nothing looked familiar and I cursed myself for obsessing over the diary when I should have been paying attention to the road.

Within twenty minutes or half an hour, the road had degenerated and it was clear I was no longer on any kind of highway. I came to a bridge over a creek that was engulfed in dense mist. I slowed to a crawl and crossed the bridge with the window open, leaning out to see, because the windshield was misted up. I couldn't hear any water.

I followed the road for another ten miles and came to a second bridge, bigger than the first, that spanned a broad canyon. Here I could hear water splashing below, and there was a sign at the entrance to the bridge that read 'Welcome to Freedom.' Beside it was another sign that read 'Barge Creek.' I knew Barge Creek and I knew it fed into the Green River. I was not too far from the highway, and probably no more than two or three hours' drive from home.

I crossed the bridge and followed a winding road up through steep hills, west along a deep valley, and then started to climb again. I had emerged from the mist, but the darkness was still intense and the stars above me were brilliant in a black sky. After a couple of miles or a little more, I began to see lights ahead. I checked my watch. It was one AM and I was beginning to get tired.

Five minutes later, I passed a gas station sitting in a pool of listless, yellow light. I glanced at my display and saw my batteries were almost spent. A moment later, I was in among a sprawl of pretty houses with large front lawns and ample backyards. The town was dotted with abundant gardens and the roads were lined with plane trees, cherries and almonds. It looked prosperous and cared for. Pretty soon, I found myself in the town square, looking at the town hall. It was a handsome, 19th century building in brown stone. The clock said it was one fifteen, and beneath it two flags hung, Old Glory and next to it a white flag bearing a green ash. I pulled into the parking lot beneath the flags and killed the engine, then climbed out to look around.

I was in a broad square, with a large garden at the center. There were scattered trees and flower beds crisscrossed by paths that radiated from a bandstand at the center. Beyond, there was a row of shops, a restaurant and, next to it, a small hotel. All the windows and shop fronts were dark. The only light came from the old, iron streetlamps and the clock on the town hall façade. The stillness and quiet was absolute, but for a small, red fox who loped across the road a hundred yards away, stopped at the intersection with Main Street, with his shadow stretched long across the blacktop, and stared at me a while. Then he turned and went on his way.

The glow from a set of headlamps illuminated the spot where the animal had stood a moment before. The traffic lights turned red and a Ford F10, bearing the sheriff's shield on the door, pulled up. Sitting at the wheel, I could see a man in a khaki shirt wearing a cowboy hat, with his arm resting on the door. He was watching me. I rested my ass on the trunk of my Zombie, pulled my Camels from my pocket and lit up while I waited for the lights to change.

He wasn't that patient. He gave his siren a single blast, crossed the lights on the empty street and rolled up alongside me. He took his time looking at me some more while I took a drag. He didn't say anything, so as I let out the smoke, I said, "Evening, Deputy. I seem to have got lost. I'm on my way to Boulder, in Wyoming. But I seem to have taken a wrong turn somewhere."

I showed him the pack of Camels. He gave his head a single shake. "Where you coming from?"

"Los Angeles."

He gave a single nod. "You took a wrong turn at the intersection with the two-forty. It happens. You'll have to go down to La Barge to pick up highway 89, via Calpet."

"Somewhere I can rest up till morning? Also..." I gestured at the hood of the Zombie. "I need to charge her up. Is there somewhere I can do that?"

He let his eyes run over the car, then looked at me.

"Charge her up? That's a '68 Mustang, Fastback. You must'a seen the gas station on your way in."

I smiled. "The chassis's a '68 Mustang. Under the hood, it has twin electric motors and lithium-ion batteries."

He raised an eyebrow. "Well, that right there is crime."

I gave a small laugh and gave my head a small twitch. "She'll do naught to sixty in one and a half seconds, top speed of two hundred miles per hour, eight hundred horsepower."

He whistled through his teeth. "That so? What's its range?"

"Five hundred miles."

He nodded a while, eyeing the beast. Then he shrugged. "Guess you'll have to talk to Jonah in the morning. He runs the gas station and the garage. He'll fix you up. Meantime, I'd best wake Missy for you. She runs the diner and the hotel 'cross the way." He jerked his head toward the establishments I'd seen earlier. "She'll give you a bed for the night. You can be on your way tomorrow."

"Appreciate it, Deputy."

Missy eventually came down and unlocked the door after the deputy had hammered on it and rang the bell for about ten minutes. She was in her late thirties, with cute, short blonde hair, scrunched up on her head by her pillow, and squinting eyes that might have been blue or green. She was wrapped in a robe and her face said she didn't know whether to be mad or confused or both. She stared at me and then at the Deputy.

"What the hell, Hank?"

Hank smiled for the first time and made a rumbling noise which I figured was a laugh. "We got ourselves a stray lamb, needs a bed for the night. Mr..." He glanced at me.

I said, "Walker, Lacklan Walker."

"Mr. Walker here took a wrong turn down at the intersection, found his way here. Car needs charging up..."

"*Car* needs *chargin'*..."

"Ne'mind that, Missy. No doubt he'll explain it to you over breakfast if he sees fit. He needs a bed for the night, and I need to get back on my rounds."

I thanked the deputy and he made his way back across the square while Missy closed and locked the door behind him. She led me to a small reception desk beside a door that stood open onto a dark living room.

"We don't get many folks passin' through Freedom."

She spun the old-fashioned register and pushed it toward me with a pen. I smiled at her and signed it. "I gathered."

"How long you stayin'?"

"Just till morning. Charge up my car and be on my way." She narrowed her eyes at me. I explained, "It's electric."

"'Lectric car? Can't be no good. Need gas in a car, not 'lectric."

I wasn't going to argue. "As long as it has a shower and a bed, any room will do."

She pulled an old chub key from a hook behind her. It had the number 14 on it. "First floor. Fourth door on the right, overlookin' the square. Breakfast's at eight. Not nine, not seven. Eight. I can do a full American breakfast—or you can have a continental."

She said all this leaning with her elbows on the counter. Her face said what she thought of a continental breakfast.

"Full American sounds great. I'll be down at eight sharp. Shall I pay you now?"

"You can pay when you leave. You ain't got nothin' to pay for yet..."

After a moment she smiled, then gurgled, to indicate she'd made a joke. I gave a small laugh. "I'll be going up then."

"You sleep well now. See in the mornin'."

The room was twenty feet square with an en suite bathroom. The walls were plain white with two small paintings of flowers hung over the bed. There was a small table with two bentwood chairs. The carpet was beige and the duvet was white with big red flowers. Heavy blue drapes hung over the window.

I dumped my bag on the table and brushed my teeth, reflecting that men make plans and the gods have a good laugh. Then I undressed and sat on the bed, meaning to send Phil a message that I might be late the next day, but there was no signal. So I put my phone on to charge, got under the duvet and fell instantly into a deep, dreamless sleep.

I was up at six-thirty, trained as best I could for an hour in my room and had a cold shower. Missy served me a full American breakfast in the dining room, where I sat alone and ate it with a pot of coffee to myself. When I was finished, I stepped out into the morning sunlight and drove the half mile to the gas station on the outskirts of town with the windows down, enjoying the cool morning breeze. I was struck as I passed the well-kept houses, parks and gardens, by how prosperous the town seemed. The people I passed were friendly; all recognized a stranger and most nodded or smiled.

I found Jonah in the shop at the gas station. He was leaning on the counter doing a crossword and looked up when I stepped in.

"Was eaten, worried and drunk, eight letters, blank, blank 'N' and five blanks."

"Consumed. Are you Jonah?"

He stared at me, then down at his paper. "I'll be darned! Not drunk as in... dog*gone!*" He sighed and filled in the word, taking care over each letter. When he'd finished, he looked up. "I thought it meant drunk, as in, in-he-bree-ated. Never thought... Yeah, I'm Jonah. You must be Mr. Walker, got lost last night. Sheriff told me you'd be droppin' by."

"The sheriff?"

He smiled, revealing an absence of teeth. "He ain't the sheriff, but we call him the sheriff. Sheriff of Lincoln County is a good thirty-five mile nor'west from here, as the crow flies, double or triple that if you're drivin'." He wheezed a laugh, like he'd thought of something funny. "He don't never show his face 'round these parts! No, Hank keeps the peace 'round here. He's a good man."

I gave a single nod. "Can you charge my car? I have the cables and the transformer. I just need a supply."

He shrugged. "I got the supply if that's all you need, but how'll I know how much to charge ya?" He didn't wait for me to answer. "Sure there's nothin' else wrong with your car? That there chassis is all of fifty year old. You want me to look at the brakes? I could look at the suspension. I don't know nothin' 'bout 'lectric cars, but I figure the suspension and brakes got to be the same."

I smiled. "No, it just needs charging up. Shouldn't take more than half an hour."

He wheezed his laugh again. "Half an hour? Don't take more'n thirty, forty seconds t' fill a gas tank!" He creased up his face and laughed some more. "Bring it on into the garage, we'll plug it in!"

I spent the next twenty minutes going over the car with him, showing him how it worked and persuading him it wasn't going to blow all his fuses. He finally plugged it in and told me to return in an hour, because he had some errands to run. By the time I got back to the town square, it was almost eleven and I went into the restaurant to find Missy behind the counter, serving coffee and pie. There was a handful of tables occupied: two elderly couples, a table of three women who looked like office workers, a mother with two kids and a guy in his late twenties or early thirties sitting alone. There was an agreeable hum of chatter, and a clatter of cups and plates. Missy saw me come in and smiled.

"Sit down, honey, I'll be right with you. Coffee and pie?"

"Sure. Blueberry. No cream. Black coffee."

I took a seat by the window, spent some time gazing out at the near empty streets, thinking about China, Russia and

Marni's diary, and then spent some more time taking in the other customers in the restaurant. I noted that the guy who was sitting alone looked tired, maybe stressed. He was eating apple pie and drinking coffee like it was his last meal on Earth, and kept glancing out the window. It occurred to me absently that he looked intelligent; maybe too intelligent. The kind of intelligent that makes you neurotic because you keep asking questions nobody can answer. Or the kind of intelligent that drives revolutionaries to get shot.

I blinked and sighed myself out of the reverie and checked my phone to see if I had signal and Missy leaned over me with a large wedge of blueberry pie, a jug of coffee and a cup dangling from her baby finger. The saucer was in her apron.

"You won't get no signal up here, Mr. Walker. This is the back end of beyond, here. Ain't nobody got a cell phone in Freedom. Closest place you'll get a signal is La Barge."

She set down the pie, then put the cup and saucer in front of me and filled it up to the brim. She winked and smiled. "I remember you like it black and hot, but not sweet."

She sashayed away back to the bar. I smiled and settled to eat my pie. Outside, I saw the deputy pull up in his Ford. He swung down from the driving seat and three more men got out with him, all dressed in khaki shirts with cowboy hats. They all bore deputy badges and they all headed for the restaurant. Their faces said they were not coming for pie and coffee. They were here on business.

I glanced around the room. Everyone had gone quiet. They were all focusing hard on their coffee, except the young man who'd been sitting alone. He was staring out the window and he had gone very pale. I looked for Missy, but she had gone in back.

The door opened and a bell clanked. The boy stood and started yammering, like he was trying to say, "No." He had his hands held out in front of him and he took a step back. His chair shifted and squeaked on the floor.

Hank said, "Now, don't give us no trouble, Noah."

"No, Hank. Don't, this is crazy…"

The three deputies who'd come in with Hank circled around behind Noah and seized his arms, and suddenly he was thrashing like a hooked marlin, kicking his legs, trying to wrench his arms free, twisting his head around in every direction, screaming in a shrill voice, "*Hank! Don't! No! Don't do this! Please!*" Then he was appealing to the other diners, screaming at them, "*Don't let them! You can't just sit there! Don't let them!*"

Nobody looked up. The depties dragged him out the door and into the street. I watched through the window as they pulled him, stumbling and thrashing, across the sidewalk and tried to shove him in the truck. He resisted, hollering and planting his feet on either side of the door until Hank drove his fist into the boy's belly and he folded up, retching onto the blacktop. When he was done, they bundled him in and drove away.

I sat staring at the empty space where the truck had been, wondering what the hell had just happened. Missy came out and her voice made me snap out of it. She was saying, "Well, who'd like some more pie? I have a fresh apple right out of the oven!"

She stepped over to my table and I frowned at her. "What the hell just happened?"

"I offered you somethin' sweet."

I pointed at the empty chair at the table where Noah had been sitting. "That young man, the deputies just dragged him out. He was hysterical..."

"Noah? Is he in trouble again? That boy ain't never gonna learn! Now who's gonna pay for his pie and coffee?"

There was a murmur around the room, and after a moment, people started to rise from their chairs and make their way toward the door, smiling at Missy and waving goodbye.

"See y'all tomorrow!" She turned back to me. "Now, you want some hot apple pie?"

I shook my head. "No, thanks. I have some things I have to do before I get back to Jonah's garage." I stood and dropped some money on the table. "Where is the sheriff's office, Missy?"

She picked up the money off the table and sighed. "It's 'round back of the town hall, but don't you go getting involved in Freedom business, Mr. Walker. Hank knows what he's doin'."

I nodded, said, "Sure," and I left.

FOUR

I STOOD A MOMENT ON THE SIDEWALK OUTSIDE THE restaurant, wondering what to do, but I didn't stand long. I couldn't afford to get involved in local problems. It was no secret that local sheriffs and deputies in remote areas often dispensed their own brand of justice, and enjoyed the support of God fearing, law abiding citizens because of it— that was why they got elected. And besides, I had bigger fish to fry, and a meeting with Phil that evening. Like I said, I could not afford get involved.

I told myself that as I crossed the gardens at the center of the square and made my way down Ash Street to the corner of 2nd Avenue. There I turned right and found the deputy sheriff's office. It was an unassuming, red brick building. It had a wooden door with a glass panel in the top half emblazoned with a five pointed star and the legend, Freedom Deputy Lincoln County Sheriff.

I pushed through and found myself in a large room paneled in wood that looked as though it hadn't changed much since the 1920s, or maybe the 1860s. There was a desk with a deputy sitting behind it, and in back there was a larger desk with Hank sitting behind that. They both looked up as I stepped in.

"Help you?"

It was the deputy behind the front desk. I shook my head. "No, I want to talk to Hank."

I stepped toward him and he leaned back in his chair. "Mr. Walker. You're still here. Ain't Jonah charged your car yet?"

I approached his desk. "He's on it. I wanted to talk to you about what happened in the restaurant just now."

He sighed.

I waited, then pointed at a chair and said, "May I sit?"

"Sure, why not? Say your piece, then I got a job to do, Mr. Walker."

"This won't take long. I want to pay his bail and pay for his legal representation. What did he do?"

He stared at me for a long time. Then he took a deep breath. "Well, Mr. Walker, I can't discuss the details of an ongoing investigation with you, but I can assure you it ain't nothing so serious that he's going to need legal representation. As to bail, well, he'll go before the magistrate tomorrow mornin' and that'll probably be the end of it."

"Well, can I see him?"

He licked his lips a couple of times and I could see from his eyes that he was getting mad. "That ain't going to be possible, either. See, he is being interrogated right now."

"Interrogated?"

He nodded.

I went on, "So this is a crime that does not warrant legal

representation, will be dealt with by the magistrate tomorrow morning, and yet he is currently being interrogated…"

He sat back, laced his fingers over his belly and nodded. "That's about the size of it."

"When can I see him?"

"I can't rightly say."

I leaned forward, with my elbows on my knees. "I'm going to go and see if my car is all charged up, Hank, then I'm going to come back here, and if you haven't arranged a meeting for me with Noah, I'm going to go away to Boston and then I am going to descend on this town next week with a team of lawyers who earn in a week what you earn in a year, plus a team of Federal agents who are going to pick over this office and this town with tweezers, until I find out what happened to Noah. Do I make myself clear?"

He held my eye. His expression was pugnacious. "You threatening me, Mr. Walker?"

I nodded. "Yes, Hank. Make no mistake. I am threatening you with the law. Not Freedom law, Federal law. I'll be back in half an hour. You better have Noah available for me to talk to by then."

I stood and left.

I walked the half mile from the deputy's office back to the gas station on the outskirts of the town. The late summer sun was overhead and it was warm. I was aware as I went of how few people there were, and those I saw seemed mainly to be of retirement age, either walking their dogs or pottering in their yards, mowing the lawn or tending to their flowers.

By the time I got to the gas station, it was twenty

minutes after twelve and Jonah was in the garage, lying with his feet poking out from under my car. I stood looking down at his boots for a moment, feeling anger welling in my gut. I suppressed it and spoke quietly.

"What the hell are you doing, Jonah?"

He was lying on a mechanic's creeper and rolled himself out to grin up at me. "I got curious after you was tellin' me about how darn fast this baby could go, so I started havin' a look, just outta curiosity. Good job I did, too!" He struggled to his feet, pulling a cloth from his overalls to wipe his hands. "Your front brakes're leakin' fluid. You hit huner'n twenny in that baby, you may as well put a .45 in your mouth an' blow your own brains out."

I stared at him. "What are you talking about? I drove from L.A. non-stop and had no problems. The brakes are new."

He made a high-pitched noise like a parrot: "Ha! You come all the way from Los Angeles, probably doing huner'n twenty clean across Nevada, you don't know what you kicked up under your chassis, do ya? At that speed, a piece of gravel, a nut, a nail..." He shook his head. "That's like a high velocity round at that speed."

I sighed loudly. "How long's it going to take to fix, Jonah? I need to be in Wyoming by tonight."

He shrugged and made a face. "If I got the bits, couple hours. If I ain't, I gotta go down to La Barge, then it won't be done till supper time."

I narrowed my eyes and shook my head. "Why do I just know that you haven't got the bits?"

"I ain't looked yet, so I don't know."

"Have you got a landline I can use? Just add it to my bill."

He pointed at the large, open doors. "In the shop. Just make a note of how long the call is, write it on the pad by the register."

I stepped out into the sunshine and crossed the fore-court to the shop. I pushed through the door, the bell clanged and the door swung closed behind me. I found the phone behind the counter and started dialing Phil's number. Halfway through, a woman's voice cut in.

"Operator, how may I direct your call?"

I think I pulled the handset from my ear and stared at it. "*What?*"

"Hello, caller, this is the Freedom operator. How may I direct your call?"

"You can't. I want a direct line. I will dial the number myself. What is this, the 1930s?"

"Caller, I am afraid that is not possible. All calls in and out of Freedom go through the operator. How may I direct your call?"

I hung up and walked back to the garage. There I found Jonah going through an old box of drawers up against the far wall. He spoke over his shoulder, without turning. "Did y'get through?"

"You have an operator who screens all calls in and out of Freedom?"

"Makes things simpler."

"How?"

"Darned if I know. I ain't got the bit. I'll have to go down to La Barge to git a new one."

"I'll ride with you."

He shook his head and turned to face me. "Can't do that."

Anger boiled in my gut, but I spoke quietly. "Why the hell not?"

"Only room for two in the truck, an' I gotta take Eddy with me."

"God dammit, Jonah, I'll ride in the back!"

"Sheriff won't allow that, Mr. Walker. I'll git fined. You just wait here and enjoy Missy's fine home cookin' an' I'll have your vee-hickle up and runnin' by tomorrow morning, eight sharp." He grinned his toothless grin at me, spat on the floor and pointed at the door. "Now I have to close up, so's I can go down and git your bits."

I had a bad feeling I couldn't place. I stared at him a moment and on impulse, I went to the back of the car, popped the trunk and took out one of my two Sig Sauers and my Fairbairn and Sykes fighting knife from my kit bag. I slipped the knife in my boot and the 9mm in my waistband, behind my back and under my jacket.

When I was done, I followed Jonah out to the forecourt. There he locked the garage with a chain and padlock and clambered into an old Chevy truck he had parked down by the side. He slammed the door, fished some keys out of his overalls and fired up the engine. I watched him do this and asked, "What about Eddy?"

He grinned his toothless grin, stuck his fingers in his mouth and emitted a piercing whistle. The he leaned over and opened the passenger door. There was a scrambling noise from the back of the garage and a moment later, a mutt with the body of a German shepherd and the face of a bloodhound cleared the old, clapboard fence and bounded into the passenger seat. As Jonah pulled away, he leaned out the window. "I never go nowhere without Eddy."

I watched him pull onto the highway and disappear south along the road which had brought me there.

I walked back into town more slowly, thinking about what had happened, and the implications. The town was practically empty but for a couple of street cleaners in luminous overalls and a handful of women I saw entering or leaving the shops on Main Street. I returned to the restaurant and found Missy setting the tables. She didn't look up as I entered, but said, "We get a bit of a rush lunchtime. They bus 'em in..."

I interrupted her. "Have you got a car I can rent?"

She looked up, startled. "No."

"How about to buy? Name your price."

"What's the matter, Jonah couldn't fix your car?"

I hesitated for a fraction of a second. "Not in time. I have an important meeting this evening. I'm not concerned how much it costs. I need a car, now."

She returned to setting the tables. "Sorry, sugar. I ain't got a car."

"Do you know anyone who might be willing to rent or sell one?"

She shook her head. "Uh-uh."

I couldn't keep the frustration from my voice. "You didn't even think about it, Missy! Think! Is there anyone..."

"I didn't think because I know." She moved to the next table. "Why would I think about it when I already know the answer?"

I cursed softly under my breath and pushed out into the street again. I loped across the square to the town hall and down Ash Street to the deputy's office. When I stepped inside and closed the door behind me, Hank was alone with his feet on his desk and his fingers laced over his belly, like he hadn't moved since I'd left.

"Good afternoon, Mr. Walker. You got your army of lawyers with you, or is it just you alone?"

"Where's Noah?"

He cocked his head on one side and almost smiled. "Well, here's the thing. I don't rightly know."

"What do you mean you don't know?"

He lifted his hands just enough to spread them and gazed around at the wood-paneled walls. "Can't say it any plainer, Mr. Walker. I don't know where that young feller is. We finished interrogating him, in the jail next door, and, wishing to be cooperative, we was bringing him over here so's you could talk to him, like you said, and on the way he just upped and smacked my two deputies in the jaw with his two fists clenched together, knocked them cold. Then he took the keys from Seth, unlocked his cuffs, and took off into the hills. Ain't nobody seen hair nor hide of him since. My boys are out lookin' for him right now."

"When did this happen?"

"Not fifteen minutes after you left." Now he smiled. "What I would suggest to you, Mr. Walker, is that you go on back to Boulder, or Boston, or wherever it is you come from, get your army of lawyers and federal agents, and come on back in a week or two. I'm pretty sure we'll have Noah for you by then, and you can all talk to him to your heart's content. Hell, I'll even give you the file and the court transcripts, so you can see we are all transparent, open and above board here, Mr. Walker."

"Is that why you have an operator screening all the calls in and out of the town?"

He laughed. "Now, you're gonna get me thinkin' you're paranoid if you keep talkin' like that!" The laughter drained from his face and was replaced by an expression of hostility that bordered on plain evil. "Was there anything else, Mr. Walker?"

"Yeah, there is. You can do us both a favor. I need to be in Boulder by this evening, but Jonah won't have my car fixed till tomorrow, and you have this town locked down so tight I can't leave even though I want to. You're so keen for me to leave, tell me where I can buy or hire a car, have one of your men drive me to La Barge."

He took his feet off the desk and stood. "This ain't a fuckin' taxi service..." He hesitated a moment. "You ain't going to buy or rent anything in this town, but I'll talk to the boys, see if any one of 'em is willing to do you that favor. Now get the hell out of my office."

I didn't move. I watched him for a long moment. I pulled my pack of Camels from my pocket, pulled one out and poked it in my mouth. He watched me do it and I said, "You're the law in this town, huh?"

"You better believe it. And you can't smoke in here."

I took a long drag, held the smoke and let it out slow. Then I dropped the cigarette on his wooden floor and crushed it with the toe of my boot. "You don't want me in your town, Hank. I don't know what game you're playing, but you better either produce Noah or let me leave..." I walked up to his desk and let him see the death in my eyes. "Because, if you don't do at least one of those two things, I'm going to take that star and shove it so far up your ass you'll die with a twinkle in your eye. All I want to do is see Noah and leave, don't make this more complicated than it needs to be."

He swallowed, and for a moment, I saw fear in his eyes. For the second time that day, he asked me, "Are you threatening..." But the question died on his lips.

I nodded. "I'll be back after lunch, Hank. Then I'd better have Noah here, and a ride to La Barge."

"Or what?"

He tried to make it sound pugnacious, but it came out uncertain and his voice caught in his throat. I looked him over and wondered what he was hiding, why he had the town battened down so tight, and whether I would have to kill him. He must have seen the thought in my eyes because he didn't push it. I went to the door and opened it.

"I'll be back after lunch."

Outside, the afternoon was turning from warm to hot. I looked up at the clear, blue sky, and something in my gut told me I would not be meeting Phil that evening. I'd be doing something else instead.

FIVE

I WALKED TO THE CORNER OF 2ND AVENUE AND ASH Street and stopped. I fished my Camels from my pocket, poked one in my mouth and lit up. I told myself again I couldn't afford to get involved in whatever it was that was going on in Freedom, but even as I was telling myself, I was aware I didn't have much choice. It was a cinch that Hank had told Jonah to disable my car. That didn't make a lot of sense on the face of it, because he was also telling me to get out of town.

I turned down Ash Street and headed toward the town square. Missy had made it clear nobody was going to provide me with a vehicle, and Deputy Hank had made the same thing clear. It was like he wanted me to go away, but he didn't want me to leave. Maybe he wanted me to walk to La Barge. I wondered vaguely how far it was and how long it would take, but something about the idea made me uncomfortable.

By the time I stepped into the square, I was considering

the possibility of hotwiring a car. It seemed to be about the only option I had left, but my mind was drawn away from that thought by somewhere in the region of a hundred men and slightly less than half as many women, milling across the gardens toward the restaurant and crowding through the door. They were streaming out of four coaches that had pulled up in front of the town hall, and seemed to be of every age from the late teens up to the late fifties.

I made my way to the gardens, found a bench out of sight beyond the bandstand, and sat in the shade of some trees.

Most of the people went into Missy's restaurant. Some emerged with take out and returned to the coaches, others sat at the tables inside to eat their food, while still others, a minority, went to the store down the road and bought sandwiches, bread and cheese. A few wandered off into the side streets.

I sat for maybe ten, fifteen minutes, smoking and wondering about this strange town, and gradually the crowd thinned out until everybody was either back on the coaches or sitting in Missy's diner. I looked for some indication of where the coaches had come from, and asked myself what Freedom had that would make it a popular place for day trip tourists. I'd lived in Wyoming a while, not far from Freedom, and I'd never heard of it. I wondered also at the fact that the one age group that was missing from these people was the very age group that might be doing day trip tourism. These people were all of working age.

In fact, aside from the fact that they had all turned up in coaches, they looked for all the world like people having their lunch break.

I was brought out of my thoughts by a voice. It was a pretty voice that made me turn and look.

"Are you Mr. Walker?"

The owner of the voice was a girl of maybe nineteen or twenty. Her skin was pale and she had a cute spray of freckles across her nose and cheeks. Her eyes were a deep green and her hair was a rich, wild copper.

I nodded once. "Yes, I am. Who are you?"

"My name is Grace. May I sit with you for a moment?"

"Sure."

She came around the bench and sat next to me, staring at the restaurant. Now I could see that her eyes were bloodshot and slightly puffy. She turned to face me and on an impulse, I said, "Is Noah your brother or your boyfriend?"

Her eyes widened. "My fiancé. How did you know?"

"You knew my name. It was a fair bet you heard I'd been sticking my nose in Deputy Hank's business, asking about Noah, and the only reason you'd have for approaching me would be if you had some personal interest in him. You've been crying. You're clearly not his mother, so that left two options."

She smiled and blinked. "You're funny."

"That's what my therapist kept telling me, only he didn't mean funny ha ha."

This time she made it to a small wet laugh, then asked, "Did you learn anything? About Noah?"

"Not much. Hank said he'd knocked out two deputies and escaped. Any idea where he'd go?"

She shook her head. "I don't believe it. I don't believe he would escape. He's..." She hesitated, then looked apologetic. "He's not that kind of man. He's very brave, but he's not physically strong. I can't honestly see him knocking out two of Hank's men."

I thought back to the man I'd seen in the restaurant, sitting alone at the table. I didn't believe it either. "He knew they were coming for him. He was anxious, like he was waiting for them."

"You saw it happen, didn't you?"

I nodded. "What's he supposed to have done? Hank wouldn't tell me."

She sighed and looked down at her hands in her lap. "He's the local schoolmaster."

I frowned. "That's not a crime—yet."

She gave a small snort. "You said it: yet. The thing is, Freedom has a very strong town council, with a rather old fashioned way of seeing things. The school curriculum is prescribed, particularly religion, history and science..."

I raised an eyebrow. "Let me guess. The Earth is flat, six thousand years old and there were no dinosaurs?"

She met my eye and nodded. "Amongst other things. Noah has different views. He believes the children should be exposed to a much wider range of ideas. The town council warned him to toe the line, *especially* in the field of religion. But in his own, quiet, unassuming way, I guess he is a bit of a revolutionary, and he refused. We had the children debating, writing speculative essays..."

"We?"

"I'm his assistant. That's how we met."

I frowned. "You're young."

"Well, as I say, this town is special. All the town council required of me was that I could spell and do basic arithmetic, cook and sew."

"You teach the kids to cook and sew?"

"The girls. The boys learn to hunt and to box."

"Those good old fashioned values, on which we used to rely."

She didn't get the reference and searched my face with eyes that looked as though they might start crying again at any moment. "I am so worried, Mr. Walker. I don't know what they've done to him. Is it true you offered to get him a lawyer and to pay his bail?"

"Yeah. I still would if I could get out of this town. But refusing to abide by the school curriculum is not a criminal offense, Grace. He might lose his job, but to get arrested by the sheriff's deputies, be locked up and interrogated, and then sent for trial..." I shook my head. "He had to have done something more serious than that."

Her hands went to her mouth. "Interrogated?"

"This morning, Hank said they were interrogating him."

"That means they have him in the lock up, next door to the sheriff's office."

"Of course they have." My frown deepened. "Where else would they have him?"

She stared at me for a long time, like she was wondering whether I would understand what she wanted to tell me. A deep disquiet stirred in me. Finally, I said, "What is it, Grace? What are you not telling me?"

She sighed and closed her eyes. "I should go. It's more complicated than I can explain. This town..."

"What about this town?"

"It has its own rules, its own way of doing things... It has its own laws."

"That's not possible, Grace."

"No, Mr. Walker, it is possible. It happens right here."
She stood and I went to stand with her, but she held out her
hand. "No. Please, don't attract attention. I shouldn't be
seen talking to you."

"Tell me how I can contact you. If I have news."

"You can't. You mustn't." She turned to go, then
stopped. "I read once, in a magazine, about a place called
Waco. Do you know about it?"

I frowned. "Of course."

She nodded, then turned and hurried away toward the
intersection where the night before, I had seen Deputy
Hank for the first time. There she disappeared from view.

I sat for a while, thinking over the things she had said to
me. The doors to Missy's restaurant opened and people
started to stream out. Soon, the square was full of people
again, like a swarm of slow-moving ants making their way
back toward the coaches, which slowly sucked them in until
after some ten minutes, the square was empty and one by
one, the big engines fired up, rumbled, and the coaches
steadily filed out of the square, one after another, leaving it
still and silent.

By the time they were gone, I had made up my mind that
that night, I would hotwire a car and drive it to my place in
Boulder, where I would arrange to have it sent back with
adequate monetary compensation. On the way, I would
phone Phil and explain. I could not stay in Freedom another
night.

Waco. I wasn't sure if I was most troubled by the
comparison itself, or the fact that she wasn't sure I'd heard
of it.

I stood and crossed the square toward the restaurant,

thinking about Grace and Noah—Noah, sitting even then in the lock up that had caused Grace such distress. You didn't need to be a genius to work out what went on in there. I dropped my cigarette butt on the sidewalk outside the restaurant and pushed my way in. Missy was leaning by the cash register, watching me.

"Don't let the sheriff see you droppin' your butts in the street like that, mister. He'll run you in before you can say Camel."

"I'd like to see him try. Also, he's not a sheriff. Am I too late for a burger and fries?"

"Nope. You want a coffee?"

I leaned on the counter. "No. I want a beer. Cold as a two dollar whore's heart."

Her eyes went wide and she screamed with laughter, covering her mouth with her hand. "My! You are some kind of *bad* man!"

"Yup. And I am in a bad mood. So give me that beer, have one yourself, and tell me about Grace and Noah. What's the story?"

The laughter drained from her face. She pulled two beers from the fridge, cracked them and handed one to me. She took a pull and sighed.

"You gotta butt out, Mr. Walker..."

"Lacklan."

"Lacklan, then. Whatever your name is, you gotta butt out. This ain't none of your business."

"Who decides that?"

"What?"

I sighed. "Who decides what is my business, what's your business, what's Hank's business? Who decides that?"

She shook her head. "You ask some damned queer questions, Lacklan."

"You know who decides what is my business, Missy?"

"I got the feeling you're about to tell me."

"I do. And I have decided that Noah and Grace are my business. You can't put a man in jail, without trial, and beat him up because he teaches kids to think for themselves and question the bible…"

She raised an eyebrow. "Is that what you think happened?"

I took my first pull on the beer and made it a long one. When I'd finished, I put the bottle on the counter and sighed. "I get the feeling you're going to tell me it wasn't."

She hesitated. Then, "Oh, boy. If anybody finds out we had this conversation, I am gonna be in so much trouble."

I felt a hot pellet of rage in my belly. "Keep talking, Missy, because if you stop, I'm going to go to the deputy's office and I am going to gut him and lynch him with his own damned colon. What the hell is going on in this town?"

"Come into the kitchen."

She turned and walked through a curtained doorway into the small kitchen she had in back. She sighed again heavily and ran her fingers through her hair. "Connie's gone. If she'd heard us… You want a burger? I haven't eaten yet."

"Yeah. Don't change the subject, Missy. What the hell is going on here?"

She opened the fridge, took out a couple of burgers and tossed them on the griddle with a couple of open buns. Then she set about slicing tomatoes and lettuce.

"It's true, Noah was the teacher at the local school…"

"Was?"

She paused in what she was doing, but didn't look at me. After a moment, she said, "Yeah, was. It's also true that he was teaching heresy to the kids." I took a breath to challenge the term, but bit my tongue and she went on. "He was teaching the kids that the world was a globe, that it was older than six thousand years..." She frowned and glanced at me. "Carbon testing?"

"Carbon fourteen."

"Whatever that is. Crazy mumbo-jumbo. What he was teaching them was all against the Bible. He was teaching the kids that the Bible was not the word of the Lord, but just any old book. I can tell you he had the Council mad as hell."

The burgers were hissing loud and she flipped them, then started buttering the rolls and spreading them with ketchup.

"He was in trouble and no mistake about that. The Council had summonsed him to the Hall and they were gonna demand he explain hi'self, and why he was defying the Council's strict instructions." She gazed at me for a moment. "That's why you saw him looking so anxious. He was goin' over to meet the Council."

"But instead the deputies turned up and dragged him away to jail."

"Some of us saw that comin'. He was real smart in some ways—too smart—but he was real dumb in others."

She put the burgers in the buns, dressed them and put them on plates. Then she took a basket of fries from the deep fryer and spilled some onto each plate. She picked them up and jerked her head toward the dining room. "Grab another couple of beers, will you?"

I did as she asked and we sat to eat. She took a bite and spoke with her mouth full.

"He should never have got engaged to Grace. We all knew that was a stupid thing to do, and we told her. They was just makin' rods for their own backs. But she was as crazy about him as he was about her. They believed if they was firm and true to each other, it would all work out. That's what she said to me."

I sank back in my chair. There was a depressing banality about it. It always comes down to sex and money in the end. "Are you telling me Hank had his eye on Grace?"

She stopped chewing and stared at me. "Hank? You think this is all about Hank? You're crazy. Hank's a happily married man! No, he's just the muscle. This town is run by the Council, and the Council is run by Mayor John Freeman."

I had seen it before, in remote Afghanistan, Colombia, Mexico and Brazil, but I was struggling to understand what she was telling me, because I had never seen it in the West. I shook my head, frowning. "What are you telling me, Missy?"

"Mayor Freeman was originally from Utah. He was raised a Mormon. But he was pretty radical and had his own interpretation of scripture. He started making a nuisance of himself..." She gave a small laugh, with more than a hint of admiration in it. "Preaching what they thought was heresy and upsetting a lot of elders, until they finally ran him out of town. This must have been, oh, forty years ago, maybe a bit more."

She paused and took a swig of her beer, then sat staring at her burger in her hands for a moment.

"Back then, this was barely even a village. We was just a

small cluster of houses back of beyond, maybe a hundred people or less. But all the land 'round here belonged to Mayor Freeman's daddy. And when old man Freeman died, Mayor Freeman moved out here with a small group of his followers and settled. He couldn't've been more than twenty-two or so, but even then, he was charismatic." Her expression became abstracted. "He had a kind of magnetism about him that made people love him, believe him, believe *in* him. Plus..." She shrugged and tilted her head in a gesture that was almost one of defiance. "He did good things for the town."

"Like what?" I remembered the coaches I'd seen a little earlier and on impulse said, "He provided work?"

"He sure did! All the land he'd inherited from his old man he turned over to agriculture, only he refused to use any kind of technology which deprived a man or a woman of a job. That's his own words. He employed every man and woman in the town, one way or another, and if anybody came lookin' for work, as eventually they did, he said, 'I'll give you a job, but you have to move here and be a part of the town, rent a house, pay taxes, help bring this place back to life.' State government, federal government, they ain't never done nothin' for us, but Mayor Freeman done every-thin' for us. That's why we named the town after him. Used to be Jonesville. Now it's Freedom."

She went quiet for a bit and I watched her eat, thinking about what she'd told me, putting the pieces together, remembering how Grace had compared the town to Waco. That comparison was now beginning to make more sense.

After a moment, she swallowed, held my eye and spoke. "He bought every house in this town, mortgaged and unmortgaged alike. He fixed 'em all up and rented them back to their owners at a minimal rent that they could afford, with the legal right to occupy them till death. He built the gardens, planted trees... He built the town hall, the school. He literally made this town what it is, and there ain't never been a crime here so long as Mayor Freeman has been mayor."

"Until yesterday, but I am struggling to see what crime was committed yesterday, and I am still waiting for you to tell me."

She sighed and put her burger down. "Yeah... yesterday."

"You said he was a Mormon..."

She nodded. "He was, but the Mormon religion cramped his style. He don't mind if you have a drink, or two, provided you don't disturb the peace. He don't object to coffee and tea, as long as you respect your neighbors and the town authorities..."

"The Council. I'm guessing they were the disciples who followed him from Utah."

"Yeah, mostly. Is that predictable?" She didn't wait for an answer. "Some of what he preaches is pretty vague and esoteric, Mary was not a virgin, Jesus *was* the son of God, though, and as such a god himself. The Earth is flat—mind you, that makes sense to me—and the world is just six thousand years old. Again, makes sense, it's what the Bible says, right? But then there's other stuff which I guess we just have to live with."

I stuffed the last of my burger in my mouth and spoke around it. "Like Freeman having more than one wife?"

She nodded. "You ain't slow, are you? Him and the senior members of the council, four men. They can pick any young woman they want to be their brides, provided they pick them before they're twenty-one. But no other man in the town can pick a bride, or get married to a woman, *before* she is twenty-one."

"So the Council get first pickings and whatever is left is for the boys. Noah broke the rules and to make matters worse, somebody on the Council had already picked Grace."

"Yeah, Mayor Freeman."

I studied her a moment, her cute, short hair, her pretty face and humorous eyes. Her body was not bad either and she had nice legs.

"How come he didn't pick you?"

"He did. But when you reach a certain age, you get pensioned off. That's how come I have the hotel and the restaurant..."

"And the guaranteed income of the farm workers who eat here every day."

She nodded. "Yeah, and that."

SIX

IT WASN'T WACO, IT WAS WACO ON STEROIDS.

I pulled my cigarettes from my pocket, fished one out and offered Missy the pack. She eyed it a moment, then shook her head.

"You can't smoke in here."

I flipped my Zippo, thumbed the flint and leaned into the flame. "So call the deputies."

She narrowed her eyes at me as I blew smoke at the ceiling. "Who *are* you?"

"Lacklan Walker."

"You're a bad man."

"Maybe so, but I don't force women into sexual slavery, and I don't incarcerate young men and beat them up for teaching science over religion, or falling in love and wanting to get married."

Her cheeks colored. "You make it sound bad."

"It is bad. This is the 21st century, Missy, not the damned middle ages."

"What are you going to do?"

I thought about it a moment and flicked ash onto my plate. "Hank can't make up his damned mind. One minute he's telling me to get out of town, and the next he's having Jonah disable my brakes so I can't leave. Either way, I have to leave today, one way or another."

Her eyes were anxious. "So you going to leave things be?"

I should have told her I would. I liked her, but I had no doubt she would report what I told her to Hank. But a pugnacious obstinacy in me made me speak. I shook my head. "No, I am going to report Mayor Freeman and his damned Council to the District Attorney for Wyoming, and I'm also going to make a report to the FBI. I am pretty sure he is in breach of several federal and state laws and he should be investigated. I don't like men who enslave woman as sex objects, and I don't like men who beat other men into submission so they can steal their wives. Hell, Missy, I am not even sure what's going on on his farms isn't some kind of slave labor. I think Mayor Freeman is a fanatical asshole and as soon as I get home, I aim to do what I can to bring him down."

Her expression surprised me. She looked sad. "I wish you wouldn't."

I stood. "You know what? If it wasn't for Noah and Grace, I'd probably move on and forget it. But I'm not going to stand by and let him abuse two nice, decent young people whose only crime is to be in love with each other and believe in their work as teachers. And neither should you. It's wrong, and you know it."

Her face contracted suddenly with irritation. "Show me

some place where there ain't injustice! Show me some place where things ain't wrong! What about your precious Federal Government, stealing people's land, shootin' folks dead for standin' up to them! Won't even let a man live on his own land if he don't live by their goddamn rules!"

I raised an eyebrow at her. "Sound familiar? In any case, Missy, it isn't a question of either or. You do what you know is right, whatever the law says, whether it's state law, federal law or Freeman's law. And you know what he's doing with Grace and Noah is wrong."

She didn't answer and I left.

I was pretty sure Hank wasn't going to produce Noah, not least because Noah was probably black and blue with bruises from head to foot right now. I was also pretty sure that Hank had no desire to keep me in the town, but what he was doing was delaying my departure to give Freeman and his cronies time to devise a strategy if I did turn up with the feds and an army of lawyers. But delay was something I could not afford right then, just as I couldn't afford to get involved in Grace and Noah's problem. What I needed badly right then was a car that would get me as far as Boulder. And that was what I was looking for.

I did the rounds of the town, with my hands in my pockets, doing my best to look like a man who was bored and frustrated and couldn't wait to go home. I walked down just about every street in the town, and found, on Mulberry Road, a small, leafy cul-de-sac a quarter of a mile from the town square, exactly what I was looking for: a Ford Focus from 2010, as new, one careful owner.

I watched him arrive home at five thirty PM, open his front door without a key, kiss his wife and go inside with his two daughters clinging to his legs as he walked. He had the look of the local accountant or bank manager. His wife was probably on a couple of committees and baked chocolate brownies for the local fetes. Most important of all, they were probably in bed early and had minimal security. And I was prepared to bet that the keys to the Focus were in a bowl beside the front door; either that or they were hanging on the cork board in the kitchen.

I wandered down a few more streets, apparently killing time, and arrived back at the restaurant at a quarter to seven. Missy was not unfriendly, but her manner had changed and she kept her distance. There was a handful of occupied tables, but they ignored me. I ordered a steak and fries and a beer, ate my meal and then went up to my room. There I got four hours sleep and rose shortly after eleven. I dressed, slipped my Sig in my waistband behind my back and my knife in my boot. There was nothing essential in my bag, so I left it in the wardrobe and slipped down to the hotel lobby. As I had expected, there was nobody there and I stepped quietly out into the street.

The square was still and silent. The streetlamps, shaded by the foliage of the plane trees, cast a limpid orange wash on the blacktop. There was a chill in the air that made me shudder briefly and I set off down Main Street and took the first turn on the left. From there I took a circuitous route, turning back on myself and doing figures of eight, watching and listening for anyone who might be following me. So by the time I got to Mulberry Road, I was pretty sure I had not been followed.

The Focus was still parked outside the house. The house itself was dark and quiet. I wondered for a moment whether to hotwire it, but opted for the key as easier, quicker and safer. I vaulted their white picket fence and sprinted across their front lawn to the back of the house. They had a kitchen door with a chub lock and French doors with a latch that yielded to my Fairbairn and Sykes in less than a minute. The room was dark, so I stood for a minute with my eyes closed, allowing them to adjust to the absence of light, while I listened for any movement in the house. All I could hear was the faint sound of snoring from upstairs.

When I opened my eyes, I could make out a couple of armchairs, a fireplace and a sofa. In the far left hand corner from where I stood, there was a door. Four long strides took me across the room. The door was ajar. The slower you open a door, the louder it squeaks. I took hold of the handle and yanked fast. It made no sound.

Now I was in the entrance hall, with the kitchen on my left. Two long steps to my right took me to a table and a mirror beside the door. I searched it with my hands for the keys. There were none. The next option was the kitchen, and after that his jacket pocket, probably in the bedroom. I shelved that thought and made for the kitchen.

The kitchen door was open and there was faint starlight filtering through the window. I could see the sink, and the stencil of the tap arching over it. I could make out the fridge and a table in the middle of the floor. I edged over to it, sliding my feet instead of stepping, feeling my way. It was hard to tell, but I couldn't see any cork boards on the wall.

I reached the table and slid my hands slowly over the surface. A fruit bowl, bananas, oranges, a pineapple, keys. I pulled them out and felt them. A couple of Yales and a car key. I turned and moved quickly down the hall to the front door, opened it, stepped out onto the front lawn and closed it behind me.

I pressed the button on the key. The car lights flashed and bleeped. The noise echoed loud in the cul-de-sac. I waited, scanning the windows and listening for movement in the house. There was nothing. So I crossed the lawn, vaulted the fence and made for the car.

As I pulled open the door, they stepped out of the pickup they'd parked at the entrance to the street. The doors slammed like a couple of gunshots and they walked toward me, in their khaki shirts and their cowboy hats: Deputy Hank and one of his boys. Hank was the first to speak.

"Well, Ned, I do believe we have us a car thief here. Ain't that Jerry Wilkins' car, parked outside of Jerry Wilkins' house? And ain't that Mr. Walker, aimin' to get in that car?"

They had come within the pool of light of the street lamp and I could see Ned more clearly now. He was six feet, strongly built like a quarterback, with a thick neck and a big jaw. He was smiling like Hank had said something really clever.

"I do believe you're right, Sheriff. You think he's gonna come quiet?"

Before Hank could answer, I spoke. "Here's the thing, Hank, Ned, I have to get to Boulder tonight, and you have deprived me of my car. So I am going to borrow Mr. Wilkins' car. Now, here's the deal: I don't believe that you boys are lawfully appointed deputies at all. In fact, I think one of the many felonies being committed in this town is impersonating an officer of the law. So I'll tell you what I am going to do. You let me get in this car and drive away, and I won't break any of your bones tonight. Does that sound like a deal?"

They looked at each other and after a moment they laughed. I knew what was coming next. It was pretty crude. They both charged me head on, aiming to grab me and drag me to the ground, where they would beat seven bells out of me. It didn't work out that way. I slammed the door open and Ned ran right into it. It didn't hurt him a lot, but it made him stagger back.

My left arm was already outstretched so I only had to reach slightly to the left to seize Hank's nose between my index and middle fingers and turn it savagely to nine o'clock. I felt the bone crunch and he tried to scream while drawing air in an inward gasp. I pulled him toward me, let go of his nose and smashed the heel of my hand into the tip of his jaw. His eyes rolled up into his head and he fell on his back.

Meanwhile, Ned was fumbling with his revolver in his holster. I backhanded him twice, grabbed him by his collar and slammed him against the Focus. There I thrust the Sig into his face.

"Don't make any sudden movements, Ned. The Sig Sauer p226 has no safety. So it could go off accidentally in your face. Then you wouldn't be your mommy's pretty boy anymore, would you? Now tell me, how did you know I was going to be here?"

"I... I... I..."

"Now you're making me nervous, Ned. And if I get nervous, I'll shoot you. I'm going to ask you again, and if you don't answer, I will shoot you in the head. Have you made funeral arrangements? Or is Mommy going to have to pay for everything? How did you know I was going to be here?"

"CCTV cameras..."

"I didn't see any."

"They're all over town. They're concealed. In the trees. They're watching you right now back at the station. They'll be on their way. Please don't shoot me."

I pistol-whipped him, dropped him on the blacktop and climbed in the Ford. I fired her up and took off fast out of the cul-de-sac, scraping past the sheriff's truck, which was half blocking the entrance. Then I was away, driving fast but not too fast, weaving through the streets, headed toward the gas station and the road out of Freedom. I opened the windows and in the distance, I could hear the wail of sirens. I wondered when the last time was they'd heard one of those in this town.

Up ahead of me, I saw Jonah's garage. I accelerated and passed it at close to a hundred miles per hour. Somehow, on the way in, I had missed the turn off for La Barge. This time, I kept my eyes peeled. Pretty soon, I saw dense pine woods climbing the slopes to my left, and after a couple of minutes, I saw a break in the trees. There, almost invisible, was an intersection with a small, wooden sign that pointed into the woods and read, 'La Barge'. For a second, I thought of driving straight on. Let them think I'd taken the turning and follow me. I'd go straight down across the two bridges and join Highway 89. But in my rearview mirror, I could see the red and yellow flashing lights of the cruisers chasing me. Two got you twenty they could see my rear lights and the glow from my headlamps.

I made the brakes complain and turned down the La

Barge road. It was a mistake. Only, there was no way I could have known it. It was a winding mountain road, densely forested on both sides, with hairpin bends and occasional steep ravines on the left. I drove as fast as I dared, not knowing the road. But I had handed the deputies an advantage, because they knew the road, they knew where they could floor the pedal and how fast they could take the corners. I had to be cautious and that meant I had to let them close on me.

It took them about five minutes, and then I saw them in my mirror, maybe fifteen or twenty yards behind me, with their lights flashing red and blue, flooding my cab. All I could do was hog the center of the narrow road and hope there was nothing coming up the hill. Because once one of them got in front of me, I was finished.

I was trusting that when I got to La Barge, they would back off. I was pretty sure they were less than legit and would be reluctant to draw in law enforcement that was not their own.

But keeping them behind me had its own problems. The truck behind me pulled up close, put his headlamps on full beam and switched on his spots for good measure. For a moment, I was blinded. I reached up and turned the mirror away, reached out the window and pulled in the wing mirror. I didn't need them anyway.

That was when he started ramming me. I accelerated to pull away from him. Screamed around a bend on the wrong side of the road and saw a second turn to the right approaching. Beyond it was a steep slope down into a wooded canyon. I took the bend on the inside, but as I braked, he rammed my trunk and sent me spinning across the road. I tried to compensate and straighten up, but the car was out of control. I hit the barrier, rolled over it, the airbag exploded in my face and next thing, the world was a spinning jumble of crashing and wrenching, and the screeching of tortured metal. I came to a halt upside down with a jarring smash against a tree.

I hung for a second, groaning and hoping the world would stop moving soon. On my left, I could see a tree trunk through the window. The fact that it was upside down made me nauseous. I felt for the seatbelt release button and at the same time, through the right hand window, I saw four pairs of cowboy boots stagger to a halt just by the roof. Then a face leered in and said, "You alive, Mr. Walker?"

SEVEN

By some miracle, apart from a few scratches and bruises, I was uninjured. I released my seatbelt, dropped to the roof and crawled out, where the four deputies kept me covered with their weapons. One of them cuffed me, took my Sig and my knife and they dragged me back up the hill to where the two vehicles were parked with their lights beating a steady rhythm of red and blue in the night.

They loaded me in the back of one of the trucks and we started back toward Freedom. On the way up the hill to the intersection, nobody spoke. When we got there and turned right, toward the town, I said, "I guess you have no crime in Freedom, huh?"

The deputy behind the wheel flicked his eyes at the mirror. "None to speak of, not till now."

"So how come a town this small, with no crime, has..." I made a rapid estimate in my mind of all the deputies I had seen since I'd arrived the day before. "I figure I've seen ten of you so far. How come you need ten deputies?"

Again the flick of his eyes. His partner stared straight ahead. "Why don't you mind your own business, Mr. Walker? We'll ask the questions when we get back to town."

We pulled up in front of the sheriff's office at the back of the town hall on 2nd Avenue. I could see lights on in the jailhouse next door. I figured that was where I was going to spend the night. The deputies climbed down, wrenched open the back door and hauled me out, with their two pals keeping their weapons trained on me from a safe distance. They dragged me across the sidewalk and shoved me through the door into the office. Deputy Hank was sitting at his desk. His nose was badly swollen and blue and he had cotton wool shoved up each nostril. He also had a big, purple bruise on his jaw. When he saw me, he smiled. It wasn't a pretty sight. When he spoke, he sounded like he had a bad cold.

"Amb I glad to see you, Bister Walker!"

I smiled back. "Where's Ned?"

"Doc's seeing to him. You hurt him bad."

The deputy who had my arm asked, "Should we book him, Sheriff?"

"Do. Just take him next door." He stood. "He's so keen to see Noah, let's introduce them."

There was some chuckling. Hank put his hat on and led the way. They dragged me out onto the sidewalk. The streets were empty, chill and quiet under the vast spray of stars. Hank unlocked the door and they dragged me through into a small office with a wooden floor, two unoccupied desks and a steel door in the rear wall. Hank unlocked this door too and we followed him through it into a narrow, dimly lit corridor that led to a flight of stone stairs that descended to what I figured were the cells below.

He went down at a trot ahead of us. The stairwell was narrow and I got the impression the place was old, older than the building above it, the remnants of some earlier, more basic construction. It was too narrow for two men to walk abreast, so the deputy who had my arm fell behind me, and after a second, I heard the click of a weapon being cocked.

"Don't do nothing smart," he said.

I sighed and continued down to where the stairwell opened out into a dimly lit space with a stone-flagged floor, maybe eighteen or twenty feet long by ten or twelve feet across. Flanking the floor there were five cells, two on either side and one at the end. The doors were old-fashioned steel bars, but the lights within each cell were turned off, and the dull light from the single bulb did not penetrate past the doors. Hank had stopped and turned to face me, with his thumbs in his belt. He was sneering, but with the cotton wool in his nose, it made him look like a caricature of himself.

"Well, Bister Walker, I guess you finally got your wish. Meet Noah. Oben it up, Bill."

This last he said over his shoulder, and one of his boys, a tall, rangy redhead with freckles, unlocked the nearest door on the left, uncuffed me and shoved me in, as somebody else snapped on the strip light in the cell.

Noah was there. His face was badly swollen and purple. His tongue protruded and filled his whole mouth. It hadn't been long since they'd hanged him, because his feet were still twitching occasionally as he swung gently left to right.

I thought of Grace, of the pain and grief that was awaiting her, and turned to face Hank. He was still leering. "Is this supposed to scare me?"

"I don't give a good goddamn if it scares you or not, Bister Walker. Toborrow you stand trial, just like he did, and I wouldn't be surprised if the judge don't pass down the self same sentence. Steeling a vee-hickle, assaulting an officer of the law, attempting to escape arrest—they're all serious offenses in this town, Bister Walker. So if you want my advice, I'd be making peace with your god tonight." He gave a small laugh. "We'll leave Noah in there with ya, so you can meditate on the dransient nature of life."

They all laughed, but I held his eye. As he reached for the door to close and lock it, I said, "Hank. All I wanted to do was get to my meeting this evening. But now I am not going to leave until I have killed you and your deputies, the Mayor and the town council. My advice to you all is, leave town while you still have the chance."

They laughed some more, slammed and locked the door and left. They left the light in my cell on so I could contemplate Noah, and the impermanence of life. I have slept in many strange and uncomfortable places in my life. I've slept in battlefields still scattered with the dead from both sides, I have slept in shallow holes, covered in leaves, with the enemy mere yards away, and I have slept in small cells, knowing that within the hour somebody would come to torture me, and always I have been able to sleep. But that night, with Noah suspended from the bars of the cell, and no way to cut him down, knowing that Grace was lying in her bed hoping that maybe next day she would have him back, that night I was unable to sleep.

Morning came after hours that seemed interminable. With no windows to show the dawn, or the changing light, each hour was much like the last, and ground past with a slowness that became almost unendurable. Until suddenly, there was the clang of the steel door upstairs, the tramping of boots descending the narrow, stone stairs to the cells, and then the single bulb hanging outside the cells snapped on.

Deputy Hank appeared with Ned and Bill. He'd removed the cotton wool from his nostrils, but his nose and jaw were still swollen and an ugly eggplant color, and when he spoke, he still sounded like he had flu.

"Pud your hads through the bars."

I did as he said and he cuffed me. Bill unlocked the door and he and Ned covered me with their weapons as I stepped out. Hank grabbed me by the scruff of my neck and shoved me toward the stairs. For a moment, I considered breaking his neck, but the risk of getting shot was high and also, I realized, I was curious to see what the trial was all about. I wanted to see Mayor Freeman and his council, and see how they operated.

Hank snarled, "Run and I swear I'll shoot you dead," and I climbed the stairs ahead of them, through the small office and out to the sidewalk. There, two more deputies covered me with their weapons and I was shoved in the back of an SUV, with an armed guard on either side of me.

We went in convoy, a truck in front and a truck behind with the SUV in the middle, down 2nd Avenue. The journey took less than a minute. We turned into a large square with a fountain at the center, administrative buildings on either side and the courthouse at the far end. It was small but elegant, made of granite, with a flight of nine steps and four handsome columns supporting a gabled portico, beyond which there was a dome that was worthy of a much larger building. Outside, the stars and stripes hung beside Freedom's own flag, depicting a green ash tree on a white background.

We pulled up in the parking lot. A small group of people had gathered on the steps to watch us. Among them was a photographer who began to snap photos as we climbed out, and as we ascended the steps, I noticed beside the photographer a woman with a microphone. She shouted to me as I passed, "Will you plead guilty, Mr. Walker? How do you feel about what you've done?"

I stared at her a moment, but passed without answering. We entered into a large, high-ceilinged hall with a stone floor bearing a mosaic with the same emblem as the flag outside, a green ash on a white background. We crossed the hall toward a set of tall, mahogany doors where two men in uniform stood guard. As we approached, they opened them and we stepped through into the courtroom. The doors closed behind us.

It was not what I had expected. At a glance, it looked like any county courtroom you might find in any county seat, but a closer look showed several irregularities—leaving aside the fact that Freedom was not a county seat. The bench was about three feet higher than you would normally expect, and emblazoned on the front there was, once again, the image of the green ash tree on a white background. And behind the bench there was not one seat for the judge, but three, with the center one raised a little higher than the other two.

The jury box, which was set on the left hand side as we entered, had only six seats. There were tables for the prosecution and the defense, set opposite the bench, but there was no public gallery. These trials were not open to public scrutiny.

I was also aware that I had not been offered any legal representation. That didn't really surprise me all that much, but it did seem to be part of a pattern—a pattern that was growing larger and more complex the deeper I sank into this mess. Like I said, this was Waco, but on steroids.

I was led down the central aisle to the defense table, where I was made to sit. Hank sat on my right and one of his deputies sat on my left. A moment later, a door opened at the far end of what I had taken to be the jury box and three men and three women filed in and took their seats. They all stared at me without expression, but the hostility was palpable. A woman I figured was the court recorder took her place before the bench. I turned to Hank.

"This is nuts. Do you seriously think you can get away with it?"

He didn't look at me. "Shut up."

The doors through which we'd come in opened behind me and I turned to look. A guy in a dark suit had stepped in, accompanied by a glamorous woman in a well cut blue skirt and jacket and a white blouse. She was carrying a file and a couple of thick books. He strode down the aisle and she tottered after him. They nodded at Hank and the man said, "Sheriff."

He nodded back. "Counselor Grumman." Then he turned to me and smiled unpleasantly. "That's the prosecutor."

I watched them sit, open the file and exchange a few words in each other's ears.

"What about the defense?"

The question was more in irony than any hope of an answer, but he snorted and said, "You defend yourself. You committed the crime, you can see to your own defense."

Up behind the bench, a court official appeared and bellowed, "All rise for his Honor Judge John Freeman!"

Everybody stood and Hank dragged me to my feet by the scruff of my neck. The court official went on.

"Presiding with His Honor, John Freeman, His Honor Gabriel Heinemann and His Honor Michael Hagan! All rise!"

He stepped smartly back and pulled open a door in the rear wall. Through it entered three men in black robes. The first of the three I took to be John Freeman, the mayor of the town. He was easily in his sixties, six-four and slim, with big shoulders and big hands. He had long, white hair brushed back, and a powerful jaw with a well-trimmed white beard. It struck me that he looked vaguely familiar, but I dismissed the thought. He moved to the central chair and sat. He glanced at me, but displayed no reaction.

Behind him was a dark-haired man in his forties, with olive skin and very black eyebrows. He sat on Freeman's right. The next man was as tall as the mayor, with red hair turning white, very pale skin and a big barrel chest. He sat on Freeman's left and the court official came down a short flight of steps to stand in front of the bench, facing the court.

"In the matter of Lacklan Walker versus the free town of Freedom, Counselor Jeremiah Grumman prosecuting for the town."

Freeman was making notes and spoke as he wrote.

"Take the plea."

The official looked at me and said, "Are you Lacklan Walker, of Weston, Massachusetts?"

I nodded. "Yeah."

"You stand before this court accused of assaulting two officers of the law, of stealing an automobile and of aiding and abetting a known criminal. How do you plead?"

I looked up at Freeman and addressed him. "I don't recognize the authority of this court and I don't recognize these clowns as officers of the law. This whole damned set up is illegal in the United States."

The three of them watched me till I'd finished, then Freeman said, "How do you plead?"

"Screw you."

Heinemann leaned over and muttered something to Freeman, who nodded and glanced down at the recorder. "Enter a plea of not guilty." He turned to the jury. "Honorable members of the Council, you are witness to the fact that the accused has not pleaded guilty, and by the laws of Freedom, he is therefore presumed innocent until proven otherwise in this court of law." He turned to Grumman. "Counselor, make your case."

Grumman stood. "Thank you, Your Honor. It is the case for the prosecution that the accused, Lacklan Walker, entered the town of Freedom two days ago at the behest of one Noah Hirsch, the convicted felon and late teacher at Freedom School. It is our contention, Your Honor, that Hirsch knew himself to be in trouble with the law and requested that Mr. Walker, a former captain with the British special forces and a known soldier of fortune, come to assist him to get away and evade justice. Walker duly arrived in a vehicle especially adapted for covert escapes, with a totally silent engine, and on the pretext of his vehicle having run out of charge, he settled himself at the Freedom Hotel. However, he arrived too late to help Hirsch escape as, at the time of their appointed rendezvous at the Freedom restaurant, Sheriff Hank West and his deputies swooped on Hirsch and arrested him, while Walker looked on, helpless to intervene.

"Proof of Walker's intentions lies in the fact that shortly after Hirsch's arrest, Walker presented himself at the Sheriff's office and demanded, with threats of physical violence, that Hirsch be released to him. The prosecution will call witnesses that will testify to the fact that it was the accused's intention to leave Freedom and return with reinforcements for the purpose of breaking Noah Hirsch out of jail, and destroying this town, its system of government and its way of life in the process. We shall further show that Noah Hirsch's fiancée, Grace O'Conor, conspired with Walker in his plans.

"Your Honor, Sheriff Hank West, upon becoming suspicious that the accused was in town to help Noah Hirsch escape, arranged with Jonah McAllen, who runs the gas station and the garage, to disable Mr. Walker's car so that he could not make his escape with Hirsch.

"Last night, seeing himself trapped in town by the sheriff's skill and cunning, Walker, in desperation, attempted to steal Jerry Wilkins', of Mulberry Road, Ford Focus, having first broken into his house to steal the keys to that vehicle. Thanks to our exceptional CCTV system in this town, the sheriff and his deputies were able to watch Walker in his theft and descend upon him as he was attempting to enter the car. It was then that Walker assaulted the sheriff, breaking his nose and causing him extensive bruising, as you can see for yourself, and also cracked Deputy Erickson's skull. Deputy Erickson is still in hospital, but copies of the medical reports on both of these injuries have been filed with the court.

"Walker then seized the Ford Focus and attempted to flee Freedom. He was pursued by four deputies who managed to stop him on the road to La Barge. The prosecution is confident, Your Honor, that the evidence adduced and the witnesses called will prove beyond any doubt that the accused is guilty of these heinous crimes, and we would call for the maximum penalty available to the court, that the accused be sentenced to hang by the neck until he is dead. Thank you, Your Honor."

EIGHT

Everybody was looking at me. I felt like I had just farted at the Mad Hatter's tea party in Wonderland. Freeman spoke suddenly.

"Mr. Walker, what have you to say in your defense? Stand when addressing the court."

I stared at him a moment, then stood.

"Are you kidding me? This is not a court of law. This is ritualized murder. You murdered Noah Hirsch and now you are conspiring to murder me. Just because you put a uniform on this ape and call him sheriff does not make him an officer of the law. And just because you dress yourselves up in black robes, and these clowns call you your honor, that does not make you a judge. What you are is a murdering thug. But let me tell you something, Freeman, you try to kill me the way you killed Hirsch, and I will defend myself."

"Is that your defense, Mr. Walker?"

I smiled at him. "No, it's a warning. My defense will come later."

Heinemann and Hagan muttered and Freeman said: "Let the record show that the defendant has declined to make an opening statement in his own defense. Mr. Grumman, you may call your witnesses."

I sat and Grumman rose. "I call Mary-Sue Freeman as my first witness, Your Honor."

A court official opened a door in the far right wall and Missy came in, dressed in her Sunday best. She glanced at me but rapidly averted her eyes and went to stand by the witness box. Freeman looked down at her and spoke softly.

"Are you Mary-Sue Freeman, of the city of Freedom?"

I expostulated, "For crying out loud! She's your wife!"

"Be silent, Walker!"

Hank turned to me. "Keep your mouth shut!"

Missy said, "Yes, Your Honor, I am Mary-Sue Freeman, of Freedom."

"Mary-Sue, do you swear, by Almighty God, his disciples and his prophets, to tell the truth as you understand it to be, in good conscience, and nothing but that truth?"

"I do swear, Your Honor."

"Be seated." He glanced at Grumman. "Go ahead, Counselor."

Grumman crossed the floor with an ingratiating smile. "Missy—may I call you Missy?"

"Everybody does, Mr. Grumman. You included!"

They exchanged a laugh and he went on. "Do you recognize the accused, Missy?"

"I do, Mr. Grumman. He was a guest at my hotel, and yesterday he had lunch at my restaurant and spoke to me about his intentions regarding Noah."

"And what did he say his intentions were?"

I thought about standing up and protesting hearsay, but I knew there was no point and my time would be better used planning how I was going to get out of this madhouse and call the Highway Patrol and the Feds.

Missy was saying: "At first, when he first arrived, I thought he was pleasant enough, but after Noah was arrested, I noticed he seemed to change. He took an unnatural interest in it and started telling me he intended to bust Noah out of jail and..." She made inverted comma signs with her fingers. "'Bring down' the Council and the Mayor. He told me he had friends back east who could help him do that."

"Did he tell you who those friends were?"

"No, but I got the impression they were adventurers and ex military types, mercenaries, you know the sort, who would do anything for money."

"Can you remember his exact words, Missy?"

She looked down at her hands in her lap. "Not all of 'em, but I remember when I told him he shouldn't put his cigarette butts out on the sidewalk, he said he'd like to see Sheriff Hank try to arrest him. Then he told me he wanted a beer, and I quote, 'as cold as a two dollar whore's heart'. After that, he said if I didn't tell him about Noah and Grace, he was gonna go and gut the sheriff and lynch him with his own intestines."

There was a murmur of horror that rippled around the courtroom. I turned and gave Hank the dead eye. Freeman banged his gavel and called for order. When silence had fallen again, Grumman said, "Missy, I have just one more question for you. Did you have the impression that the accused, Mr. Walker, was speaking metaphorically, or did he mean what he said?"

She shook her head. "Oh no. He definitely meant what he said."

If it had been a real court of law, there would have been lawyers screaming objections from the rooftops. But it wasn't, there weren't and I didn't care. She was right. I had meant it and I meant it now more than ever. Grumman turned to face me. "I have no further questions for this witness at this time. Mr. Walker, your witness."

I stood and showed my cuffed hands to the judge. "I get to question the witness with my hands cuffed?"

He raised an eyebrow and smiled. "It is your wrists that are cuffed, Mr. Walker, not your tongue. If you have questions, ask them."

I looked at Missy. She wouldn't meet my eye. "Missy, what were we doing when I said those things to you?"

She frowned and shrugged. "I don't know what you mean."

"It's a simple question. What were we doing? Isn't it true that we were sitting at a table having lunch together in your restaurant?"

"Yes..."

"But that wasn't where the conversation started, was it?"

"What do you mean?"

"You having trouble understanding plain English, Missy? Isn't it true that the conversation started at the bar, when I asked for a beer as cold as a two dollar whore's heart?"

"Yes..."

"And I asked you to tell me about Noah and Grace?"

"Yes..."

"And then we went into the kitchen while you cooked us lunch?"

Her eyes said she was sensing a trap, but she said, "...yes..."

"Because you wanted to tell me the real reason Noah had been arrested while you cooked."

Her face went pale. "No!"

"And the real reason was that this creep," I pointed at Freeman, "wanted Grace for himself so he needed Noah out of the way. Isn't that true?"

"No!"

"Then maybe you can explain to your judge and husband how I happen to know that."

There was real terror in her eyes now and she sat forward. "*No!*"

Freeman was very silent, watching Missy. I snapped, "No, don't bother. Just answer me this instead. When you told me that the Council would kill you if they knew we were having that conversation, were you speaking metaphorically or did you mean it!"

"*You're making this up! It never happened!*"

"Then perhaps you'd like to explain to the court what we *did* talk about in a conversation that went from the bar to the kitchen while you cooked, and then continued while we ate at the same table in the restaurant."

"It's a lie! *It's lie!*"

"My final questions, Missy. You told me that the Mayor considers you too old to perform your conjugal duties, so he put you out to pasture with the hotel and the restaurant while he went after younger women. Part of that settlement is the guaranteed custom of the workers who get bussed in every day for lunch. So here are my questions: where do they work, and what do they do?"

She stared at me open mouthed. The silence lasted only a couple of seconds, but seemed to go on for a long time. Then Grumman stood. "I object, your honor. The accused's line of questioning is irrelevant."

Heinemann and Hagan muttered and nodded. Freeman stared at Missy a moment longer. She turned and stared back. He blinked, then turned to me. "You will withdraw the question, Mr. Walker."

I sighed and dropped into my chair. "Screw you. Get this charade over with."

He grunted. "The witness is excused. Mr. Grumman, call your next witness."

"I call Sheriff Hank West, Your Honor."

Hank, sitting next to me, stood and walked to the witness box, where he was sworn in and sat in the chair Missy had occupied moments before. Grumman approached him, pursing his lips and studying the toes of his shiny shoes.

"Sheriff, would you please relate for us the events of last night, starting from the point where you and your deputies noticed the accused leaving his hotel at close to midnight."

He recounted how they had seen me, by means of the CCTV cameras they had installed out of sight throughout the town, approach Jerry Wilkins' Ford Focus on Mulberry Road, how I had examined the car and then entered his house. At that point, they had hastened to the address to prevent me from committing some heinous crime, but as they had arrived, I had been exiting the house and had attempted to enter the car. He then described how by use of trickery and lies, I had managed to overpower them and beat them senseless. When he had finished his narrative, Grumman turned to the jurors.

"Members of the Council, it is your duty to decide upon the matters of fact in this case, and I would pause at this point in the proceedings and ask you, whatever you may have heard before, can the word of our own sheriff be in doubt against the word of a supposed American who sold his loyalty to the British crown and has since become a mercenary and an adventurer?" Then he turned to me. "Your witness, Mr. Walker."

I didn't stand. I leaned back in my chair. "Where do those people who get bussed in and out every day work? And what do they do? What racket have you got going?"

Freeman glared at me. "That question has already been ruled irrelevant!"

"Irrelevant? You know as well as I do, Freeman, that it is the very reason I am here in this courtroom. And it's the reason you plan to kill me. It's at the heart of this whole damned charade and you know it."

"Be *silent*, Mr. Walker! The witness is excused."

Hank stood and returned to the table, grinning at me. Grumman said, "Your Honor, the prosecution's last witness is Grace O'Conor."

I felt a knot twist in my gut as the door opened and she was brought in. That knot turned to a cold rage as I saw the condition she was in. Her face was swollen and bruised, her wrists were cuffed behind her back and she had her ankles chained. I watched her led to the witness box and saw

Freeman turn to look at Hank. He looked like a man whose Ming vase has been damaged.

"Was this necessary, Sheriff?"

Hank gave his head a small twitch. "She was out of control, Your Honor, threatening to tear our eyes out. She had to be restrained and that weren't easy."

Freeman turned back to Grace. His tone was that of a kind teacher. "Grace, I hope this has been a salutary lesson to you, to respect authority and abide by the rules passed down by your betters."

She nodded once. "Yes, Your Honor."

"Do you understand why you are here?"

"Yes, Your Honor."

"Now, Grace, in the full understanding of where you are and why you are here, do you swear, by Almighty God, his disciples and his prophets, to tell the truth as you understand it to be, in good conscience, and nothing but that truth?"

"Yes, Your Honor, I do swear."

"Be seated."

She sat and I saw her lower lip curl in and she started to sob, silently. Grumman stood and crossed the floor to stand in front of her.

"Grace, I am pretty sure there are lots of questions that the Council here would love to ask you. I know there are a few I'd like to ask you myself, like what induced you to get engaged to a man who spread the word of Satan, and wanted to teach *our children* the ways of the Devil. But we are going to save those questions for your trial, tomorrow. But I want you to be aware, Grace, that what you say and do here today will greatly influence the Council's view of you, and the sincerity of your repentance, when you do come to trial. Do you understand that?"

"Yes, Mr. Grumman."

"Good, now, take a good look at the accused and you tell me if you recognize that man."

She looked at me and her face was twisted with grief and with pain. Her cheeks shone with tears. I scowled at Freeman and snarled, "For God's sake, Freeman! Let the girl go! All she wanted was to know if her fiancé was safe!"

He hammered his gavel and shouted, "*Be silent!*"

I stood and bellowed at him. "*For crying out loud! You're going to kill me anyway! Why does she have to suffer any more?*"

"*Silence!*"

Hank stood and smashed his fist into the small of my back. "*Siddown!*"

The pain was intense, but I swallowed it and snarled at him, then I sat. Freeman pointed at me. "One more outburst and I will have you taken down to the cells, Mr. Walker..."

His meaning was clear, and there was nothing to be achieved by getting my bones broken. The court went silent. Grumman gave me a look that said he'd be in the front row at my lynching and turned back to Grace. "Grace, do you recognize the accused?"

She looked at me and I gave her a small nod and a smile that said it was OK. Her voice was almost inaudible.

"Yes."

"When did you meet him?"

"Yesterday, in the town square, while the workers were going for lunch to the restaurant."

"What did you talk about?"

"About Noah."

"Now think very carefully, Grace. Think what is at stake here. What, exactly, did you discuss in regards to Noah?"

She closed her eyes and took a shaky breath. "His teaching methods, the fact that the Council were not happy with him. I was worried because he had been arrested. I knew Mr. Walker had witnessed the arrest and spoken to the sheriff. I wanted to know if he had any news."

"Is it true, Grace, that when you introduced yourself to him, the accused already knew who you were?"

She met my eye and her face was a mask of grief and self-recrimination. I remembered asking her if she was Noah's sister or his fiancée. She had told them that and they had twisted it. I gave her a small smile of encouragement and she said, "Yes."

"And what did the accused say his intentions were with regard to Noah Hirsch? Is it true that he intended to get him out of the jail?"

Again I gave her a small smile of encouragement and a small nod. She closed her eyes. "Yes."

Grumman turned to me and offered me the kind of smile a snake offers a mouse just before it swallows it whole. "No further questions, Your Honor. Your witness, Mr. Walker."

I stood. "Grace, did you often discuss Noah's educational philosophy with him?"

"Yes, all the time."

"And is it true that you advised him repeatedly that it was unwise and a bad mistake for him to pursue that philosophy?"

There was gratitude, and a little bit of irony in her eyes when she answered. "Yes, that is true."

"But he persisted, in spite of your advice?"

"Yes."

"One more question, Grace. When I approached you in the square yesterday..."

Grumman was on his feet. "Objection! The witness has stated in interrogation that it was she who approached the accused!"

I cut in fast. "Your Honor, the witness gave that version of events because I had threatened to do harm to her and her family if she told the truth about what happened. It was I who approached her."

Freeman frowned at her. "Is this true, Grace?"

She hesitated, eyeing me. I snapped, "Tell the truth, Grace. You are under oath!"

"Yes, that is true," she said.

"Now, when I approached you, is it not true that you told me that Freedom had its own rules and its own laws, that Noah had fallen foul of those laws and that I should leave and not interfere with the workings of the town?"

She nodded. Her voice was choked and she could barely talk for sobbing. "Yes, that is true."

Grumman was on his feet again. "Your Honor, the accused is leading the witness..."

But Freeman was happy to have this witness led. He cut Grumman short and addressed me.

"Explain yourself, Mr. Walker. Why are you incriminating yourself like this?"

"Because my fate is sealed. You have proven me guilty and I must take my punishment. But this child has done nothing wrong, even by your crazy laws. The prosecution are trying to frame her and she doesn't deserve it. I used her and I threatened her, but I happen to know that she was opposed to what Noah was doing, in spite of the fact that she loved him, and was trying to set him on what she considered to be the right path. The kid is innocent. She had no part of what me and Noah were doing."

He raised an eyebrow at me. "Do I understand, then, that you are changing your plea to guilty?"

"Yes. Let's get this damn charade over and done with."

Grumman spoke again. "Your Honor, as we now have a guilty plea, I move that the Council proceed to sentence."

Freeman conferred a moment with Heinemann and Hagan, then turned to the Council. "Members of the Council. The accused has, of his own free will, entered a plea of guilty, having originally entered a plea of not guilty. You have heard the evidence against him and you have heard his defense. Have you reached a decision on sentence?"

A woman with gray hair, a white frilly blouse and a mouth like a slash from a razorblade, spoke for the other five. "We have."

"And what sentence have you decided upon?"

"Death by hanging."

"Very well, the court so rules. Mr. Walker, this court has found you guilty on all counts and sentences you to be taken immediately to a place of execution and hung from the neck until you are dead."

NINE

GRACE SCREAMED AND FELL ON HER KNEES, sobbing. Hank and one of his deputies seized my arms and dragged me to my feet. Freeman stood and looked down at me like Jehovah scowling down at Adam.

"May God have mercy on your soul!"

I didn't resist. I knew right then, it would accomplish nothing. But I met Freeman's eye and snarled at him. "Yeah, put in a word for me, John. You'll be meeting Him before I do."

"Take him away. We shall foregather in the cells for execution of the sentence."

They dragged me across the courtroom, with Grace screaming behind me, across the main hall of the courthouse and out into the sun. There was something surreal about the sunny day, where life was proceeding in its mundane, banal way, while I was being dragged away to be killed. A few passers-by glanced over at me as I was bundled into the back of the SUV, and Hank and his deputies climbed into their trucks. Ned got in the driver's seat and Bill climbed in beside him on the passenger's side. We reversed and pulled out of the lot like we were in a hurry, and I tried to focus my mind. I figured I had maybe half an hour, if I was lucky. My wrists were cuffed in front of me, which was an advantage, but I was not going to get many opportunities between now and when they hung me from the ceiling of the cell.

We would arrive, I'd be bundled through the front office and down the narrow stairs. The guests would arrive and I would be lynched. I couldn't see any windows of opportunity coming up. One thing was clear, though. If I waited till we were in the cells, they would be at their strongest in numbers, and I would have at least one steel door to get through. Once inside, any attempt at escape could turn very quickly into a protracted battle of attrition, a battle I would almost certainly lose.

If I was going to act, it had to be now.

I didn't make any sudden movements. I just leaned forward like I was going to say something to Ned. Instead, I smashed the middle knuckle of my right fist into Bill's left temple. My wrists were cuffed, so it was a double-handed blow. That gave it extra strength, but it made it less accurate, too. It was meant to be a death blow; instead, it stunned him badly and he leaned over to the side, groaning and holding his head. Ned yelled, "What the—?"

But by then, I had looped my cuffs over his head and around his bull neck, planted my feet against the back of his seat and I was heaving back with all my strength. The car swerved violently. I could see his cheek turning purple and his hands were flapping. Then he was clawing at the chain that bit into his neck, ripping at his skin with his nails. His legs began to flail. We swerved violently again and the truck behind us screeched and smashed into our trunk. The impact made me lurch back and I felt something give under the cuffs.

The truck in front had braked hard on seeing the chaos behind them and now we were driven into its trunk. There was a horrible sound of screaming, rending steel and Ned was hurled through the windshield in a shower of shattered glass. I was rammed against the back of the driver's seat and then the SUV was slewing sideways. It teetered and rolled on its side.

I lay still for a second, maybe two, stunned but telling myself I had to react. I had to move. I struggled into a kneeling position. Outside, I could hear voices shouting. I reached around the front of the driver's seat and unhooked my cuffs from what was left of Ned's throat. He'd been practically decapitated and there was blood and gore all over my hands. I wiped them on his shirt, twisted around and reached down between the seats, into his pocket for his keys. It was hard, and an awkward position, and outside, I could hear the shouting coming closer. My fingers touched the keys. I fumbled them out and managed to fit one into the cuffs, one side, then the other. The cuffs dropped away and I pulled his .38 revolver from his holster just as a deputy looked down at me through the passenger side window.

I shot him through the eye. He staggered back and disappeared from sight. I didn't hang around to find out what happened next. I rolled into the back of the SUV, kicked out the rear window, a couple of feet from the buckled hood of Hank's Ford pickup, and clambered underneath that vehicle as several guns suddenly erupted and the SUV was riddled with bullets. I crawled on my belly to the back of the Ford, scrambled to my feet and peered around in the general direction of the SUV. I saw Hank and four of his deputies approaching the wrecked, riddled vehicle with slow steps and their weapons held out in front of them. They thought I was still in there, looking like a bleeding colander.

I turned and looked back the way we'd come. Five cars had stopped and I could see gaping faces behind the windshields. I figured the nearest was forty or fifty feet away. It was a VW sedan. Behind it was a Dodge truck.

I leaned around the Ford, took aim at the nearest deputy, who was just coming up to the overturned SUV, and put a .38 slug in the back of his head. I didn't wait to see the result. I sprinted toward the VW with the .38 held out in front of me, trained on the driver. All the way I screamed, "*Get out of the car! Get out of the damned car! Now!*"

I knew that behind me, Hank and the deputies had dived for cover and I had about four seconds to reach the sedan and get the hell out of there. I used almost three of those seconds arriving at the car. By then, the woman driving it was out and backing away with both her hands held out in front of her, saying, "Don't shoot me! Please don't shoot me."

I snarled, "Get the hell out of here!"

By the time I'd climbed in and put it in drive, Hank and his three remaining deputies were running at me with their weapons drawn. I floored the gas, driving straight at Hank. When I was ten feet away, I slammed on the brakes and spun the wheel hard left. The car fishtailed and the trunk slammed into one of the deputies and knocked him sprawling across the blacktop. Then I hit the gas again and accelerated away with a hail of bullets chasing me down 2nd Avenue.

I drove crazily, with no direction, taking practically every corner I came to regardless of where it led. Often I went in circles, or turned back on myself, but steadily I moved toward the northern end of Main Street, where it led out into the wooded hills above Freedom. This was the direction I had seen the coaches take. If Hank and Freeman thought I was on the run, they had another think coming. The golden rule in any form of combat is that the best defense is a good attack. And my gut was telling me that the farm, or whatever it was, where the people on those coaches were employed, was Freeman and his Council's Achilles' heel. I meant to find out what it was all about, and what they did there, and when I had found out that, I planned to destroy them all.

I slowed at the intersection of Cherry Blossom Lane and Main Street, turned north and accelerated away out of town. I hadn't heard any sirens behind me and I figured Hank and his men were regrouping, tending to the injured and licking their wounds. They'd be after me soon enough, and their knowledge of the territory would give them an edge, but for now I had a short breathing space.

Pretty soon, I had left the town behind me and was climbing fast up a snaking road with thick pine forests towering over me, making a shaded green tunnel of the blacktop; a tunnel whose wooded walls sped past with no turnings to left or right. As I drove, I thought. The coaches had come this way. They would not have been able to turn left or right either, therefore logically I was still on the right track.

I eventually broke out of the cool, green tunnel into

bright, glaring daylight. Now, gentle hills and highland plains spread out to right and left, with scraggy lines of trees forming a distant, broken patchwork. And then I saw the road—a twisting, broad dirt track that wound through low hills to a tall white wall with a gate. I slowed as I approached the intersection where the track started, came to a halt and looked around for somewhere to dump the car and lay low until the initial hunt had died down.

There was nothing. Everything I could see was open and exposed. So, with my heart beating fast and hard, I turned the car around and sped back the way I had come, toward the forest. The tunnel of trees was now a black maw in a wall of woodland, yawning open as I approached. I hit a hundred before I started to brake, expecting at every moment to see the deputies' trucks come hurtling toward me.

The tires complained and the car slewed sideways as I slowed to fifty, thirty, then twenty, then eased off the road, crawling my way in among the trees toward an area of dense undergrowth, bushes and ferns. When I was certain it was hidden from the road, I made my way back to the roadside and lay concealed, looking and listening for any sign of the chase. There was nothing to see and nothing to be heard, so I sprinted across the blacktop and plunged into the deep tree cover on the far side.

I picked my way through the woods, heading steadily east toward the wall I had seen from the road. The forest was dense, mainly towering pines creating a thick, whispering canopy thirty feet above my head. Limpid green light filtered through, but the deeper I went into the woods, the more difficult it was for that light to penetrate, and the shade that lingered among the trunks, bushes, saplings and dense ferns became eventually a heavy twilight of gloom. I have a pretty good internal compass, but it wasn't long before I had lost my bearings and was unsure whether I was heading east, southeast or northeast—or worse, just walking in circles. I told myself that if I kept left of downhill, I'd be going in roughly the right direction. But even that wasn't so easy with the uneven terrain, the density of the trees and the vast areas of ferns that grew among them.

After twenty minutes, maybe half an hour, however, the trees began to thin out and the ground began to level off, gently but steadily. Soon I was able to break into a rifleman's march, walking five steps and running five steps, all the time seeking a path that was slightly to the left of the slope—or, as I hoped, slightly north of east.

Finally, the trees gave way to clearings and open ground. The massive trunks were increasingly replaced by young saplings, small bushes I could not identify, and broad areas of rough grass and shrubs. And in the distance, perhaps half a mile away, set in a broad, shallow valley, I saw the farm—or as I had begun to think of it, the Farm.

It was vast. It was hard to estimate the size because it seemed to be spread across several square miles, but there was no doubt in my mind that it covered many thousands of acres. Not too far away, I could see a perimeter fence that ran roughly east to west and was lost to view in the distance. It didn't look too challenging: about seven feet high and made mainly of wire mesh affixed to metal poles set into the ground. I figured it was probably electrified. Beyond it, not far from where I was hunkered down, I could see cattle grazing, but they seemed to keep their distance from the wire.

Farther up the slope, going back in the direction of the

road, I could make out acres of neat, regimented green-houses glinting in the sun. Some were comparatively low, no more than eight or ten feet in height, but others were more than double that.

All the land I could see along the outside of the fence was exposed, which made an approach risky. I couldn't see any people, but that didn't mean they weren't there. How many, and how well armed, was a moot point. I didn't even know what the hell they were doing in there. I just had a strong hunch it was bad, and involved the exploitation of the people of Freedom.

I smiled without humor at the name. Orwell would have enjoyed it.

I lay in the cover of the bushes, observing the farm, and took stock of my situation. I was on the run and being hunted by an indeterminate number of men. As far as my arsenal was concerned, I had one .38 with four rounds left in it. My knife and my Sig were back at the jailhouse. I had nothing in the way of equipment and no visible means of getting into the Farm.

I withdrew a couple of hundred feet back toward the woods, where the tree cover was thicker, and there were low bushes and ferns to hide among. There I settled with my back against a tree and began to think.

My obvious course of action was to wait till nightfall and make my way on foot to La Barge, which as the crow flies was about seven or eight miles east, if my reckoning was right. There I could call for help, and get on with the task in hand of meeting with Phil and Cyndi.

But there was a major problem with that plan, and that was Grace. Grace went on trial the next day and her life was in serious jeopardy. I had a hunch Freeman was keen to save her and keep her for himself, but it wasn't a hunch I was ready or willing to gamble on. Besides, being saved by Freeman could well wind up being a fate worse than execution. So I had to get back to Freedom before he and the Council passed sentence on her. But before I did that, I needed to find out what was going down at the Farm, because that information might just give me the means to bring down this bunch of lunatics.

So, the bottom line was, I needed to break into the Farm, find out what the hell was going on in there, then get back to the village, find out where Grace was, bust her out and head back to Weston with her. That was the plan.

And along the way, I'd have a little chat with Hank and Freeman. All the gods in Freeman's heaven were not going to save him from that.

So my first question was, how? How was I going to get in? One thing was clear—I would have to wait till it was dark. So I would use the hours between now and nightfall to reconnoiter the fence and the wall at the front. The simplest point of entry, given my lack of equipment, might after all be the main gate.

TEN

I HAD SPENT THE AFTERNOON EXAMINING THE perimeter fence from the cover of the trees. Sometimes I'd had to break cover and crawl on my belly to the crest of a hill in order to get a better, closer look. But by dusk, as visibility was failing, it had become clear to me that not only my best point of entry, but my only point of entry, was going to be the front wall, and probably the main gate.

There was not much security. I figured that the last thing Freeman and his Council had ever expected was a pain in the ass like me to come snooping around. That having escaped from execution, that pain in the ass would then actually try to break into the ranch seemed not to have crossed their minds at all. They had a couple of guys with rifles at the gate, what looked like a CCTV camera and that was about it.

I had also seen that just to the left of the main gate, on the inside of the perimeter wall, there was a large area where I could see five coaches parked and, about three hundred yards east of that, there was a large, sprawling house. The house was accessed by a gravel driveway that wound through lawns and gardens dotted with ponds, weeping willows and rose gardens. At the back and to the side of the house, there were stables, a pool and tennis courts—all the necessary trappings of a charismatic prophet of the Lord. The question it brought to my mind was, where was the money coming from to pay for all this luxury? One thing was certain: it wasn't beef or barley.

Finally, a few hundred yards from the rear of the house, beyond some wooden corrals, were the huge greenhouses.

The sun had set in a blaze of blood-red and fire-orange across the western horizon, and I was lying on the crest of a small hill, in the cover of some low bushes, running over in my mind how I was going to get through the gate. That was when I saw the column of headlamps winding through the growing dusk, along the dirt road that led to the Farm. There were three of them, and as they drew closer, I was able to make out a Range Rover in the lead, followed by a dark Audi saloon and a Toyota Land Cruiser. They drew up at the gate. The boys with the hunting rifles went to talk to the driver in the lead truck, then stood back and the Range Rover and the Audi filed through and made their way toward the house. The Land Cruiser followed, but turned and parked beside the buses, to the left of the gate. Four men in suits climbed out and by the look of it, they were carrying assault rifles.

Definitely not beef or barley.

I smiled to myself. Entry to the Farm just got a lot more difficult, but my gut feelings about Freeman's operation just got confirmed beyond any doubt.

There were now six guys on the gate, which equated to

four assault rifles and two basic hunting rifles, while I had a noisy revolver with four .38 rounds left. The only real advantage I had was surprise. I'd have to use that to maximum effect, and the odds were I'd die doing it. But what the hell, I told myself, if Freeman's thugs didn't get me, the Camels and the whiskey would, sooner or later.

I chose a path down the hill that would keep me in the deep shadows of the dusk, and avoid creating a silhouette against the skyline. Alternating between crawling and sprinting, I made my way silently down to the perimeter fence where it met the wall that fronted the farm. There, I lay on my belly, pressed up close against the white-washed façade, and crawled, one inch at a time, toward the large gate. The sky shifted from dull gray to deep blue, and dusk turned to dark.

When I was thirty or forty feet away, one of the two original guards stepped out. Limpid, yellow light lay on his back. I could see the glint of his rifle slung over his shoulder. A cigarette glowed red for a moment at his mouth, then went dark. He exhaled and a plume of smoke caught that yellow light from the gate for an instant, then dispersed. He turned his back to me and started to walk slowly away. I crawled a few feet closer. His form was gradually engulfed by the dark.

One thing was clear, these guys were not on red alert, and they were not expecting an imminent attack—from me or from anyone else. That suggested that they were pretty sure I had gotten away. Their worry was, then, as I had thought, that I would come back with the Feds or a team of lawyers in tow. Their worry was *not* that I would come back in the night armed with a .38 revolver and four rounds left in it. Their mistake.

I slid quietly forward. The tread of the invisible boots ahead of me stopped. I saw the glow of his cigarette and heard his boots start to crunch the ground again, growing closer. He came into sight, bathed by the soft glow from the gate. He stopped five or six yards away and stood looking in for a while, smoking.

Inside, I heard the grind of an engine in low gear. There was an exchange of greetings and a moment later, a truck emerged. There was a middle-aged guy with a mustache at the wheel and a couple of girls in the back. There were some goodnights exchanged and the truck drove away toward the road.

The guard watched the tail lights disappear, then turned and looked in through the gate. After a moment, he called, "So, y'all know what this meetin's about?"

There was a murmured reply from within. The guy on patrol dropped his cigarette and trod on it, shaking his head. "That boy's long gone, man, I'm tellin' ya. I heard they tried him, found him guilty and were gonna hang him, but he broke free, stole a car and hightailed it outta here. He weren't gonna hang 'round waitin' to be lynched. That boy's in Cheyenne b'now, if he's got any sense."

There was another murmured reply and the cowboy took his time spitting on the ground. When he spoke, there was a clear edge of menace to his voice.

"Keep your panties on, Boris. I take my orders from Mr. Freeman, not from Mr. Yeltsin."

At that, he turned and kept on walking. He passed within seven feet of where I lay motionless in the shadows. When he was two feet behind me, I rose silently and moved in on him. He never knew he'd died. I smashed the heel of my hand into the base of his skull, where it met his vertebrae. That probably killed him instantly, but for the sake of completeness, I wrapped my arm around his neck, squeezed hard, lifted and gave a twist to the side. I felt his vertebrae crunch and lowered him softly to the ground.

His rifle was no use to me, but he had a Colt .45 semi-automatic, which I took and slipped into my waistband behind my back. I didn't want to use a firearm unless I had to. But I was pretty sure I was going to have to before very long.

I returned to the deeper darkness by the wall and covered the last few feet to the gate in a couple of swift, silent strides. The dull light from inside was laid across the grass just a few inches in front of me. I dropped to my belly, inched forward and peered carefully around the massive gatepost. There was a prefab guards' hut built up against the wall. The door was open and there was a guy in an Italian suit leaning against the jamb, looking in with his back to me, smoking and talking quietly with whoever was inside. A couple of feet from the door, there was a window. Through it, I could just make out a couple of bodies. One was wearing a suit, the other was the dead guy's cowboy buddy.

Two suits in the hut, one live cowboy and one dead cowboy; that left another two suits unaccounted for. My bet was they were patrolling the gardens in front of the house, or the perimeter fence. It was a risk I'd have to take.

I snaked around the gatepost and stood as the guy leaning against the jamb flicked ash and put his cigarette in his mouth. I took a stride and smashed my elbow into the back of his neck at the base of his skull. Like the cowboy outside, he never knew he'd died. As his body dropped, his ghost was probably still leaning on the doorjamb, talking and smoking. The other suit and the cowboy were frowning at his body as I stepped over it and into the confined space. They looked up at me in astonishment.

If you face imminent death often enough, you learn to use all kinds of things as weapons. I took a stride, snatched up a ballpoint pen from the desk, smashed my instep into the cowboy's balls and as the suit watched him double over, I rammed the pen into his windpipe. He wasn't about to alert anybody to my presence. He was too busy clawing at his throat with his nails while Roy Rogers writhed on the floor, clutching what was left of his family jewels.

I drove my fist into the suit's solar plexus. Blood spurted out around the pen and he went down on his knees. I broke his neck with the blade of my hand and stepped past him to Roy Rogers. I rolled him on his back, knelt on his chest and pressed the muzzle of his friend's Colt against his chest.

"I'm only going to ask you once. Where are the other two suits?"

He was really pale. His voice came out as a wheeze. "Patrolling the gardens. Who the hell are you?"

"How many in the house?"

"Freeman, the Russian guy, Peter Kuznetsov and his lieutenant, Joseph Vasiliev, six other guys I don't know. Please, mister, don't kill me. I need a doctor."

"What about Freeman? He must have men with him. Is the sheriff here?"

He shook his head. "Uh-uh... You the guy they're looking for?"

"I need a knife. Do you have a knife?"

He went the color of bread dough and stared at me a moment. "What for...?"

"Not for you. Don't ask questions. Cooperate and you'll live."

"Jacob had a huntin' knife in his drawer, in the desk. Mister, I need a doctor real bad."

"I know." I stood and went to the desk. I opened the top drawer and saw a large, bone-handled hunting knife in a leather sheath. I took it out. The blade was serrated on one side and razor sharp on the other. I looked down at Roy Rogers. His eyes were glazed, he was pale and sweating and his pupils were dilated. He was hemorrhaging badly from his testicles. I knelt beside him, placed my left palm over his eyes and cut through his carotid artery. Death was painless and came in a matter of seconds.

I fixed the knife to my belt and slung the suit's AK-47 over my shoulder. I found the other suit's rifle leaning against the wall and took his magazine. Then I switched off the lights and waited, pressed up beside the door.

It didn't take long. First, I heard a shout of inquiry not far away. It sounded like Russian. I angled my face away from the door and shouted an answer, some inarticulate noises that might have been words. I waited again and heard another shout, irritated, like, 'What the hell are you saying?' Only it sounded more like, '*Shto, short vadni, ty gavarish?*

I put a smile in my voice and shouted again, into the room, half covering my mouth with my hand, "*Com vis mudak!*" which means something like, 'come here, shit head.' It worked.

I heard feet tramping and a second later, a large body stepped through the door. I used the knife like a bayonet. I drove it home into the side of his neck, through the carotid artery and the jugular vein, and out the other side. His body went rigid and he quivered. I left the knife in place, grabbed hold of him around his chest and walked him a couple of steps into the hut, then laid him carefully down on the floor, across his buddies' legs. By the time I pulled out the knife, his heart had stopped pumping and there was very little bleeding. I switched on the light, left it a couple of seconds, switched it off again and swore in Russian, not violently, just like I was annoyed. The performance didn't have to make a lot of sense. It just needed to make the guy outside curious enough to investigate. It did.

Thirty seconds later, he stepped in, speaking loudly in Russian, demanding to know what the hells was going on. He never found out. The bayonet thrust severed his spinal cord just below the base of his skull. He died in utter silence.

I took his and his pal's magazines, switched the lights back on and set off at a gentle jog toward the house. I didn't go in—not yet. Before that, I needed to see what was in those greenhouses.

I kept close to the wall on the right, where it connected with the tall, wire fence, and followed it down for ten minutes at a half run. I covered about a quarter of a mile and left the house and its floodlit gardens behind me. I was in among the series of wooden corrals I had seen from the hill, which I figured were used for bronco breaking, branding and anything that required the isolating of some animal from the herd.

From there, hunkered down and staying in the shadows, I could see a single guy standing on the back steps of the house. It didn't look like any kind of alarm had been triggered yet.

I turned and crawled under the wooden fence of the corral and headed for the nearest of a series of ten huge greenhouses, about seventy yards away. I covered most of the distance at a crouching run, until I was able to slip down the side of the thirty-foot-high glass structure. I saw a door about halfway down—some thirty-five yards away—and sprinted the remaining distance. I turned the handle and stepped in.

It was like stepping into a forest of tropical Christmas trees. It was hot and humid, and there were trees everywhere. Each one was at least twenty feet high, with a trunk five or six inches across. The foliage was dense, with leaves well over a foot in length and diameter. A fine mist was being sprayed intermittently from tubes that crisscrossed the ceiling overhead, emitting a rhythmic hissing sound in short bursts. A stark, white light permeated the vast nave. The smell of boiled cabbage was overpowering.

A network of paths intersected the 'forests' every thirty or thirty-five feet, like long avenues through a dense woodland. Only this was not woodland and these were not trees. They were as big as trees, but they were cannabis plants of a vast size such as I had never seen in my life. They towered above me, weighed down with buds as thick my fist, as long as my forearm, oozing and sticky with white, milky threads. There must have been tons of marijuana in that greenhouse alone. I had no idea how many other greenhouses he had, but I had counted ten that were within my sight. At three thousand bucks a pound, the street value of what he had here must have run into many millions.

It begged two important questions: who was he selling this much weed to, and what the hell was in the smaller greenhouses? I wasn't sure which of the two was the more important.

I took photographs and video footage on my cell phone and stepped outside again. There I waited a while in silence, listening. I couldn't hear anybody, so I ran the fifteen yards to the next row of greenhouses. These were the smaller ones, only about ten feet high, and I had a strong feeling I knew what I was going to find inside. I stepped up and opened the door.

It was dark. There was a faint, sweet, musty smell, and the sound of trickling water. I closed the door behind me and hunkered down. Shielding my cell with my hand, I switched on the torch and by its light, for a count of three seconds, I took in my immediate surroundings, and saw what Freeman was growing there: poppies.

White poppies.

ELEVEN

I SAT A WHILE ON THE FLOOR WITH MY EYES closed, allowing them to adjust to the darkness. After a minute, I opened them to a world of shadows overlaid with darker, amorphous forms. But what was clear, and now easily distinguishable, was the vast, pale glow of the sea of poppies.

I rose and took a walk. It was a plantation the size of an aircraft hangar, complete with a controlled irrigation system and narrow walkways to allow access for whoever was tending the crop. There must have been tens of thousands of them; it was impossible to calculate, but again, the street value once they were converted to opium and heroin was well into the tens of millions. The ranch taken as a whole was capable of generating hundreds of millions of dollars' worth of product.

I came to what I figured was the eastern extreme of the greenhouse. Through the thick, opaque glass panels, I could just make out the dull glow of the moon. Looking back, the far end was lost in shadows. On my left, there were a couple of white, plastic drums and beside them a door. I tried the handle and found it unlocked. So I pushed it open.

It didn't lead to the outside. It lead to a room. It was very dark, and so it was impossible to gauge its size. From what I could see, there were no windows; no light filtered in from outside. I closed the door behind me, hunkered down and switched on the torch on my phone again. Shielding it with my hand, I took in what was immediately around me. There were benches up against the walls, but they didn't hold plants and I dismissed my initial idea of a nursery. The benches seemed to hold electronic equipment, computers, scanners...

I removed my hand and played the beam farther around the room, searching for windows. There weren't any. So I felt on the wall behind me, beside the door, found a switch and flipped it.

The room was some kid of lab. Benches lined all the walls and ran down the center of the room, which was about thirty feet square, maybe ten feet high and painted white. The strip lights on the ceiling gave a stark, dead glow that reflected off the banks of electronic equipment, as well as test tubes and other apparatuses that I associated with chemistry rather than electronics.

I didn't know much about electronics, but I knew absolutely nothing about chemistry, except that it played an important part in turning the sap from white poppies into heroin. I also knew that in recent years, more addictive and more lethal variations had been developed.

I looked for handwritten notes, logs, clipboards—anything that could provide some kind of concrete information about what was going on in this lab, what it was used for. I didn't find anything. I switched on a couple of the computer consoles, but wasn't surprised to find them password protected. I was about to give up when I saw a glass jar which was doubling as a pen holder beside one of the terminals. Sitting in it were a bunch of pens and pencils, some paper clips, an eraser and at the bottom, almost invisible among all the junk, was a pen drive. I shook it out and put it in my pocket.

I came, finally, to the far end of the lab. There I found another door. This one was locked, but the key was in the latch. I unlocked it and stepped inside. The light slanting in from the lab lay angular across the floor, with my shadow distorted at the center. It showed a room twenty or thirty feet long, but only half that width, and lining the walls were cages, to a height of some twelve feet.

I flipped on the light and walked slowly down the aisle formed by those cages, examining each one as I went. They were occupied mainly by monkeys, though some held dogs. Each one of the animals was dull, listless, and watched me with incurious eyes. All of them were scarred over their faces and their bodies, like they'd been involved in vicious fights.

When I came to the end, I found a couple of large rubber trash containers and, stacked around them, large, black refuse sacks. With a sinking feeling of nausea, I opened one of the sacks and looked inside. It contained two dead monkeys. But they weren't just dead, they had been dismembered, not as a result of vivisection. They were not surgical cuts. These animals had been torn apart, literally ripped limb from limb.

I took photographs and footage, resealed the sack and

returned the way I had come. I switched off the light, closed the door and locked it.

After that, I examined the lab again, trying to make sense of what I had just seen. Whatever way I looked at it, it didn't form a coherent picture. One thing did strike me. Most of the equipment—at least the electronic equipment—was Russian, like the suits at the gate. My mind went back to what Roy Rogers had said to me just before he died, when I'd asked him how many people were at the house. He'd said, "Freeman, the Russian guy, Peter Kuznetsov... Joseph Vasiliev..."

Russians. It still didn't make a lot of sense, even ignoring the lab animals that had been dismembered. Taking it as a simple drugs operation, the question remained, who the hell were they selling the stuff to? The Mexican cartels had everything sewn up from El Paso to Boston, the Gulf to Seattle. There was simply no room in the States for an operation of this size.

I grunted. There was one simple way to find out. The Audi had brought Kuznetsov and Vasiliev and, presumably, a driver and a bodyguard. The boys in the Land Cruiser had stayed at the gate. Two got you twenty those in the Range Rover were guarding the back of the house. That meant I had four guys, a driver and a bodyguard to get through before I could beat some answers out of the three clowns in the house. It was doable.

I stepped out of the greenhouse and made my way silently back toward the house. A quarter of the moon was rising in the east and was filtering thin, turquoise light into the sky, but visibility was still negligible. I thought for a moment of my kit bag in the back of the Zombie. There I had night vision goggles, an HK416, my orange osage take down bow...

I put the thought from my mind and focused on the task in hand: identify and locate the four targets outside the house. The one I had seen earlier was still standing on the steps, silhouetted against the bright light streaming from the open French windows. That left three more.

I had arrived at the flat area where the corrals had been located, and was lying on my belly. Between me and the house, there was an expanse of lawn. Over to the left, there was an area of dirt which eventually led to the fence. On the right was the swimming pool and beyond it some tennis courts. Surrounding them was an area of trees. What lay beyond that, I had no idea.

It was pretty clear in my mind that security was basic. The greenhouses had been unguarded because Freeman did not see me as a clear and present threat to his physical safety. He saw me as a long-term threat to his operation. So he had a couple of boys here as a sensible precaution, and the suits were obviously the praetorian guard of his Russian visitors.

So I lay, allowing my eyes to adjust to the dim light, and slowly scanned the area, not for human shapes, but for movement. Moonlight will warp and distort shapes, blend shadows and create suggestions of things that are not there, or hide the things that are, but movement will always stand out and tell you pretty precisely where someone is. That night was no exception.

The first giveaway was the red glow of a cigarette over on my right. Like I said, security was not on red alert. It burned bright for a second, then swung down and died out. I stared at the area and slowly began to make out his shifting, fidgeting form. He was standing on the grass, forty or fifty feet from the guy at the French windows, at a 45° angle to him, jerking his knees and shifting his shoulders. And two got you twenty his pal was symmetrically placed on the other side. Thirty seconds of careful observation and the limpid glow of the rising moon brought him to light, too.

The fourth guy appeared shortly afterwards. He climbed the five broad steps from the lawn to the French windows and stood smoking and talking quietly to his pal on the door.

I had identified my targets. Now I had to decide how to take them out. A stealthy approach was out of the question. They were all in view of each other and I'd be dead before I got to first base. My only option was to storm them.

A man taken by surprise will take about four seconds to respond to unexpected violence. A trained man on orange alert can take as much as three. These guys were on orange at the very maximum. They were not expecting an attack, so if I kept it tight, I figured I had a chance. I took it.

I decided I'd go for the guys in the dark first, then close in on the two framed in the light of the doorway. I lined up the guy with the cigarette on my right, because if you're right handed, it's easier to pan left with a rifle than it is to pan right.

It was impossible in those conditions to go for a precise shot, so I waited for him to suck on his cigarette again and then aimed just below, at the middle of his thorax, and let off a burst of three shots, keeping the grouping tight. I didn't wait to see if I'd hit the mark. I swung left and let off another three shots into that guy's body too. Then I swung up to the French windows. They were both standing, legs straddled with their weapons at their shoulders, aiming vaguely in my direction. Their weapons flashed and spat. The logs above me splintered and the dirt around me erupted in showers. I kept it steady, opened up once and the silhouette in the doorway did a little dance and fell. Then I was up and running as bullets tore into the ground behind me. I still had the AK-47 at my shoulder and as I ran, I was aiming it at the guy who was bounding down the steps toward me, screaming. I took him out with two short bursts, which caved in his chest and made his legs wobble. He fell on his face and lay still.

I ran up the steps and burst through the French doors. I took in the room at a glance. It was empty, large and elegant. Two walls were bare stone, the others were wood-paneled. The ceiling was exposed, dark wooden beams. On the far right, there was an open fire with large logs burning in the grate. Directly in front of me, a big, overstuffed cream sofa and two overstuffed armchairs were arranged around a coffee table. There was a standard lamp, paintings on the walls, books in bookcases.

No people, but across from where I stood, in the opposite wall, there was a door, and beyond it, I could hear running feet. I dropped to one knee, put the rifle to my shoulder and lined up the center of the door.

It burst open and two big Russians in Italian suits ran in. One had an Uzi, the other had an HK416. I put three rounds through each of them, ripped kindling out of the door behind them and sprayed it with blood and gore. I closed the French doors, locked them and moved forward. I took the 416 and slung it over my shoulder, stepped over the two corpses and found myself in a wide entrance hall. The white marble floor was dotted with palms in huge, fat pots. A white marble staircase with a white, wrought iron banister curled up on my right to a second floor.

No people.

Diagonally on my left, there were double doors, eight feet tall in walnut, with large, brass handles. Something about them said 'dining room'. Keeping the AK-47 at my shoulder, I moved fast and silent across the hall to a door at the foot of the stairs. There was nobody on the landing. I opened the door. It gave on to a library-cum-study which was also empty.

My gut and my watch told me they were in the dining room, and had been having dinner while they talked. I wondered where the staff were and decided they had left in the truck I had seen depart, leaving Kuznetsov, Vasiliev and Freeman to talk business. They, with their two remaining gorillas, were now probably barricaded in the dining room.

I pulled out the .45 I'd taken from the cowboy and put four rounds through the lock. The reports echoed loud and jarring around the marble hall. Then I took a run at the doors and gave them a two-footed flying kick. They burst open. I hit the floor, rolled and came up on one knee with the AK-47 at my shoulder. The two bodyguards tried to track me with their handguns, but I was moving and they were static—and I'd already tabbed them as I landed. They each took a double tap to the chest and the show was over.

Three men stood against the wall beyond a twelve-seater mahogany table laid with ornate silver candelabras, fruit bowls and Delft crockery. They'd been dining on roast lamb and roast potatoes, with broccoli and Vichy carrots. Now they were standing in a row, in front of the sideboard beside the fireplace, staring at me. As I stepped toward them, their hands went up.

There was Freeman, looking somewhat less awe-inspiring than he had in his courtroom. Next to him was a tall, lean Russian with short hair, maybe in his late thirties. He was wearing a light gray, five thousand dollar suit and a watch that cost about as much again, and I figured he was probably Peter Kuznetsov. He was scared, but trying not to show it. Next to him was the guy I guessed was his second in command, Joseph Vasiliev. He looked twice as strong and half as smart, with a broad Slavic face and a dark five o'clock shadow. He also looked mad. I knew he was dangerous.

Freeman was frowning hard. "I thought you'd got away..."

I cut him short. "Get on your knees. Facing the fire. Put your hands on your head. Hesitate and I'll blow your kneecaps off."

He didn't hesitate. He got down on his knees, facing the fire, and laced his fingers across the top of his silver head. I turned and jerked my head at the tall, lean guy. "You Kuznetsov?"

He swallowed. The Slav glanced at him. It was good enough for me and confirmed my guess. I waved the Colt. "On your knees in front of the fire. You." I jerked my head at Vasiliev. "Stand over there, hands against the wall."

He curled his lip, but did as I said.

I rested my ass against the table and spoke to Freeman. "Who's in the kitchen? What staff have you got? Lie and I'll hurt you."

He babbled, "Mrs. Doyle, she's the cook. Ruth and

Miriam, the maids, Abigail helps Mrs. Doyle in the kitchen. That's all. But they they've all gone home..."

"That's fine. Now, we are going to talk. Bullshit me and I will cause you a lot of pain. Try to escape and I will kill you. You have to realize you are not dealing with an amateur. I will not hesitate. Are we clear on this?"

Freeman nodded. "Yes, yes, we understand."

"Kuznetsov, let me hear it."

Kuznetsov nodded. "We understand. What you want?"

"How about you start by telling me what the hell is going on here?"

He swore elaborately in Russian, but aside from that, made no answer to my question.

I shot Vasiliev through the head. A plume of blood and brains sprayed across the cream paint. He sagged forward, his cheek and right eye creased against the wall, and he slid awkwardly to the floor.

I turned to Freeman. "Do I need this clown? Can I get the works from you? Am I wasting my time...?"

Kuznetsov was talking before I had finished.

"No! You don't kill me! We can work out deal. No more killing, please!"

I pushed myself off the table and stepped behind him. I paused a moment, then put my foot between his shoulder blades and shoved hard. He cried out, flailed with his hands and fell face first toward the fire. His right hand grasped the marble surround, but his left had no place to go except the iron grate. He screamed as he gripped it and pushed himself back, squeezing his scorched hand under his armpit. I kicked him again and again he fell toward the fire, but this time, he managed to right himself and scramble to his feet. As he stood, I pistol whipped him and kicked his feet from under him. He landed with a whoosh on the floor and curled into the fetal position, still clutching his hand under his arm.

I knelt and shoved the .45 in his mouth. "Get on your knees, in front of the fire. Next time I get attitude from you, I'll shove your damned head in the flames. Do we have an understanding, Kuznetsov?"

He nodded. "Yes, yes, I understand."

I stood and rested my ass against the table again. "Let's start again. What has a Russian gangster and a self proclaimed Wyoming prophet sitting around a table together dining on roast lamb, at a ranch with a couple of square miles of giant cannabis trees and white poppies growing out on the range? What the hell have you two got going down here?"

Freeman shook his head. "You couldn't in a thousand years begin to understand..."

"You may not have noticed, Freeman, I am not a man endowed with a great deal of patience. If I have to tell you boys one more time, I am liable to do something you will regret."

It was Kuznetsov who answered. "We are developing new strain of cannabis. It grows more abundant, it contain LSA, is like natural LSD, it have hallucinogenic properties. The effect of smoke is more powerful, also more addictive."

"And the poppies?"

"For production of heroin, but also we have small lab where we are develop variations what are more addictive, more powerful for less quantity. More profit for less product."

"What about the monkeys and the dogs?"

He glanced over his shoulder at me. "For testing…"

I shook my head. "You have acres of the stuff here. There must be several tons of marijuana and raw opium out there, where the hell do you plan to sell it?"

Freeman shrugged. "L.A., Frisco, New York… everywhere! Later we'll move into coke farming up in the mountains, maybe Colorado."

I laughed. "And you think the Mexican cartels are just going to sit back and let you steal a multi-billion dollar market from them?"

Kuznetsov craned around to look at me. His expression was one of curiosity. He shook his head. "No. We will destroy Mexican cartels."

TWELVE

WE WERE SITTING MORE COMFORTABLY IN THE living room. I had them seated on the sofa with their ankles bound to each other, and I was sitting on the arm of a chair opposite. The fire was burning low and I had just laid another log on it. I lit a Camel and inhaled deep as Kuznetsov began to speak. I had my cell on the table beside me, recording as he spoke.

"The *pakhan* of our *bratva* have notice, in last year, maybe two, there is..." He made an eloquent gesture with his hands, indicating a hole. "Emptiness at center of Western power..."

I was interested. I said, "A power vacuum?"

He spread his hands and nodded. "A power vacuum, yes. In America, in Europe, is like chicken with no head, running this way and running that way, like sheep when the shepherd is gone. Europe disintegrating, American politics like civil war. Everything going in pieces. Nothing holding West together no more. This is opportunity for us. So we make move for more power."

I frowned. "You're always making moves for more power. That's not news."

He gave a smile that looked somehow predatory. "Opportunity is new. Nobody is saying to *Pakhan*, 'No, you cannot go here, you cannot do that.'" He shook his head. "The field is open, empty."

I narrowed my eyes. "Nobody, like who?"

He shrugged, spread his hands. "*Pakhan* not talk to me about this. Only, 'U.S.A. is open now, go, take territory, make money."

I grunted, thinking. "So how does that bring you to a town like Freedom, Kuznetsov?"

"We hear, through grape vine, that there is man in this town who is very holy man." He looked at Freeman and grinned. "Who is believe in Old Testament, and he is looking for partner to make business."

"Business? You mean like cannabis and heroin?"

"Yeah, this kind of business." Kuznetsov laughed suddenly, a big, Russian laugh. "You know how many people in Washington getting rich from Sinaloa? From other cartels too! You know how high influence from Mexico going in American government? You think only Russian government is corrupt with crime? Difference is our organized crime is Russian, yours is Mexican. Only difference. Many judges, many cops, many Congressmen and woman making many millions from Sinaloa."

He paused, laughing softly. "But always *Pakhan* saying to us, we gotta respect Sinaloa territory. We don't make war on Sinaloa. Then, year ago, maybe little more, things begin to change. Chaos beginning in system which is working good since end of Second World War. At first, we do not know what it means. No control, no direction, chaos. How do we interpret this? But then *Pakhan* realize, and tell us, there is power vacuum at heart of West. People who are controlling, gone. West in chaos.

"So they are send me here, and one of my boys hear about Mayor Freeman." He shrugged again, made a face. "It was luck. We come and we visit him. We are make proposition to him, but he is make better proposition back to us. We can make big plantations on this ranch, he is control his town and his workers real good: sheriff, law, telephone, no signal for cell phones... Is total control, and the people, they will do anything for God, and for prophet, Mr. Freeman."

The room was quiet, apart from the crackle of the logs in the fire. I flicked ash into the ashtray.

"Explain to me how you plan to shift all this product. Who are you going to sell it to?"

It was Freeman who answered. He laughed. "You know why things don't get done in this world, Mr. Walker? Because people don't do them. It's that simple. And you know why people don't do things? Because they don't believe they can. Freedom, Mr. Walker, is a state of mind. And the only thing standing between you and what you want is your belief."

"Save it for the self help book you're going to write from prison, Freeman. If I want half-baked philosophy, I'll read Kant. Give me the facts. The Mexicans own the market. You are facing serious reprisals if you muscle in. So how are you going to sell this stuff?"

He laughed again and shook his head. "What do I need?

Muscle? Professionals who are not afraid to get their hands dirty? Ruthless killers? Is that what I need? OK, I have it, right here." He gestured at Kuznetsov, then gave him a look you wouldn't want to see on your girl's face after your first night together. "Though I have to say their performance tonight wasn't exactly awe inspiring."

I narrowed my eyes at him. "You are planning to start a turf war between the Russian mob and the Mexican cartels? Even you can't be that stupid. Nobody wins a war like that."

He sighed, like it was exhausting that everybody was less intelligent than he was. "It is not simply a turf war, Mr. Walker. The U.S.A. is the biggest single drugs market in the world, and I can supply from Alaska to Miami, *without passing through a single border control.*" He gestured out toward his ranch. "I rear beef, beans, all those household products that we produce here in Wyoming, all legitimate stuff. And I have a small fleet of trucks and vehicles that we use to distribute them. As well as that, I have a workforce of devoted—and I *do* mean devoted—disciples who can deliver my merchandise nationwide, and all over Canada. I can out-price and out-deliver the Mexicans and the buyers will simply stop buying. And where protection is needed, I can provide it."

I gave a short laugh that told him all about my incredulity. "How long do you think it will be before the Feds storm this place? The Mexicans produce their stuff in the mountains of Sinaloa for a reason."

"I'll tell you. They will *never* storm this place. Because nobody but my most trusted followers will ever know where it is produced. The buyers will have no idea, the distributors will have no idea. They will assume it is coming from somewhere in Latin America. My own people would rather die than tell. And as you have already seen, my little town is on lockdown twenty-four seven, and they love it that way."

"Sure, especially Noah and Grace."

He seemed not to hear me. "We can supply the distributors with cheaper, better merchandise. Our deliveries will be more reliable because the risk factor involved will be minimal. All those distributors who had an allegiance to the Mexicans will simply shift, and the demand for Mexican produce will dry up. There will be no turf war, but where muscle is needed, the Russians will provide it. And..." He smiled and for a moment, I had the feeling I was looking at something truly evil. "...Along the way, we will step into the shoes of the Sinaloa and the other cartels and pick up their retainers, all the way from local law enforcement right up to circuit judges and Congress. They will be taking *my* dollar and playing *my* tune."

"You're out of your mind."

I said it, but I was aware of my own lack of conviction, and his smile told me he was too.

"Why?" he said. "It's been done before. The Mexican cartels effectively invaded the U.S.A. using precisely the method I am talking about. Only they were cruder. They relied entirely on violence. You know why it *will* work, Mr. Walker? Shall I tell you why I will be successful? Because I am a man of God. Because I *believe* in what I am doing, and those people who follow me *believe* in me. Belief is infectious. We are doing *much* more than trafficking drugs! The drugs will merely finance the operation. Mr. Walker, I am going on TV! I am going on *TV!* To spread the Word, to spread the word of *God!*" He laughed out loud. "Freedom was just the first tiny step. I *am* a prophet, Mr. Walker, and the Lord is guiding my steps. Have you *seen* the trees we are growing? Have you ever seen anything like that? We created that plant, with the Lord's guidance. When we unleash that drug on the market, when people start smoking that stuff, judges, politicians..." He sat back and his face was radiant, he was grinning like an idiot child. "It will be a revolution—a true revolution of faith."

I sighed. "Ginsberg and Leary already tried that, remember? Kerouac, William Burroughs? That experiment ended up with the South American cartels selling heroin and cocaine all across the western world, and Paul McCartney getting a knighthood from the Queen of England."

He snorted. "The beats and the hippies. They were following the bankrupt philosophies of the East. I bring them the Word! The very Word of God, and I offer them a way to hear it, and transcend to the Lord, and lie in his bosom."

"Sure, while you select their prettiest daughters and lie in theirs."

He sat back and observed me a moment with dead, blue eyes. "Join us."

Kuznetsov glanced at him, then at me with questioning eyes.

Freeman went on. "I can offer you power, riches beyond your wildest dreams, women, luxury undreamed of. You will be a prince among men." I raised an eyebrow at him and he laughed. "Look at what you have done! I do not want you as an *enemy*, Mr. Walker! I would much rather have you as an ally!" He sat forward, his eyes alive again. "Look at what *I* have done! Look at what I have achieved! I am a king! A king in my small kingdom! You know what Milton says in Paradise Lost—the Mind is it's own place, and can make a hell of Heaven and a heaven of Hell! I have fashioned my own paradise from my mind, and the people have come to me from far and wide, to follow me and live in my paradise. This is the power of my mind. Think! Think what we, you, I and the military power of the Russian Bratva, could achieve! Come, Lacklan! This is surely your destiny! You could have anything you dreamed of!"

I smiled, shook my head and asked, "Anything?"

I watched his pale eyes turn predatory and he leered. "*Anything!*"

I nodded. "OK, let's start with one small thing. Give me that and I will seriously consider your offer."

His eyes became cautious, but he said, "OK, name it."

"Grace. I want Grace."

"As your woman?"

I nodded. "One of them."

He grunted. "I have not yet tasted her. I had my heart set on her. She is lush."

I studied the .45 a moment and spoke absently.

"I think we're done here."

He laughed and held up his hands. "Slow down, cowboy! Let's not be hasty. You shall have Grace..."

"Damn right. Where is she? She in the jailhouse?"

"No." He gave another, smaller laugh. "It struck me Sheriff West was getting a little too enthusiastic with his fists. He does enjoy beating up on women. So I removed her to somewhere a little safer."

"Where?"

"The hotel. She's in one of the rooms. My wife, Missy, and one of my servants are looking after her."

I stared at him a moment. "Your wife and one of your servants..."

"Do not judge, Mr. Walker, lest ye be judged also."

"I'll take my chances. Where is Hank? What's he doing?"

He looked surprised and shrugged. "I imagine he's at home in bed. We figured you'd got away. That's why Kuznetsov is here."

"You were going to have his people hunt me down?"

"Of course..."

I smiled. "No need now, huh? Come on, let's go."

I had Kuznetsov tie Freeman's hands behind his back using his shoelaces. Then we walked out to the Range Rover parked out front. I shoved Freeman in back and told him, "Lie face down on the floor." Then I turned to Kuznetsov. "Let's be clear, Boris, I think there are too many men like you in the world. One less would be nobody's loss. So you try anything smart, and I won't kill you. I'll be sitting right behind you, with my foot on Freeman's head, and I'll shoot you through your lower spine and paralyze your legs. And that will just be the beginning of the nightmare. Drive me to the jailhouse in Freedom, no detours. Clear?"

He nodded. "We are clear."

"Get in and drive."

I sat as I had promised, right behind him, with one boot on the back of Freeman's neck. We drove through the gate under the rising moon, past the guards' hut with its gruesome occupants, and up the long dirt track to the main road. There we plunged into the black tunnel of trees, with the beams from the headlamps barely penetrating the darkness, making ragged monsters out of the pines that seemed to reach down for us with knotted, twiggy fingers, flash past and vanish, back to their world of nightmares; a world I would never leave, a world where I belonged.

The town, when we arrived, was still and silent. We moved through the pools cast by the amber streetlamps, which bathed the parks, empty sidewalks, and blacktop with dull, lurid light. We moved among the sleeping houses with windows like hollow eyes and doors like yawning mouths, until finally, we pulled up outside the jailhouse.

I climbed out with the Colt trained on Kuznetsov. "Get out."

He swung down and I waved the gun at the back door, which I'd left open. "Get him out."

He helped Freeman out and I waved them toward the jailhouse. A .45 round through the lock opened the door, and five minutes in the front office found the electronic key for the steel door at the top of the stairs. The keys to the cells, in true Freedom fashion, were big, old iron chubs.

I shoved Freeman and Kuznetsov through the top doorway and down the stairs. The clatter of their feet made a deathly echo under the stark, strip lighting. Once we were down, I grabbed Freeman by the scruff of his neck and kicked his feet from under him. He went down on his knees and I threw Kuznetsov the key to the nearest cell. "Open it."

"What are you going to do?"

"Don't ask questions! Open the damn thing!"

He unlocked the door.

"Leave the key in the lock. Get inside."

"No..."

I lined up his right knee, but he was already moving into the cell, yammering, "No! No, don't…"

I kicked the door closed and locked it. He clutched at the bars, staring at me. "Now what?"

"Now we wait."

I stepped over to Freeman where he was kneeling in the middle of the floor, grabbed a fistful of his collar and laid him down on his face. Then I shoved the Colt in the back of his neck and snarled, "When he comes, you say, 'Hank, come and help me.' Say anything else and I will not kill you, Freeman, but you will wish I had."

He nodded. His face was gray and his calm was beginning to crack. There were beads of sweat on his brow. "Hank, come and help me. Got it."

I took up my position to the left of the entrance by the stairs, out of sight.

We didn't have to wait long. Ten minutes later, two sets of boots entered the office upstairs at a run. They paused, then clattered down the steps. Another pause and I heard Hank's voice. "Mayor!"

I lined up the back of the Mayor's right knee, but he lifted his head and gasped, "Hank! Help me, for God's sake!" He said it like he meant it and a moment later, Hank and one of his deputies stormed in.

THIRTEEN

THE .45 ROUND FROM THE COLT TOOK OFF MOST OF the top of the deputy's head. The report was deafening. Hank shrank into his shoulders and the deputy's legs folded like he was going into the lotus position. Then he just slumped to the floor. I waited a couple of seconds for Hank to take in what had happened. When he finally turned and stared at me, I said, "Drop your belt."

He undid his holster and let it drop to the floor. I tossed him the key to the cell. He fumbled and dropped it, then picked it up, staring at it like he didn't know what it was. His hands were shaking.

"Open the cell, leave the key in the door, go in and lean against the wall. You too, Kuznetsov."

They did as I said, I locked the door and put the key in my pocket. Kuznetsov watched me do it. The only hint of an expression was the incredulity in his eyes.

"You will not escape. We can find you. We will find you wherever you go, and we will kill you."

I gave something like a smile. "Yeah? I already found you, Kuznetsov. That's why you're in the cell, and I'm out here."

I grabbed Freeman by his neck again and dragged him to his feet.

"Let's go see Grace, wise guy."

I shoved him back up the stairs. Behind me, Kuznetsov was screaming.

"*We will find you! We will find you and you will suffer hell!*"

I pushed Freeman out into the street and into the passenger seat of the Range Rover, and we drove the short distance to Missy's hotel. There was a surreal feeling to the scene as we climbed out of the truck in the empty town, as though we were playing out a scene on a stage. Only nobody knew it was a play.

We crossed the sidewalk, I hammered on the door and leaned on the bell. After a moment, I saw a light come on inside, and feet hurried downstairs. A moment later, the door opened and Missy stood staring at me, then at Freeman and then back at me again. She gave a slow, delayed gasp and went pale. I leaned past Freeman, pushed the door open and shoved Freeman through. Then I stepped in and closed the door behind me.

"Good evening, Missy. Nice to see you again. I've brought your husband with me. Let's go into your living room and have a chat."

She wasn't looking at me. She was looking at Freeman. "John... what...?"

"Do as he says, Missy. Have faith in the Good Lord, this will soon be over."

She glanced at me, turned and led the way past the reception desk to the living room. Once inside, I shoved Freeman on the sofa and stood, looking into Missy's eyes. "Go and get Grace, Missy. I know she's here. Go get her."

She frowned, looked at Freeman, then back at me, shaking her head. "She's not here." Again she looked at Freeman. "John...?" Back at me. "She's not... I don't know..."

I pointed at the sofa with the Colt. "Sit next to him." She moved over and sat by Freeman's side. "Hold him."

"What?"

"Hold him! Hug him. He's going to need that support in a moment."

He turned a pasty gray and her eyes went wide with horror. I trod on his foot and placed the muzzle of the Colt against his kneecap. They both screamed. He went frantic and started trying to kick his leg free. I knelt, slipped the gun off his knee and rammed it in his crotch. He froze. Beads of sweat stood out on his brow. The pouches beneath his eyes had turned blue as the blood drained from his face. I spoke very quietly.

"What do I need to do to make you understand that I am serious? What do I need to do to make you understand I will go the full nine yards, and then some? I don't like you, Freeman. I have done real bad things to people I've liked and respected. Now, what do you think I am capable of doing to a piece of shit like you?"

I let him think about that a second. Missy was making a strange, involuntary warbling noise in her throat and I knew she would break easy.

"I am going to ask you a question. If I get anything but a straight, clear answer, I will blow one of your legs off at the knee. We don't want to go there, Freeman, so give me a straight answer." I looked at Missy. "We on the same page?"

She nodded.

"Where is Grace?"

It was Missy who answered. "There's a small apartment over the restaurant next door. She's there."

"A prisoner?"

"Locked in. She can't get out. There is a door upstairs. It connects the two buildings. I take her food. I've been tending to her bruises. John asked me to care for her. He wants..."

"What?"

She glanced at him. "He wants her ready for conjugal duties in a couple of weeks."

"I'll bet he does. Go get her. Bring her here." I held her eye. "Don't do anything you'll regret, Missy. Don't make me prove I'm serious."

She looked at Freeman. Freeman nodded to her. He said, "Kuznetsov is locked up in the jail. So is Hank. We have no choice but to cooperate. Go and do it, Missy."

She rose and left the room. I stood and went to the fireplace, where I could cover him and the door. I also had a view of the street through the bow window. We heard Missy's feet tramp up the stairs. I pulled my cigarettes from my pocket and lit one. Freeman asked me, "What are you going to do? I thought we had a deal."

I studied him a moment without expression, letting the smoke trail from my nose. There was a faint smile on his face, which I might have imagined, but once again, I had the feeling that his face was oddly familiar. I dismissed it and replied.

"Who says we haven't? You're a liar and a cheat. So I'm covering my bases, Freeman. When I know you need me alive, I'll let you go free. Until then, I'll keep you where you can't hurt me."

"That makes sense, I suppose."

Upstairs, I heard the faint clunk of a door. I saw Freeman swallow. I took another drag. "You understand what will happen if she doesn't bring Grace?"

He nodded. "She's going to bring Grace."

I thought about going up after her, but Freeman was my trump card and I didn't want to risk losing him by leaving him alone, and I was pretty sure Missy wouldn't risk getting him hurt, but a tightness in his face was telling me I was overlooking something.

"What's going on, Freeman? Are you aware what's at stake here for you?"

"Of course I am! What's going on is that I am terrified."

That might have been it, and it might not. Either way, I didn't get time to think about it. I heard the door open and close upstairs again and a moment later, two pairs of feet descended the stairs. I covered the door with the Colt and a moment later, it opened. Missy came in with Grace. They both looked terrified, but there was a tension in Missy's face that was absent from Grace's, but echoed Freeman's.

I reached out my left hand toward her. "Grace, come here."

She came over and I held her. She clung hard to me and started to sob. I spoke quietly, keeping my eye on Freeman and Missy. The more I watched them, the more certain I was that something was wrong. "Take it easy, Grace. We're getting out of here. Everything is going to be all right."

I waved the Colt at the telephone on the side table by the sofa. "Call Jonah, the mechanic. Tell him I want my car working and ready, here, at the door, in fifteen minutes. For every minute over fifteen that it takes, I'm putting a .45 round in the mayor. And, Missy? You better understand something and explain it to Jonah. I'm taking Freeman with me. If anything goes wrong with the car, your mayor dies. I'll make damn sure of that. So make the right choices."

She sat and picked up the telephone. She dialed and waited.

"Good evening, Carol..." She paused and sighed. I could hear laughter and a voice chattering on the other end. Missy interrupted. "Carol, listen! Please listen. I'm sorry to disturb you so late..." Another burst of chatter. "Yeah, I know. Listen. This is an emergency. I have the mayor here with me... I can't explain, Carol, not now, but can you just put me through to Jonah McAllen? Please, don't ask questions... I'm sorry to be like this... Thank you."

We waited in silence, all of us staring at Missy. I felt Grace tighten her arms around my waist. Missy spoke suddenly.

"Jonah! I know it's late, forgive me. I'm here with the mayor and Mr. Walker..." She sighed again and closed her eyes. "Please, don't talk, Jonah. Just listen to me, will'ya, please? Mr. Walker insists you gotta fix his car and have it here at the door of the hotel in fifteen minutes. The mayor is tied up and he is holding us at gunpoint. Please, Jonah, do exactly as he says. For every minute over fifteen he's threatenin' to... in his words, 'put another .45 round in the mayor.' Please, Jonah, I beg of you, hurry and do exactly as he says."

She hung up and looked at me without expression. I pulled out my cell and set a timer. I showed it to them. "I said it and I will do it."

We waited, then, in silence. I was watching Missy, who was staring at her hands in her lap. I kept running over her conversation with Carol at the exchange. Something about it had unsettled me. Something about it was wrong, and I couldn't place what it was. Five minutes passed. Grace let go of me and went to sit in an armchair, hugging her knees.

I ran through the conversation again, Missy's expression, the chattering voice, Missy interrupting. Then, somehow, it dawned on me.

"That wasn't the first time you'd spoken to Carol this evening, was it?"

She stared at me. Her face was rigid and there was real terror in her eyes. I repeated the question. "*Was it?*"

Her eyes flicked over to Grace. I looked at Grace and she spoke with her eyes glued on Missy. "She spoke on the phone in the apartment, before she came to get me from the bedroom."

"*Grace!*"

Grace turned her eyes on me. "She did! I don't know who she called, but she must have spoken to Carol..."

I felt a hot rage welling in my belly. "You alerted Kuznetsov's men."

"I had to."

"What the hell do you mean, you *had* to? Are you out of your mind?"

"He told me to."

I stared at Freeman. His face was impassive. "When I told her Kuznetsov and Hank were in the jail, she understood what she had to do. I knew she would. It is futile, Mr. Walker. There is no way out for you, but it is not too late for you to join the fold." His eyes turned to Grace. "And there can still be forgiveness and redemption for you, Grace. You know what you have to do. Obey your conscience."

She buried her face in her knees and covered her ears, screaming, *"Shut up! Shut up! I will not listen to you!"*

I took aim at his head. The impulse to shoot him was powerful, but I needed him alive for us to get away. I checked the timer on my phone. Three minutes. "Where are they coming from? I swear, Freeman, lie to me and I will hurt you for the sweet pleasure of revenge. You need to keep me on side, man. You do not want to put me in a corner."

He swallowed hard. "They are based at Rock Springs."

He might be telling the truth, but I had no way of knowing. Rock Springs was about a hundred and sixty miles away, seventy or eighty as the crow flies. Three hours by car, maybe more. I glanced at the timer. One minute thirty. I looked Freeman in the eye.

"Things are about to get real ugly for you, Freeman."

I turned to Missy. Her bottom lip was curling in and she was beginning to sob convulsively. "Please don't hurt him…"

I snarled, "It's a shame Noah didn't have somebody like you to plead for him, isn't it, Missy? Get on the phone to Jonah. I want him to hear this."

Freeman had closed his eyes and seemed to be praying quietly under his breath. Missy was blinking away tears and keening as she dialed. I felt nausea in my belly, but I knew I had to do what I was about to do if I was going to get Grace out of here.

"Carol... Please don't talk, Carol! Just listen to me. Put me through to Jonah. It's *urgent!*"

She stared at me with wet, swollen eyes, stifling her sobs. I looked at the timer. There were fifteen seconds to go. I took aim at his ankle. His face was gray and his eyes were closed. Missy's face screwed up like a fist. She spoke in a strangled voice, "*Answer! Please, God, answer!*"

I watched the last seconds tick away and began to squeeze the trigger. A squeal of tortured rubber outside made me stop. I glanced at the window and saw Jonah scrambling out of the Zombie. I felt a jolt in my chest. I turned to Missy. "Open the door. Let him in."

She staggered to her feet and ran for the door, crying, "Oh, God! Oh, thank God! Jonah! *Jonah!*"

I grabbed Freeman by the collar of his shirt and dragged him to his feet. "Get up!"

I heard the front door open, Jonah yammering about getting here as fast as he could, Missy sobbing, still thanking her god. I looked at Grace. "Come on, let's go."

I shoved Freeman out into the lobby. Jonah and Missy stared at us. I shoved Freeman again and he staggered toward the two of them. I was calculating in my head that it was about fifteen minutes since Missy had called Kuznetsov's people. If they were coming from Rock Springs, they were at least an hour away.

As I came level with Jonah and Missy in the open door, I reached for Jonah's collar with my left hand and dragged him toward me. At the same time, I shoved the muzzle of the Colt into the back of Freeman's neck.

"You listen to me, Jonah. I'm taking this piece of shit with me. If my brakes fail, if anything happens to the car, he will be the first to die. And then I'll be back for you. Now, if there is anything you need to tell me, this is the time to do it."

He shook his head. "Car's workin' fine, mister. I was only late getting here 'cause I couldn't work out how to start her. But I fixed the brakes OK. You heard 'em squeal!"

I dragged Freeman out onto the sidewalk and pulled open the door of the Zombie. Grace was right behind me. I said: "Get in the passenger side," and she ran around and climbed in. That was when I heard the chopper.

I looked up at the sky. There was nothing visible, but I could hear the throb of the rotor. I stared over at Jonah. He held out both hands in front of him and backed away. "I never done nothing. I only did what I was told to do. Don't hurt me..."

Then he turned and ran into the night. I scowled at Missy. Her eyes were wide with terror. I shoved Freeman toward the open door of the car. "Get in the back!" The chopper was getting closer, beating the air. The glow of a spotlight illuminated the sky to the east. A terrible scream like a banshee tore the night in half and a searing pain tore into my face and my neck. I turned and Missy's face was an inch from mine, twisted with madness as her nails clawed for my eyes. I put my hand on her nose and mouth and shoved. She stumbled back and fell sprawling on her back. Freeman thrashed and twisted and tore lose from my grip. Missy was up on her feet again, screaming like a madwoman, hurling herself at me, and Freeman was running, bellowing over his shoulder, "*Kill him! Blind him! Tear his eyes out! Kill him!*"

And as I tried to shield my face, I could hear Grace

screaming, too. *"For God's sake, Lacklan! Let's go! Leave them! Let's go!"*

Like a giant, black insect, the chopper rose over the bowing, thrashing trees, making a ghastly stencil of the rooftops and the chimneypots. Its spotlight panned across the square and found us. Missy raised her arms, shielding her eyes. The downdraft tore at her hair and her clothes. She backed away, running for the hotel door. Flames spat from the black silhouette of the helicopter. I ducked and slugs ricocheted off the blacktop, the roof of the Zombie and the sidewalk.

I ducked in. Grace was screaming. I slammed the door, hit the ignition and floored the pedal. The beast surged forward. The only sound was the tortured howl of burning rubber, and in one and a half seconds, we were doing sixty down Main Street, in absolute silence.

FOURTEEN

I FISHTAILED INTO FREEMAN AVENUE. GRACE HAD her head in her lap, covered with her arms. The chopper was yawing over the rooftops, playing the beam of the spotlight over the road. I straightened up, accelerated, was crushed into my seat, braked, spun the wheel left, oversteered, rectified and floored the pedal again, surging down First Avenue West, climbing in five seconds to a hundred miles per hour, streaking down the broad, empty street without making a sound, leaving the chopper behind us.

I started to brake and felt the inertia wobble the vehicle, but managed to hold it. I turned down Gospel Road and then sharp right onto the La Barge Road. Again I floored the pedal. I knew I had a couple of miles of pretty straight road and I let the beast climb to a hundred and thirty. Behind me, I could hear the thud of the helicopter's rotor, and I could see the spotlight getting brighter in my mirror. From what I'd glimpsed, it was an Airbus 155, capable of close to two hundred miles an hour. The Zombie could do two hundred without breaking a sweat—in a straight line. On a mountain road with dense pine woods on either side and the head-lamps off, I might as well stick my .45 in my mouth and blow my brains out. The most I could hope for on dark mountain roads was sixty miles per hour, and that was a risk.

The chopper would match that easily, and the only thing it risked colliding with was nocturnal bugs. Plus, it had the advantage of height. I needed to lose it, fast, because the moment it sat on us, the assault rifles would come out again, and we'd be sitting ducks. I had to lose them, and that meant staying in the forests and heading for the canyons north of Calpet.

For a second, the cab was flooded with bright light. Grace screamed. I looked in the rear view and saw the chopper surge forward along the gash of night sky between the black walls of the trees. Ahead, I spotted a small gap in the trees on the left. I floored the pedal and we jumped from sixty to a hundred and ten. I felt myself crushed into the seat by a ton weight. Grace gasped. The chopper accelerated after us. A wall of trees at a right-hand bend in the road ahead hurtled at us. I slammed on the brakes. The tires screamed. The chopper overshot us. I spun the wheel left. We fish-tailed, drifted, the Zombie tilted onto its right wheels and settled, facing a narrow dirt track that wound in among the woods.

I gently accelerated and we slipped into the shadows of the forest. Here I could take it easy, make steady progress and stay out of the chopper's spotlight. We eased along the track, enfolded by a tunnel of trees. Looking up through the wind-shield, I could see the distant glow of the searching spot. The track wound and weaved. The surface was uneven and pitted. We crept forward, bumping, rolling, moving steadily downhill. Ahead, half a mile away, the glow of the search-light made a luminous blue crest over a wooded peak. I pulled in close to the trees and stopped. The glow grew brighter. The thud of the rotors grew louder.

And then the chopper was over us, swinging out to our left. I didn't wait for the guns to open up, I hit the pedal and we were away, with a shower of dirt kicking up behind us. The rocks and potholes meant my speed was limited, but I weaved right and left, doing forty, fifty miles an hour, seeking the cover of the huge pines. He trailed me, keeping close, a mere forty or fifty feet above me, showering us with bursts of automatic fire. The chassis was bullet proof—I'd taken that precaution long ago—but the windows weren't. Slugs smacked and whined off the trunk, the roof and the hood, and it wasn't long before the rear windshield shattered.

Then suddenly we were on a broader, flatter road. It was still dirt, but it was well kept. That meant I could accelerate, but it also meant we were more exposed. We surged from forty to a hundred. The chopper stayed with me, but he couldn't brake the way I could. I skidded on the dirt and he overshot me again by a hundred yards, then had to bank left to come back to me. I accelerated hard toward the tree cover on the left, searching the darkness, and the steep banks left and right for better cover than the trees.

I found it. A deep gorge ahead on the right. In the wash of the chopper's spotlight, I saw steep, jagged rocky cliffs, stony outcrops and sheer walls. I weaved violently back and forth across the road. Spouts of dust erupted around us. The front windshield exploded, showering us with glass. Grace screamed and covered her face with her arms. I shouted: "*Are you hit?*"

She stared at me wide-eyed, paralyzed by fear, but didn't answer.

I had no idea if there was a path into the canyon, but I knew the chopper couldn't get in there. So one way or another, that was where we were going. I hurtled toward it, spun the wheel, skidded, and lined up the hood with the entrance. Then I accelerated and braked almost instantly as we surged forward along a narrow track barely wide enough for the car.

I fought to control the speed. Rocks smashed into the front wheels, smashed and raked the sides. Branches battered at the hood and the windows. The cab was flooded with glaring light. Slugs smacked against the roof and the trunk. Then the sheer sides of the canyon were rising steeply on either side. The chopper rose vertically and veered away. The noise and the glaring light were gone.

Grace was trembling, whimpering and muttering, "Oh God... Dear Lord, oh God..."

I ignored her. I was thinking ahead.

I slowed to little more than five miles an hour, picking my way carefully along the track, climbing steadily, even as the walls of the canyon grew steeper and higher. Soon, after about five minutes of climbing, the path widened into a kind of clearing. To the right, a stream cascaded over rocks among the pine trees, catching and reflecting the starlight from the vast sky above. On the left, twenty or thirty feet above us, there was a large rock shelf that overhung a cluster of boulders below. The cascading stream snaked across the clearing, making the soil soft and grassy, then veered east, into shadows, seeking the lower ground.

I pulled over among the rocks under the overhang and popped the trunk. I turned to Grace and took hold of her wrist. "Listen to me. The body of this car is bulletproof..."

Her eyes were wide. She shook her head and said, "Why?"

I frowned, ignoring the question. "Stay in the car. You understand me? Stay in the car and wait for me. I'll be back."

I climbed out and closed the door. I could hear the chopper nearby, getting closer. I was asking myself how it had found us, how it had tracked us, even with the headlamps off, through the trees, even into the canyon. I was pretty sure I knew the answer.

I wrenched open the trunk, pulled over my kit bag and found my HK416. I rammed in a magazine and slung the rifle over my shoulder. I fitted my night vision goggles and scanned the trunk. It only took me a few seconds to find it. A simple cell phone. They were tracking the GPS. I grabbed it, ran toward the clearing and threw it over arm, like a grenade. It landed in the grass, about thirty yards away. I ran back and took up a position among the boulders, waiting.

It took maybe thirty seconds for the chopper to appear. It came over the crest of the hill, a black mass low in the sky, half hidden by the glare of its own searchlight. I pushed the night vision goggles up onto my head and, squinting, took aim into the heart of the glare. I let off three rounds and the glare died.

The chopper banked, rose, came around. I knew what was coming next and ducked behind the rock. At least three assault rifles opened up in a hail of hot lead. They didn't know exactly where I was, so they sprayed the whole area. Slugs thudded into the earth behind me, splintered the rocks, ricocheted, whining into the night. I closed my eyes and, through the storm of fire, I focused on the sound of the rotors, holding its position in my mind. The fire stopped, I counted one and...

I straightened with the 416 already at my shoulder, trained it at the base of the rotors and opened up: three short bursts. Then I ran and hurled myself behind the next boulder as they rained fire where I had been moments before. I didn't wait this time. They weren't shooting at me. They were shooting at where they thought I was. Now I stood, took careful aim, gave myself the luxury of two and a half seconds, and fired, six short bursts of four rounds each, all focused on the base of the rotors, where the engine housing was. I heard a nasty grating of tortured metal. The chopper started to rise, writhing like it was in pain. I shifted my aim to the shielded tail rotor and emptied the magazine into the small blades.

Suddenly the helicopter was going wild, spinning crazily in circles. It jerked up violently, went nose down, with its tail in the air, and plunged. By then I was already running back to the Zombie. I wrenched open the door, threw the 416 on the back seat and climbed behind the wheel.

Grace was staring in horror, through the gap where the windshield should have been, at the mangled wreck of the Airbus. A lone figure crawled out and staggered to its feet, a tragic, dehumanized silhouette. It staggered toward us as I began to reverse. Then, with a dull thud and a whoosh, the chopper, and the figure, were engulfed in flames. Grace covered her mouth with her hands. But in her eyes, I saw the dancing flames of that figure's personal hell as he fell to his knees and died.

I turned the car around and we snaked our way slowly back down the canyon to the broad, dirt track. There, I turned back the way we'd come. The moon was rising in its first quarter and cast a thin, silver-blue light on the road. The air was turning cold and Grace had started to shiver badly. I knew she was in shock. I pulled over and climbed out, found a blanket in the trunk and wrapped it around her shoulders. I had hoped to make it to Boulder that night. It was less than a hundred miles away, but in these mountain roads, that could take a couple of hours, and with the state she was in, we needed to find some hot coffee and a bed where she could sleep and recover.

Twenty minutes later, we'd found our way down to Route 189 and were headed north toward Big Piney. Another twenty minutes after that and we'd arrived at the town and pulled in to the motel opposite the All American gas station. I got a double room, packed Grace into a bed, made her some hot coffee and let her sleep. Then I called Phil. I got his voicemail, which was just a robot voice that said, "Leave a message."

"It's Lacklan. Something unexpected came up. I don't need to tell you it was serious. I'll be home early in the morning. I'll call you then."

I called Cyndi and left pretty much the same message, but before I could hang up, she came on the line. "Lacklan. What the hell happened to you?"

"I drove into the Twilight Zone."

"Don't joke. I was worried."

"Yeah, I was pretty worried myself. Where are you?"

"At your house. Where are you? I tried to call you and just kept getting your answering service."

"It's a long story."

"You OK?"

"Just about. Listen, I'll get home to Boulder tomorrow early. I'll call you again. I should be in Weston in a couple of days. You got any friends in the FBI?"

"What do you think? Of course. Why?"

"I'm about to call them. It's a pretty crazy story, but I need them to act fast. Likewise the Wyoming Highway Patrol. They need to act tonight."

"Give me the facts."

I gave her the gist. When I'd finished, she asked the obvious question. "Is this Omega?"

"No..." I hesitated. "Not exactly. It's exactly why I wanted you involved in the next job. Omega dies and immediately the Russians start jockeying for power with Sinaloa. Before long, some Islamic terrorist group will be involved, the Triads... When we pull this off—if we pull it off—we need to have some serious input into what takes Omega's place."

She was quiet a moment. "I hear you. OK, give me ten minutes, then call Assistant Director Aaron Solomon. I'll send you the number."

I gave her twenty and my phone rang.

"Walker."

"Mr. Walker, this is AD Aaron Solomon. I just had an interesting conversation with Cyndi McFarlane. She speaks highly of you, which is why I'm calling, otherwise I'd dismiss a story like this as a fantasy."

"Yeah, that makes two of us. But I have the fiancée of the

hanged man right here with me, bruises and all. And if you act now, you can take the ranch with its crops and its lab before they have a chance to dispose of the evidence. They are hurting badly right now, and my guess is they are devoting their manpower to hunting for me. But before long, they're going to realize I've gone and they'll focus on sanitizing the scene and destroying what evidence they can."

"I've contacted the Jackson field office. Just run through the story from the start for me, will you? Let me see if I have it straight. Where are you right now? I'd like to meet."

"I'll be in Boulder, Wyoming, early tomorrow. Then I'm returning to Weston, Boston."

I went over the story for him and agreed to meet with him once I got back to Weston. After that, I called the Wyoming Highway Patrol Department and was put through to a Detective Jim Hansen, who had just gotten off the phone with the Jackson FBI field office. By three AM, I finally hung up and settled in the chair to grab a few hours sleep, with the Colt .45 on my lap.

I slept for maybe an hour.

Then my eyes opened. I wasn't aware of having heard anything, but some sixth sense had woken me and told me something was wrong. I remained motionless, waiting, listening. The window, with the thin drapes closed, was a faintly luminous square in the darkness, washed by the lamps in the parking lot. The dappled shadow of a tree danced across it, tossed and was still.

And then there was the shadow of a man.

FIFTEEN

I ROSE, STEPPED ACROSS THE ROOM AND FLATTENED myself against the wall beside the door. There was a soft rattling and after a few moments, the lock clicked. Nothing happened for fifteen seconds. Then, the door opened just fast enough not to squeak. A warped oblong of limpid light stretched across the floor, bisected by a long, black shadow. The shadow twisted and a large body stepped in, just a few inches in front of me. I put the muzzle of the Colt against the back of his head and spoke quietly. "Freeze. Move and I'll..."

He moved, fast. Suddenly, he was facing me and the Colt was pointing at empty darkness. He smashed his forearm into my elbow and electric currents of pain shot through my arm. Then his two fists pounded my floating ribs, my lungs were in spasm and I was going down.

My head was reeling. I saw his boot coming for my face and caught it, fumbled and twisted. He should have fallen, but it didn't work. He was still standing and his fists were pounding at my head. I covered myself with my forearms, caught his rhythm and as his left pounded my shoulder, I smashed my right fist into his balls. It should have killed him.

He staggered back and grunted, and as I staggered to my feet, he came at me again. I kicked his right knee hard, rammed the heel of my right hand into his jaw and connected two right crosses to his head. He fell back a step, then powered at me with two uppercuts that, if they had connected, would have torn my head off. Instead, I stumbled back with my arms aching and bruised, wondering who the hell this guy was.

I knew the Colt was on the floor, but I had no chance of finding it. He charged at me in a side kick. I managed to take it on my arms, but the force threw me out the door and I sprawled on the asphalt in the parking lot. He didn't give me a chance to recover. He came after me and leapt in the air with his knees bent. I rolled and he came down with his heels where I had been a second before. He didn't stop. He lashed out with his foot and I sprawled on the asphalt. That was when I noticed the other two guys approaching from the Ford pickup. They weren't running, but they were walking fast, wearing khaki shirts and cowboy hats.

A sick, empty feeling crawled through me, telling me I was going to die. I got to my feet. My arms were hurting badly. The guy was coming at me through the door. That was the first time I saw his face.

"*Hank?*"

He lashed out at me with his foot. I ducked and rolled, and as he turned, I was running for the room, for the open door, for the Colt. If I was going to survive this attack, I needed the damned gun. The two deputies were charging me, aiming to cut me off. But before they got to me, I felt two arms like a vise wrap around my legs and I went down hard. A boot kicked me in the ribs. Another stamped on my back. A fist grabbed the back of my shirt and dragged me to my feet. Shafts of pain pierced every part of me. A powerful arm wrapped around my neck, cutting off my airway. One of the deputies came at me. There was no emotion in his face. He balled his fist and closed in for a right hook to my floating ribs.

I rammed my right thumb in his left eye, grabbed his ear with my fingers and squeezed. He screamed and thrashed as blood and slime oozed through my fingers. I kicked him hard in the balls and dragged him toward me. My lungs were screaming for air. He fell against me, slobbering and whimpering over my chest. My left hand found his revolver and pulled it from the holster. Then I let go of his head and he fell to the ground, pawing his face and sobbing.

I could feel my face swelling and I was losing focus. The second deputy was coming at me with that same, weird lack of expression. I put three rounds in his chest at point blank and he fell on his back, rigid. Hank was staggering back, trying to lift me off my feet. I knew I had seconds before I blacked out. I slipped the revolver behind my back, pressed it against his belly and pulled the trigger. It exploded and I felt the hot gasses burn my back. He didn't let go. Pulled again, and then again. His arm began to slacken. I dropped the gun, grabbed his wrist with both hands, wrenched his arm away from my throat and staggered away, wheezing noisily, dragging air into my lungs.

I turned. My legs were trembling. He was still on his feet, but his belly was an ugly mess and his pants were drenched with thick, oozing blood. I yelled a horrible, inarticulate noise and rushed at him, hammering at his head with both fists until he finally fell to the ground. Then I took his piece, went to the guy I'd blinded and blew his brains out point blank.

I stood a moment, staring at the three bodies, then I turned and walked unsteadily back toward our room, still wheezing badly through my bruised throat. I stood in the doorway, leaning on the jamb. Grace was sitting up, hugging her knees and sobbing.

I rasped, "Get up. We have to go. Now."

She didn't move. I crossed the room, took her arm and gently pulled her from the bed. I picked up the Colt from the floor and we made our way to the Zombie. I helped her into the passenger seat, wrapped her in a couple of blankets from the bed and got behind the wheel. We pulled out of the lot and back onto Route 189, headed north.

I drove through the small, dark hours. The road was empty and barely a light glimmered in the vast darkness. Above, through the shattered windshield, a billion stars were visible, like luminous dust in the turquoise sky, and beyond them, black, empty infinity.

After two huge, sobbing yawns, Grace had fallen into a deep sleep. Shock will do that. It will make you shut down, sleep and try to heal. But this was a shock, I thought bitterly, from which she would never recover. These ugly parasites had taken this good, valuable person and damaged and soiled her, brutalized her for their own greed, in the name of a god they had created in their own image.

I drove on, with the cold, pre-dawn air battering my face, thinking about Hank and the two deputies, wondering what the hell was going on. I had seen guys take that kind of punishment while they were on angel dust. But this was different. Hank and the deputies were not on angel dust. There had been no frenzy in them, no raving, no screaming. They had been almost robotic, mechanically impassive. Except that all three had been flesh and blood when I had shot them. They had all bled red, human blood.

So how did Hank turn from a clumsy thug into an almost indestructible killing machine?

Eventually, I came to the intersection with Route 191 and turned right, south and east. Fifteen minutes later, at five AM, just outside Pinedale, I stopped at an all night service station and pushed through the plate glass door into the stark light of the shop. I bought some bread, cheese and ham, other groceries, a pack of Camels and a pint of Irish. I also bought a thermos flask and filled it with hot coffee.

Then I stepped back outside into the cool dark and returned to the car. When I climbed in, Grace was awake. I handed her the flask. She stared at it a moment, then took it and unscrewed the top.

I showed her the whiskey. "You want to lace it with some of this? Doctors will tell you it's bad for shock. Soldiers will tell you the doctors are wrong."

She nodded and I poured in a generous measure. Then I took a swig from the bottle. I peeled the pack of cigarettes and lit up, took a deep drag and sat looking at the long, empty road in the dark, empty landscape. A pair of head-lamps sighed past and disappeared. Dawn would come in an hour. She sipped the coffee and shuddered. I fired up the engine and slipped silently onto the road. We were just ten miles from Boulder, and my house. Cold wind fingered through the broken windshield.

"That was Hank, and two of his deputies," I said. "Back at the motel."

She looked at me, but didn't answer. So I went on.

"You're in shock, and you don't need to hear this, but it looks like, even here, away from Freedom, both our lives are seriously at risk, Grace. A lot more than I'd thought at first. If we're going to survive, I need to know what the hell is going on."

I looked at her. Outside, the dark, flat fields slipped by. She blinked, swallowed, and looked away. The wind whipped her hair across her face.

I growled at her, "I shot Hank three times in the belly, and he didn't go down. I'm a trained killer, Grace. I was ten years with the best special forces unit in the world. In Freedom, I broke Hank's nose and knocked him half unconscious without even trying. But this morning, whatever I did to him, he just kept on coming. He was killing me. How did he do that?"

She didn't answer. After a while, I realized she was sobbing. I didn't pursue it. I knew that pressing her would do no good.

Boulder is little more than a gas station and a restaurant surrounded by a cluster of houses, a general store and a motel. That was why I'd chosen it when I got back from England. It was the kind of place where you could do your own thing and, if you were courteous and left your neighbors alone, your neighbors would leave you alone.

I turned onto the 353 at the gas station and a couple of minutes later, I pulled into the yard outside my house. There

I sat, staring at the dark windows and the locked door, listening to the dawn chorus getting started in the cottonwood trees that surrounded the building. I hadn't been there since Marni and I had spent six months there, together, as man and wife, pretending we were alone in the world, and there was no such thing as Omega.

It couldn't have lasted. Lies never do.

Grace was staring at me. She sniffed. "This is where you live?"

I smiled. "This is my house. It's not where I live." I climbed out, among the crazy chatter of the pre-dawn starlings. I opened the garage and drove the Zombie inside, parked it where it had sat, long ago, in another life, when Ben had rolled up in his Cadillac CTSV sedan, sent by my father to beg me to go and find Marni; to protect her from Omega. Now I had found her, I had all but destroyed Omega, according to his wishes, and Marni was lying, dying in her bed in my father's house in Weston.

Full circle.

I helped Grace out of the car and we went in from the garage directly to the kitchen. She took the blankets with her. The house was dark, chill and silent. It smelled musty and the atmosphere was heavy and close. I pointed to the living room through the kitchen door. "Make yourself comfortable on the sofa. I'll get some wood from the shed."

She didn't sit. She dumped the blankets on the sofa, and while I brought in the wood and built the fire, she made toasted cheese and ham sandwiches and brewed coffee. Outside the kitchen window, the horizon turned from black to gray. Dawn slowly broke, and we sat around the fire and ate, and drank black coffee laced with whiskey. And finally, then, she began to talk.

"The mayor, Mr. Freeman, it's hard for an outsider like you to understand. He is..." She paused, staring at the rich, orange flames. "He was everything to us. This may seem odd to you, but most of us never left the town. We had no need to. We had everything we wanted right there. He provided everything for us. Meat, vegetables, milk... We even brewed our own beer!"

"What about clothes, electrical goods, car parts, magazines, books...?" I shook my head. "There is a lot more to life than food and beer."

She smiled. "Of course there is. But he had a system set up."

"What kind of system?"

"Warehouses. It was run by the members of the Council. It was carefully calculated. How many washing machines we would need in a year. How many light bulbs, vacuum cleaners, fan belts—all those things we could not make in the town—and believe me, we made an awful lot of the stuff we needed, from brooms and mops to roofing tiles, chairs, wardrobes and window frames..." She nodded and smiled. "We even had our own book publisher who printed all the school books and Freeman's Bible."

"Freeman's Bible? Are you serious?"

"It was handed to him by the Lord when he left Salt Lake City."

"You believe that?"

"No, Mr. Walker, of course not. But there was a tacit agreement in Freedom that you did not question the Faith. Because if you did..." She went pale. The sandwich she was holding in her hand she laid down on her plate and picked up her mug. "Well, you saw yourself what happened to Noah."

"Did that happen often?"

"Often enough. Maybe once every couple of years. Sometimes it was just a beating. Other times, it was an execution."

"How could he stay off the radar this long? The IRS, the county sheriff..."

She snorted. "He was smart. He made sure the county and the state received just enough money and information from us—about us—to stop them from getting curious. He had people like Counselor Grumman and a couple of others to take care of that. They were the town's respectable face." She shrugged. "And where necessary, officials were bribed to look the other way, but on the whole, that wasn't really necessary, because we were nothing more than a small, remote town that kept to itself and never gave anybody any trouble." She shrugged again. "When we did need anything that we couldn't make and didn't have in the warehouses, there was a handful of trusted people..."

"Like Jonah."

"Exactly, who were tasked with going to La Grange and getting it. The rest of us knew that we were to stay within the geographical area of Freedom. And to be fair, Mr. Walker, most of the people in town had no real inclination to go anywhere else. It was beaten into us at school that the world was an ugly, dangerous place. Noah explained it to me. If you feed people an emotional diet of alternating fear and cozy, secure comfort, even if that comfort is provided within a prison, they will happily stay in that prison and even thank you for keeping them there. More than that, in the end you can entrust those people, and their children and their children's children, to keep that prison going. They'll even run it and maintain it for you."

"That's true enough. What can you tell me about the ranch?"

She gazed down at the hearth and for a moment, she looked forty years older than her age. Her cheeks were hollow and the pouches under her eyes looked dark. She took a deep breath and sighed. "That was another one of the reasons the mayor wanted Noah removed. Noah was..." She seemed to search for a word among the flames. The orange light flickered on her face. Then, a distant smile dispelled the haggard look of just a moment earlier. "He was *intelligent!* You can't keep a good mind down, however hard you try. He asked questions. First he asked himself, then, after we'd met, he asked me and we used to talk about the things we did not understand. Like, how did the economy of the town work?"

"Explain."

"He said, and he was right, that there was no way the town could generate the kind of wealth it was enjoying. The mayor kept up every house and every building in the town, to a high standard. You saw that. Everything was clean, the streets were clean, the houses were painted once a year, the parks were maintained, the shops were always stocked; and yet, what industry did we have?" She held up her index finger. "One ranch. One ranch where most of the men in the village worked, but received a nominal wage. You were right when you said it was a kind of slave labor, because every worker owed Mr. Freeman far more than he could ever pay him back. Sure, we had small, local industries like carpenters and iron mongers, but they barely generated enough wealth for one family. And nobody paid taxes, except the minimum required by the state. I mean, the town hall was paying for the upkeep of the town, but nobody, as far as we could see, was paying for the upkeep of the town hall. So, where was that money coming from?"

I was frowning and shook my head. "He sells marijuana and heroin, but that's only a recent thing, in the last year, if that."

She gave a short, dry laugh. "Oh, no. The recent thing is the association with Peter Kuznetsov. The ranch has been producing drugs for a long time."

"Where did he sell them?"

"I'm no expert." She paused, looking into her mug of coffee. The fire crackled and spat a shower of sparks onto the hearthstone. "I think the amount he was selling was comparatively small, and he was targeting areas where he was not going to find powerful opposition, where crime levels were comparatively low, but there were enough kids, gangs..." She shrugged, looking at me a little helplessly, telling me with her face that she didn't really know what she was talking about. "You know the sort of place?"

I knew and I nodded. "He stayed clear of major urban areas like New York, Chicago, L.A., and sold to dealers in smaller areas that were of less interest to the big cartels."

"I guess that was it. Noah believed that it was part of a long term plan that he had been working on for a long while." She smiled. It was a sad expression. "It sounds crazy, Mr. Walker, but he has his sons educated at home. When they are old enough, he has them sent away to university.

They have studied mainly law, politics... and chemistry. He has them working at the ranch."

"How many sons has he got?"

"Six, they are all part of the Council."

I rubbed my face with my palms. Suddenly, I was exhausted. She watched me a moment. "I guess something like this must seem insane to you."

I smiled. "Not as much as you might think. People like Freeman crop up occasionally. You were right when you compared it to Waco, only it's on a much bigger scale."

"This is the farthest I have ever been from Freedom."

"What about Noah? How come he was so aware?"

"His parents came to Freedom when he was seven years old. Before that, he was in Salt Lake City, where Freeman grew up before he received the Book..." She gave a small laugh. It sounded oddly ashamed. "Noah used to get mad at me when I said things like that. Old habits are hard to change. I should say, before he *says* he received the Book. After that, neither of us ever left Freedom."

I spoke half to myself, half to the flames in the fire. "I'm not so sure, Grace, that we aren't all living in Freedom, and we just don't know it."

SIXTEEN

My cell had started to ring. I pulled it from my pocket and thumbed the screen.

"Walker."

"Lacklan, it's Phil. What the hell happened to you? I was seen knocking at your door."

"Who by?"

"Somebody in a tractor."

"Anybody else?"

"No."

"Then don't worry about it. I got arrested."

"What? What for?"

"It's not important. We need to meet, soon."

"Where? I shan't return to Boulder."

I tried to think. I was exhausted, bruised, worried about how long I had been away from Marni. Suddenly, I had a craving to be home with her.

"Tomorrow, in Rawlins."

"Wyoming?"

"Is there another?"

"Maryland."

"No, Phil, the city in Wyoming. Roses Lariat, a Mexican diner on East Cedar Street. Be there at two-thirty PM. It should be quiet at that time."

"Don't stand me up again."

"I didn't stand you up, Phil. I got arrested by..." I sighed. "Never mind. I'll be there."

I hung up and the phone rang.

"Yeah, Walker."

"Good morning, this is Special Agent George Ramirez of the Jackson field office of the FBI."

"Good morning. I already spoke to Agent Solomon..."

"Mr. Walker, I'm just calling to let you know that we are at the ranch in Freedom right now, and that units from the bureau and the Wyoming Highway Patrol have moved into the town and are securing the jailhouse and the telephone exchange. Freeman is in custody and we are holding his family."

I sat on the arm of a chair, stared a moment at the fire, then out at the gray morning, turning slowly to blue.

"Thank you. That's good to know. Did you find..."

"We found the greenhouses, just as you described them. Mr. Walker, it would be mighty helpful if you could come here and talk me through exactly what happened, what you saw..."

I interrupted him. "Did you find the lab, with the animals?"

He hesitated for a fraction of a second. "Yes, we did."

"But it wasn't what you expected."

"There is a processing plant, where the opium is turned

into heroin. But there is, aside from that, a fairly sophisticated lab."

"A couple of his sons are trained chemists…"

"Mr. Walker, do you know something you're not telling me?"

"Just what I found out this morning."

"As I was saying, it would be really helpful if you could come and go over this with us. Honestly, I have never seen anything quite like it. I can send a car…"

I sighed. "I'm sorry, Agent Ramirez, I can't. I have to go to Boston. It's something I can't postpone."

"How soon will you leave?"

"I need to sleep. Midday, I guess. I'll be seeing Agent Solomon in Boston. I'll give him my statement."

"Yeah, I know." He sounded unhappy. "It's not quite the same thing, though, is it?"

"I'm sorry."

"Yeah…"

He hung up.

Grace had stretched out on the sofa and covered herself with the blanket. She was breathing softly and her eyes were closed. I put another log on the fire and stepped outside. The morning air was fresh. The sun was a couple of inches over the eastern horizon. In the old cottonwood in the yard, sporadic bursts of birdsong erupted among the rustle of wings.

Nothing moved on the roads or in the fields. Weariness threatened to close my eyes. I ignored it. A quarter of a mile away, small and silent in the distance, a white truck rolled along the track by the creek, raising a motionless cloud of red dust in its wake.

Nothing. Nothing threatened, except the stillness and the emptiness itself. I told myself I should sleep. I needed rest. I needed to be sharp. But there were still things to do.

I returned indoors, crossed the kitchen and entered the garage. From the back seat, I took the Heckler and Koch, and from the kit bag I took my spare Sig. I replaced the 416's magazine and rammed an extended magazine into the butt of the Sig.

I did the rounds of the house, checked every room and double-checked every window. I kept telling myself Hank was dead, Freeman was in custody. I could relax—I *should* relax, do what I came here to do, then get some sleep before the long drive this afternoon. But even as I told myself that, I knew it was wrong. It was wrong because Hank shouldn't be dead.

So instead of getting some sleep, I called J.R. at the local mechanic's.

"J.R. Motors, and how may I help you this fine morning?"

"J.R., it's Lacklan."

"Lacklan? Shoot. Y'all back in town?"

"Yeah, briefly. Listen, I need the front and rear windshields replaced on the Mustang."

"That weird-ass old electric thing a'yours?"

"Yeah. Can you do it this morning? Whatever it costs, J.R. I'll pay you double. I need it by lunchtime."

"'68 Fastback ,weren'it??"

"Yeah. Can you bring your truck over and do it here?"

He was quiet a moment. "Sure, I can do that. Y'all good?"

"Yeah. Just had a rough night. I appreciate it, J.R."

"I'll be there in ten or fifteen minutes."

When I'd hung up, I woke Grace. It wasn't easy. I took her upstairs and put her to bed in the spare room. I told her, "You've got four hours. At twelve, we're out of here."

She nodded, closed her eyes and went to sleep.

Ten minutes later, J.R.'s old truck rolled into the front yard. I went down to open the garage for him. He swung down from his cab and watched me with sharp eyes.

"You look like hell. I guess city life don't agree with you."

I managed a smile. "Don't ask, J.R. You don't want to know."

"Guess you're right at that." He said it with no special inflection, then stepped into the garage and had a look at the car. "What in the name of tarnation did you do to this thing?"

"It's a long story."

"Somebody been shootin' at you." He ran his hand over the roof and the hood, then leaned in the back, pulled out a couple of slugs and held them up for me to see. He was grinning. "That's from a goddarn assault rifle."

"Like I said."

"Welcome to the cowboy state. Yeehaa!" He laughed.

"Listen. I need to get some sleep. Anybody shows up, or looks like they're snooping, give me a shout. And, J.R.? Do me a favor, park your truck across the garage door, will you?"

He was still grinning. "Sure thing."

I climbed the stairs to my bedroom, reflecting that nothing earned you more respect in Wyoming and Texas than getting shot at—except perhaps shooting somebody yourself. Maybe, I told myself, that was why I felt so at home here.

With J.R. fixing the windshields and, more importantly, keeping watch for me, I pushed into the bedroom I had shared with Marni. There I opened the drawer of my bedside table and pulled out her diary and stood by the window, looking at it. It felt like another lifetime. Buddhists talk about dying and 're-becoming' in a new life, in a new body. They say that some people can recall those earlier lives. This felt that way, as though I had died and re-become, and what I was looking at was something that belonged to that earlier life.

I sat on the bed and opened it. The earliest entries were from when she was very young. They referred to us. I was Skywalker and she was Princess Leia. We had been close. So close we had excluded the world. Neither of us had had much time for anybody else. We were enough, *contra mundum*.

The entries were sporadic. They stopped and started, with gaps, sometimes of several years. Her handwriting evolved and matured, as did the nature and subject matter of the entries. Then the entries, as such, had stopped. The last one said, *Skywalker has gone.*

There was a gap, then, of five years. The next entry said, *Went to see Lacklan. He said no.*

She had come to see me in London. I had been with the Regiment for five years by then. She had asked me to come back. She had wanted us to build a life together. I had said no. No because I could not subject her to what I had become. Skywalker had died, murdered by my father, and in escaping from him and everything he represented, I had become a killer. I had loved her too much to make her a part of what I had become, so I had said no.

After that, what entries there were, were notes and thoughts on her post-graduate work and her thesis, about climate as a chaos model, the structure and dynamics of the Greenland ice sheet, and, increasingly, reflections on her father and his work in the same field. Occasionally she mentioned him, how she missed him. It was strange to read that now, knowing that she had looked on my father as a surrogate, that it had been my father who had killed hers, and that in time, she would kill my father.

It was almost a Greek tragedy, almost Freudian.

And somewhere in these pages, concealed by her father before he died, was his research: research that would have, if we had found it, brought down Omega. I took the pages and flicked through them, spraying them past my thumb, wondering how it was concealed in this small book, and, at this stage, with Omega all but finished, why was his research so important? I found no answer.

I put the diary in my bag, lay down and slept. I didn't dream. Time seemed not to have passed at all, but there was a voice calling me. I opened my eyes. I felt rested. There was a voice: J.R.'s, calling up the stairs.

I stood, put the Sig in my waistband and stepped out onto the landing. J.R. was at the foot of the stairs.

"Yeah?"

"You'll want to come out. There's some guys here in an SUV. Say they're from the FBI. They want to talk to you. I told 'em they could wait in the yard. Your windshield's done, front an' back."

"Come on up."

He climbed the stairs. I took two hundred bucks from my wallet and gave it to him. "That cover it?"

"Should do."

"Come with me. I want you to meet my sister."

I knocked on Grace's door. When I went in, she was sitting up in bed, rubbing her eyes. She frowned at me, like she was trying to remember. As she did, grief started to creep into her face.

"Grace, this is J.R. He's a friend. He's going to take you down to the car. I want you to get in and wait for me there. OK?"

She glanced at J.R., who was frowning at her bruises. "Where will you be?"

"I'll be out front, talking to some guys. I'll be five minutes. You do as I say and everything will be fine. Got it?"

She nodded and climbed out of bed. I turned to J.R. "See her into the car. Then come out through the front door, tell me the plumbing is fixed and be on your way."

"You got it."

"You're a pal. I owe you."

"No sweat. You know I ain't got much time for the federal government."

We shook hands and I took the stairs down two at a time, then stepped out into the front yard. There was a dark Chevy SUV with Wyoming plates, and there were two men wearing dark suits and dark glasses, leaning against the hood. I smiled like I thought I was funny and said, "What is this, the Men in Black?"

They didn't smile, like they didn't think I was funny. There wasn't much to tell between them, but the one who stood and showed me his badge looked more Hispanic, maybe in his early thirties. The other was a bit younger, paler and broader in the shoulders.

"Special Agent George Ramirez. We spoke on the phone."

"I remember. It wasn't that long ago. What can I do for you?"

"I'm going to have to ask you to come with us."

"You already did that, Agent Ramirez, and I gave you the same answer then that I am going to give you now. I can't. I am going to Boston, and when I'm in Boston, I'm going to talk to AD Solomon. I am afraid you've wasted your time."

He shook his head and looked at my boots. "I'm afraid you don't understand, Mr. Walker. I need you to come back with me, either of your own free will or as a material witness. Or, if need be, in custody under the Patriot Act."

I raised an eyebrow and smiled. "You are going to arrest me under the Patriot Act? Are you out of your mind? I called you, remember? I called Senator Cyndi McFarlane to ensure I didn't get caught up in red tape when I reported this business."

His face hardened. "Nevertheless, Mr. Walker, if you're not willing to come with us voluntarily, I'm going to have to take you in by force."

I narrowed my eyes. "Let me explain something to you, son. You arrest me, you try to take me in by force, and I'll have your job." I gave him a moment and held his eye. "I will have so many lawyers crawling over you, you'll think you're a jelly sandwich at an ant convention. There will be lawyers and private dicks investigating your parents' political allegiances, who they smoked hash with at college, who you bought your weed from when *you* were in college, who you screwed, who screwed you, who your friends are, what kind of porn you download to your computer. There will not be a single aspect of your life or your family's life that they will not know about. And then, when they have it, they will start to use it." I shook my head. "This is not what the Patriot Act was intended for, Agent Ramirez. So you take your threats, you make a neat little ball of them, and you shove them up your pretty ass. I hope I am not being too subtle for you."

His face had drained itself of all its blood and was busy going tight with injured ego. I saw his hand twitch toward his jacket and turned to his pal, who'd taken his elbow off the hood of the SUV and had stepped up close.

"Explain to your partner, Special Agent, that he has no grounds to make an arrest here. Explain to him that, just by breathing, I make more money in one hour than he makes in a year, and that if he tries to arrest me, before breakfast tomorrow morning, the FBI will be flying me home in a private jet while *he* is putting his pen holder, 'I'm the Champ' mug and his photo of his mommy in a carton and vacating his desk."

I took a step toward Ramirez and pushed my face really close to his, though I continued talking to his partner. "Explain to him also that if he wants me to cooperate, he needs to be polite and say please, and if he reaches for that piece under his arm..." I allowed myself a wolfish leer. "Well, this is Wyoming. So first I'll tear his arm off, then I'll shove his Glock down his throat and after that, I'll blow his ass off with it. And I have twenty witnesses right here in this town who'll testify they saw it happen and it was self defense. After that, for good measure, I'll sue the FBI for trespass and assault." I narrowed my eyes and cocked my head. "Tell me, am I getting through to you?"

I turned then and looked at his friend. I put my finger on

his chest and shoved. "And you, next time you set foot on my property, you identify yourself and show me your goddamn badge! What's your name?"

"Special Agent Calabrio."

"My attorneys will be filing complaints against both of you. Is there anything else I can help you boys with today?"

Calabrio shook his head.

"Then get the hell off my land."

Behind me, the door opened and J.R. emerged. He waved and called, "Your U-bend's all fixed, Mr. Walker. Anythin' else I can do for you?"

"I'm all good, J.R. These gentlemen were just leaving. They had the wrong information. Ain't that right, boys?"

They stood a moment, trying to give me the dead eye. Then they turned and pulled open the doors of the Chevy. As they were about to climb in, I said, "Hey, Ramirez."

He turned to face me. "What?"

"You still got Freeman in custody?"

"Screw you."

I nodded. "That's what I thought. See you around."

J.R. was pulling out of the yard. Ramirez turned his truck around and followed him out, then overtook him and sped down toward the gas station, where they turned right onto the 191, north and west, toward Freedom.

I walked back to the house and locked up. I collected the HK416 from my bedroom and made my way down to the kitchen. There I went through to the garage and found Grace waiting for me in the Zombie. I climbed in, pressed the button on the dash and the garage door began to rise. As we slid silently out, Grace spoke without looking at me.

"Who were those men?"

"Feds."

"Why didn't you let them talk to me?"

"I don't know."

"You're lying."

I sighed, then nodded as I turned onto the road. "Yeah, I am."

"Why, then?" Now she turned to look at me. "Why won't you let the FBI talk to me?"

I was silent, cruising under the clear blue sky toward the intersection where Ramirez had turned north and west. When we got there, I turned south, onto the long, straight road that would carry us the ninety miles to Rock Springs and the I-80, which would in turn take us to Rawlins, and Phil; back to the task in hand, the murder—the assassination —of the final Omega cabal, now that the madness of Freedom was over.

Grace's voice broke into my thoughts.

"Why?" she asked, and then again, "Why would you not let them talk to me?"

"Because you've been through enough. Ramirez is an asshole. You need to rest. Back in Weston, you can talk to AD Solomon, after you've rested."

"You're still lying to me, Mr. Walker."

I didn't answer.

She went on. "You know why I loved Noah?"

"He was a special kind of guy."

Outside, the endless, flat plains sped by. I saw the needle climb to a hundred.

"Yes, he was. In a town full of men who thought they were better than me because they happened to have testicles and penises, he respected me and didn't treat me like a little woman who needed to be protected. He treated me as an equal. He respected me as an intelligent person. Now you have rescued me, for which I am very grateful to you, but you have rescued me and now you are treating me the same way that Freeman and all his cronies did, as though I was some kind of helpless, blonde idiot."

"You're a redhead."

"Don't be facetious!"

"I saved your life because they were going to murder you, Grace. I don't need to play this damned PC, feminist game. If my behavior offends you, you can get in line. There are plenty of other people, men and women, black and white, gay and straight, who all find me offensive. Hell! Sometimes I even find myself offensive! That's just who I am."

Her voice came bitter and twisted. "Is this your way of making sure I rest and don't get upset, because I have been through so much? And you think *Ramirez* is an asshole!"

"Cut it out, will you! I didn't want Ramirez to talk to you and that's all there is to it."

She clenched her fists and shouted at me. "*Why are you lying to me? Why would you not let those men talk to me? Stop patronizing me!*"

I glared at her.

She glared back. "*Kindly* keep your eyes on the road, Mr. Walker!"

"Because..." I turned away and sighed. "Because we do this my way. End of story."

SEVENTEEN

SHE DIDN'T SAY ANYTHING FOR THE NEXT FORTY-five minutes.

After five minutes, her head began to nod forward and pretty soon she had fallen asleep, and she stayed like that, with her arms crossed and her chin on her chest, until we were approaching Rock Springs. Then, as we entered the outskirts of the town and moved through the industrial parks, she lifted her head suddenly and turned to look at me with sleepy eyes.

"You're out of your mind," she said flatly.

"Thanks."

She sighed, then yawned. "He was everything to us in Freedom, like a god. But outside of his small pond, he was nobody. If you're going to start buying government officials, you need real power, real money. He didn't have that kind of power or money."

I frowned at her curiously. "Are you continuing a conversation you were having in your dreams?"

"Maybe." She said it like she found the idea depressing. "Weren't we talking? I think you have the wrong idea about him. Maybe he was a bit crazy, but he was no master criminal."

"Are you kidding me? What I saw at the ranch was millions—tens of millions of dollars' worth of merchandise! Hell! Maybe more even than that. He was in bed with the Russian Mafia, Grace. Freeman had the power *and* the money to buy himself a whole bunch of government officials if he needed them. And Kuznetsov had the muscle to enforce any deals they made. Believe me, Freeman was well on his way to becoming a major player."

She rubbed her face. "Sorry, I'm feeling confused."

"I'm not surprised. You're probably still in shock."

We passed under the bridge and took the I-80 turn off at the lights, headed east now toward Rawlins, a hundred miles away. When we were safely out of town, I glanced in the mirror and put my foot down, and watched the needle climb to a hundred and twenty.

She spoke suddenly, like she was answering something I'd said.

"That's a recent thing."

I glanced at her. "What is?"

"He never had that kind of power before. Or that kind of wealth. Everything he had he invested in the town. This thing with the Russian Mafia, it's all recent."

"Yeah, I got that from what they said. The last year or so. You told me Noah thought he'd been planning it for years." I said it more to myself, knowing it was important and wondering why.

She glanced at me, like she was reading my thoughts. "Yeah, maybe."

We made it to Rawlins in less than an hour. We came off the Lincoln Highway at the intersection and took West Spruce Street into the town. Then took Colorado Street south as far as East Cedar and left the car out of sight at the back of the parking lot.

I turned to Grace before we got out. "You're going to walk a few paces ahead of me, like we're not together. You walk into the restaurant and you take a table at the back. Order whatever you like."

"I have no money. It's all back in..."

"I'll cover it. Don't worry about it. You sit and have your lunch. Don't look at me. Don't be aware of me. OK?"

She nodded. "OK."

"I'll be right behind you, I'll be keeping an eye on you. I'm going to sit at another table with another guy. Ignore him too. When we get up to leave, you leave too and make your way to the car. Got it?"

"Got it."

I followed her across the lot, looking at my phone like I was checking my messages. I scanned the cars and the street in all directions, but didn't see anybody that caught my attention. I watched her go into the restaurant and take her seat at a table at the back. I saw Phil sitting at a table nearby, working at his laptop.

I stood on the sidewalk a while, looking up and down, then went inside and sat with Phil. He looked up at me as I sat down.

"Couldn't you find anywhere more public? Did you

alert the media? Perhaps we should tell them Robert Downey Junior will be joining us. Just to make sure, you know, that we get the attention."

"You done?"

"I've barely begun."

"Stop making a scene and maybe we'll get by without anyone noticing us."

"What do you want? Are you aware I am agoraphobic?"

"I had kind of guessed, Phil."

"Well? What do you want?"

The waitress came over and I ordered two burgers and two cups of coffee. When she'd gone away again, I said, "I told you we're finishing the job."

"Yes, you told me that."

"There is only one pillar left, and we aim to bring it down."

"I don't think much of your metaphor, but I understand what you're saying. I'm still waiting to hear what you want from me."

"Take it easy, will you, Phil? The more antsy you get, the more attention you attract. We're a couple of old pals who've run into each other and we're having a burger and a coffee and a good ol' chinwag. Now relax."

He sighed. "Fine." He produced an ugly rictus which was meant to be a smile. "What, for the third time, do you want?"

"I'm coming to that. Just hear me out. When we took out..." I paused. "When we went to Africa, we dealt with the personnel, but we didn't deal with their accounts, not in the same way we did with Europe. Are you following me?"

"Of course I am following you, Lacklan. You are making it plainly obvious."

"Good. Now, when we deal with China, we need to apply the same methods, and the same ordnance, that we used in Europe."

He closed his eyes. "Oh, dear God. I was dreading you would say that." He shook his head. "I told you then I would not do it again. You know what the risks are. It was a miracle it was contained that time. A second attempt..."

His words trailed off and he shook his head. I laughed like he was saying something amusing.

"Take it easy, will you? You need to reframe this thing." I shrugged, still smiling. "You're balancing a risk against a certainty. If the Chinese corporation gets on the market, we are toast, my friend. That's a certainty. There is another thing you need to consider, Phil. If you don't supply the goods, I'll have to get them elsewhere. Now ask yourself, is there anybody you trust more than yourself?"

He shook his head. "No." He stared for a long time at the table top, then looked up at me. "You'd do that?"

"My father told me you were the go-to guy, remember? But if you are abdicating from that post, then you're not the go-to guy anymore, and I'll have to find somebody else who is. I don't know much about what you do, Phil, so I may not make a well-informed choice. But the clock is ticking and I need to do something fast, because the departure date for China is approaching fast. Now, will you provide me with the ordnance, or not?"

I asked it like I was asking how the wife and kids were, and he looked at me as though he thought I was insane.

"You're not leaving me any choice."

"That is correct. That is the idea. Because," I said with a laugh, "I need you to do it, and soon."

His hands were trembling and he kept swallowing. The waitress appeared with our coffees. She set them down and went away. When she was gone, Phil said, "What do you want, the same as last time?"

I shook my head. "A little different." As I spoke, I laid my cell on the table. "While we talk, download the photographs and video from that onto your laptop. Yes, I want pretty much the same thing you gave me for Europe, but I want you to see if you can make a small modification."

His eyes were wide, but his pupils were pinpricks. He fiddled with his keyboard. "Your Bluetooth is on?"

I nodded.

"What modification?"

"Africa must have dealt with China, right? It makes sense."

"I guess."

"So their computer networks would have connected at some time."

"That would make sense, yes."

"Would it be possible to trace those contacts and find a way for the..." I hesitated. "For the infection to spread into the African network?"

He went pale. "What you're asking for is not only almost impossible, it elevates the risk level exponentially."

"I'm not asking you to do it. I'm asking you to think about whether it is possible."

He ran his fingers through his hair. "Of course—of *course* it's possible..."

"Hey, chill. You're standing out like a fluorescent dildo

at a convent. Relax. I'm worried that the whole infrastructure of Africa is intact. It's a fertile breeding ground. We need to remove it before somebody else takes over."

He stared at me, then at the screen. "Download is complete."

"Cool." I reached in my pocket and pulled out the pen drive I'd taken from the lab. "This goes with it. See what you can make of it, will you?"

He took it, stared at it a moment like he didn't know what it was, and dropped it in his pocket.

"This is not good," he said.

"I have to agree with you, Phil. None of it is any good. That's why we're trying to fix it. Now, can you do it?"

"I'll try."

I shook my head. "Try is not enough. This is the end game. We make it happen or we go down. Are you in?"

He nodded. "Of course."

The burgers turned up and the waitress told us to enjoy them. In my peripheral vision, I could see Grace picking at a small bag of fries. Phil did the same thing with the fries on his plate while I bit into my burger. He leaned forward. His face was ashen, his eyes were wide and his pupils were contracted. I found myself wondering if he smoked dope. He spoke in a whisper.

"Lacklan, what you are asking for is a virus that will infiltrate every computer on a network that could contain thousands—tens of thousands of terminals. When it has finished spreading, it will erase all the data from those computers. In Europe, miraculously, all of the Omega computers were hermetically isolated from contact with the wider net, otherwise the consequences would have been apocalyptic."

"I know, Phil."

"But this time you are asking more. Because you want this virus to trace memories of networks that have made contact in the past, and follow those pathways back into those other networks. But imagine if just one of those computers has connected with the London Stock Exchange, or Wall Street, or a major investment bank..."

"I know, Phil. You need to stop talking..."

"*There would be no way to stop it spreading!* Because every network on the Internet has connected with some other network on the Internet and the virus will *never stop spreading!* It could take hours, days, weeks or months, but one day, every single computer on Earth would just crash. Air traffic control, world banks, stock markets, supermarket stock controls, university libraries, hospitals... It just goes on and on, Lacklan. Our entire world is run by computer. Have you *any conception* of what would happen? You would be doing their work for them!"

I stared him hard in the eye. "Stop talking."

He stopped for just a moment. Then, he said, "Have you taken in what I have said to you? Have you assimilated the meaning of what I am saying?"

"Yes, Phil, and I am hoping that I am the only person in this restaurant who has. Stop talking."

"So?"

"So we need to do it anyway."

Over his shoulder, I could see the street outside through the window. Across the road, a dark Audi saloon had pulled up in the empty lot and two guys got out. One was in a suit. The other was in jeans and a hat.

I smiled at Phil. "Leave now. Don't ask. Just get up and go. We'll be in touch in a day or two."

"But..."

"Go now, Phil. Right now."

He closed his laptop, stared at me for a second, stood and walked out. Through the window, I saw him turn left. The guys across the way were leaning against their car, apparently waiting for somebody. Then I noticed that the guy in the suit was talking on the phone. I looked to the back of the restaurant. The only doors were the restrooms. I stood and went to the bar. The waitress smiled at me.

"Is there a rear exit?" I gave her my most winning smile. "There's a guy out there I really don't want to talk to..."

She glanced out the window. He was still talking on the phone, but now they were both crossing the road. I could see clearly now it was Ramirez.

The waitress was saying, "Sorry, we have to take the trash out the front each night. But I don't want any trouble, mister..."

I made my face more reassuring than it felt. "No trouble."

I went and sat with Grace. "Ramirez is here, with one of Freeman's deputies."

She studied my face a moment. "That doesn't make sense..."

"Yeah, not much about Freedom does."

As I said it, the door opened and the cowbell hanging above it clanged. He looked straight at us and said, "Yeah, they're here."

Then he hung up, put the phone in his pocket and crossed the room with a cowboy behind him who looked like Man Mountain McCoy on steroids. They sat at our table and stared at us. The waitress came over and Ramirez said, "Coffee," without looking at her.

The cowboy looked at her and smiled, the way his momma had taught him. "And a slice of blueberry pie, miss, if you have any, with cream."

I said, "What do you want, Ramirez?"

"You know what I want, Mr. Walker. I want you to come back to Freedom with me. You are a material witness to what happened there and I need your statement so that I can carry out my investigation."

I gestured at the cowboy. "And this gentleman is?"

"Samuel O'Brien, the new deputy of Freedom."

I looked at the big slab of granite he used for a face. "What happened to the old one?"

His pale blue eyes narrowed. "He was shot."

I nodded once. "Really?" I looked back at Ramirez. "I understood he was in custody."

"He escaped."

"With the FBI and the Wyoming Highway Patrol swarming all over Freedom and the ranch? How did that happen?"

The waitress brought the coffee and the pie. She set down the cups and the plate, smiled and withdrew. Ramirez stared at his brew for a moment like he was really mad at it.

"I'm not here to answer your questions, Mr. Walker. I'm here to take you to Freedom."

"And I'm going to give you the same answer I gave you before, Ramirez. You're wasting your time."

"Are you going to force me to arrest you?"

"It would be interesting to see you try." I pulled my cell from my pocket and thumbed my contacts.

He frowned. "Who are you calling?"

"Senator Cyndi McFarlane. She arranged for AD Solomon to call me." I smiled. "I have her on speed dial."

"Don't do that."

I smiled. "Really? Give me a good reason why I shouldn't."

He sighed. "I have information you can use."

I didn't answer for a moment, wondering what the hell he was talking about. Then, I put my cell in my pocket and crossed my arms. "What information?"

He pulled his own cell from his pocket, pressed his speed dial and after a moment said, "Sir, you'd better come in."

He hung up. I looked at O'Brien. He was absorbed in his pie. Ramirez was watching me, like he was trying to figure what I was thinking. I said, "How did Hank West escape, Ramirez?"

"That doesn't concern you."

"When the first thing he did was come after me and Grace and try to kill us, I figure it concerns me."

For the first time, his eyes shifted to Grace. "Grace O'Conor... Some folks back in Freedom are saying you kidnapped her."

I raised an eyebrow. "*Some folks back in Freedom?*"

O'Brien finished his pie and wiped his mouth on the back of his hand. "Yes, sir, that is just what some folks back in Freedom are sayin'."

The cowbell over the door clanged and I heard Grace give a small cry beside me. A tall man in an expensive suit had stepped in. He had striking white hair and a gaunt, handsome face. I looked at him and went cold inside, not because I hadn't expected it, but because it was exactly what I had expected.

Freeman saw us and smiled, and moved toward us.

EIGHTEEN

RAMIREZ AND O'BRIEN WENT TO STAND. HE placed a hand on each of their shoulders.

"That's all right, boys." He smiled at Grace. "Hello, Grace. Are you OK? He hasn't hurt you, has he?" He didn't wait for an answer. He turned and signaled the waitress for coffee, pulled over a chair and sat opposite Grace. He turned his smile into a small laugh. "My! We haven't seen this much excitement in Freedom since... well, *ever!* Ain't that so, Grace?"

She didn't answer. I spoke to Ramirez. "What the hell are you playing at?"

"What am I playing at? Seriously?" He gave a snort that might have been a laugh. "Let me tell you something, Captain Walker. I pulled your file. You're an interesting guy. British special forces, your name linked indirectly or vaguely to a whole bunch of incidents from Europe to Latin America via New York and L.A., where a whole bunch of people seemed to wind up dead. Your connection? No connection ever proven, but you just happened to be there. And you know what? I think you've somehow got the idea that you are above the law, that you can just do what the hell you like and your billion dollar bank account and your senator friends will keep you out of trouble." He shook his head. "But not this time."

"Really." I pointed at Freeman. "How about this guy? Will his billion dollar bank account and his Russian Mafia friends keep him out of trouble? How about his cannabis and opium plantations?"

Freeman chuckled. Ramirez leaned forward. "It's not enough for you to just say they were there, Walker. They have to actually *be* there."

"What are you talking about? You can't hide ten hangar-sized greenhouses full of giant cannabis plants! There must have been tens of thousands of poppies. You really think the Bureau isn't going to follow up? You really think there won't be an inquiry? You think they won't find traces of these plants, and the lab?"

Ramirez had closed his eyes and he was shaking his head. "What I have, Walker, is a town full of people, many of them who work on that ranch, who are willing to testify, under oath, that there is not now, and never has been, any production of illegal substances on that farm."

I laughed. "But what about the *tons* of cannabis and opium?"

He shook his head again. "What cannabis? What opium?"

I sank back in my chair. "You're actually going to try and do this."

"This is why I need you, Mr. Walker, to come back to

Freedom with me. Show me where these plantations are, because I have not been able to find them."

"How about the Highway Patrol?" I asked. "Have they been to the ranch?"

"That's none of your concern. Now, how's it going to be? You going to come willingly, or do I have to take you in?"

"Neither, Ramirez. I told you before. I am going to take Grace to Boston, and there I am going to make a statement to AD Solomon. The only thing that's changed is that the statement will now be more detailed."

Freeman placed his hand on Ramirez's arm and turned to Grace.

"Grace, child, what happened? Was Freedom not good to you? Did Freedom not care for you?" He held up a hand and closed his eyes, like he was stopping her from answering. "I understand if you want to leave, but before you do, just answer a couple of questions for me. Can you do that?"

She sighed. "Yes."

"Did I provide your mother with a home?"

She glanced at me. There was real anxiety in her eyes. She looked down at her lap and licked her lips. "Yes," she said.

"Did I maintain that home in good order?"

She nodded. "Yes..."

"Did I provide her, all of you, with food, and warmth in the winter?"

Her voice seemed to shrivel in on itself. "Yes..."

"Did I provide your father with work, and a stable income?"

"Yes..."

He leaned forward, reached across the table and held out

his hand to her, palm up, like he was beckoning. "Did you ever need or want for anything? Did I ever demand anything in return? Did I ever ask for a single cent in payment?"

"No…"

"Was it, perhaps, too much to ask that you, like so many young girls before you, do your duty by the village, according to our sacred tradition? Did I ask more of you than I have asked of so many girls who have gone before you?"

Her voice had become almost inaudible, little more than a whisper. "…no…"

"Then give me your hand, child, and come home. Come back to the fold where you belong, where you will be safe and cared for."

She looked at me. Her face was wet and shiny. Her eyes were wide with grief and terror. I saw her hand rise from her lap and reach out toward his. I shook my head.

"Grace, you don't want to do that." I reached behind my back and pulled my Sig Sauer from my waistband. I kept it under the table and leaned forward with my elbows on my knees, holding the piece with both hands.

"Freeman, the nice waitress told me, when these two assholes were crossing the road, that she didn't want any trouble. I don't want any trouble either. So I'll tell you what I am going to do for you. Right now I have a p226 Tacops trained on your balls. I won't pull the trigger if you and your two gorillas leave nicely. But before you answer, I would ask you to remember what happened to Vasiliev last time you doubted the seriousness of my intentions."

Ramirez sneered. "You going to shoot an FBI agent and a sheriff's deputy, too? You know what will happen to you?"

I smiled sweetly. "Yes. And it will be better than what's about to happen to you." I looked at Freeman and raised my eyebrows. "The clock is ticking, Freeman. I don't want to do this. Don't make me."

He sighed. "He's serious. I believe he'll do it." He looked at me and held my eye. "This doesn't change anything, Mr. Walker. It just delays the outcome, and makes it worse for you."

"Sure."

He went to stand.

"Freeman."

He paused.

"You're insane. What makes you dangerous is that you're rich and you can buy yourself assholes like these two. But that doesn't change the fact that you're insane."

"Thank you."

"Answer me a question."

"Will you shoot me if I don't?"

"Perhaps." I watched his face carefully. "What do you know about Omega?"

He frowned, then shrugged. "Omega? The watch?"

"Never mind. Get the hell out of here."

They stood. Ramirez gave me the once over. "We'll see you again before the day is out."

They left and I watched O'Brien and Ramirez cross the road, while Freeman turned right and disappeared from view. I slipped the Sig back in my waistband. Grace took a couple of paper napkins and blew her nose, then wiped her eyes.

I said: "OK, let's go and get you some clothes."

She looked up at me like I was nuts. "What?"

I paid at the counter and Grace followed me out onto the street. The cowbell clanged behind us and the door clunked closed. I scanned the street. There was no sign of the Audi. Nothing struck me as out of place or wrong. I gave Grace my arm.

"Come on, let's stroll. It's six blocks down from here."

"Why are we buying clothes? I told you I have no money."

"Don't worry. It's on me." I winked and smiled. "I want you to look nice when I introduce you to the folks."

She gave a small, wet laugh, then said, "You're bullshitting me again."

"I know. Let's get the clothes and I'll explain in the car. We have a thirty hour drive ahead of us. We'll have plenty of time to talk."

Ten minutes later, we pushed into a clothing department store. We must have looked pretty rough, because the assistant looked alarmed and stepped toward us like she was going to advise us to go elsewhere. But I smiled at Grace and said, "This lady will take care of you. Get whatever you like." To the assistant, I said, "You take AMEX Black, don't you?"

She stopped, her knees turned in slightly, and she smiled at Grace. "Of course. Such pretty hair! What did you have in mind, honey?"

While Grace did her shopping, I stood outside and smoked a Camel. I still saw no sign of Freeman or his men. It was clear the chopper had tracked us from Freedom using Jonah's cell in the trunk. But the only way Ramirez could have tracked us to Rawlins was if Grace had some kind of tracking device in her clothes, or her shoes.

I took a drag and inhaled deeply, flicking ash, trying to

make out Freeman. I had told him he was insane, and I did believe that. But I had to admit that insane didn't quite cover it. He was insane the way Ben had been insane, the way the Omega cabals were insane. They were out of touch with what most people would call reality, but at the same time they were so focused on what they believed, in what they wanted their reality to be, that they created a whole new reality to suit themselves—a reality where they were sane and the rest of us were nuts. Who was it who said that reality was just a psychosis we all agreed upon?

I stood another couple of minutes thinking about Freeman, then flicked the butt onto the road and went back inside. I found Grace dithering with the assistant over two blouses. One was red and the other was mauve.

"We'll take both. Did you get shoes?"

Grace looked embarrassed. "Shoes? The ones I have are fine..."

"Pick two pairs of shoes, or boots, both, whatever. And underwear. But make it snappy, Grace. We're on the clock." I smiled at the assistant. "We have a long drive down to San Diego." To Grace, I said, "Go get changed. Everything. Let's go."

Fifteen minutes later, we stepped out of the shop and into the late afternoon sun. Grace was dressed in her new clothes—jeans, boots and a sweatshirt—and we had two full bags. One held a change of clothes, the other all her old clothes and her shoes.

We made our way up Cedar Street, back to the parking lot behind Rose's Lariat. There I slung Grace's old clothes in the trunk and spent five minutes scouring the Zombie for any sign of tampering. I didn't find anything and we climbed in and headed out east, along the I-80.

An hour out of Rawlins, we came to Laramie. Late afternoon was turning to dusk. At the intersection with Highway 287, I came off and parked by the entrance to the Ramada motel. I booked a room, dumped Grace's old clothes on the bed and we continued on our way. It wouldn't put them off our scent. They knew who I was and they knew where I was going, but it might delay them for a while. And, I told myself, as we sped into the growing darkness, with the capabilities of the Zombie, a small lead was all I needed.

That, and a plan.

But the more I thought about it, the more I realized it was hard to make a plan. Because what I didn't know about Freeman could fill volumes, and what I knew I could write on a postage stamp. Freeman to me was a whole bunch of questions: what made him tick? How did he get that way? Was he insane? Was he a sociopath? Did he believe the shit he spouted? Did he really believe he was chosen by God? Why the hell did the Russian mob take him seriously? How the hell did he put together that ranch without anybody noticing? And, how the hell did he get to Ramirez and Calabrio?

And that was just for starters. Then I had deeper questions relating to his connection to Omega. Was it my imagination, or were there hints that he and Omega had links? My brain told me it was too much of a coincidence that I should return home from a meeting with Jim and just happen to run into an Omega sapling in Wyoming. But my gut told me that the whole story about the power vacuum in the West had Omega writ large all over it.

Like I said, what I didn't know could fill volumes.

It had grown dark outside. We had just left Cheyenne behind and we were speeding under a vast sky toward Nebraska. Grace spoke suddenly and her voice seemed loud in the confined space of the car.

"I think you're a good man, Mr. Walker."

"Thank you. Call me Lacklan, will you?"

"Thank you. I think you're a good man. But I wish you would understand that I have just had my fiancé murdered, I have been arrested, kidnapped and..." She paused, hesitating. "What is this? A rescue? Or also another kidnapping?"

I scowled at her, then laughed. "It's a rescue, Grace! It's not a kidnapping! You are free..."

"I understand," she interrupted me. "What I am trying to say is that though my life until now may have been very sheltered, in the last few days, perhaps weeks, I have experienced a great deal."

Half my mind was still on Freeman and Omega, the other half was trying to understand what she was saying to me. I couldn't, so I said, "What's your point, Grace?"

"I think you should tell me what's on your mind. I think I have a right to know. This may be your business. Maybe you are, as you say, a professional killer. Perhaps whatever is going on is a part of your life. But it was my fiancé who was murdered, and it was I who was kidnapped and almost tried. This is my life that is being thrown into turmoil."

I sighed. "I can't argue with that, Grace. And..." I shrugged and sighed again. "I wish I had an answer for you, but I am sitting here, driving, and trying to work out what the hell just happened. Who *is* John Freeman? How can he be *that* rich, that powerful, and yet nobody has ever heard of him? How can he own that ranch, control federal agents, and never have shown up on anybody's radar? I don't know." I glanced at her. "I can't tell you what I am thinking, because I don't know."

She was quiet for a while, gazing at our ghosts in the window, illuminated by the dials on the dash.

"Noah had friends outside. Sometimes they would send him magazines and newspapers. They weren't forbidden, but they were discouraged." She glanced at me. "The Council believed it was good to have some idea of what was going on around us, just so long as we saw through the lies and the glamour to the wicked truth within. That's how I saw the article about Waco."

She stopped talking for a moment, then returned to gazing out the window at the vast fields speeding past in the dark. "Noah used to let me read those magazines and newspapers, and one of the first things I noticed was just how many men, and women, there are out there who are just like Mayor Freeman."

I stared at her. What I felt was something like astonishment. We didn't talk again until we stopped for the night just outside Williamsburg, Iowa. It was three AM.

NINETEEN

THERE WAS NO SIGN OF FREEMAN OR RAMIREZ that night or the next day. We set out at seven thirty AM, having slept four hours, and as we pulled back onto the I-80 and accelerated east, the road behind us and the sky above us were both clear. It was tempting to believe we had shaken them, or that we were too far from home for them to take action, but I knew that wasn't true.

I called Cyndi. When she answered, her voice was sleepy.

"Lacklan... For God's sake, where are you?"

"Not now, Cyndi. Just listen to me. This is complicated. I need you and Solomon to meet me."

"Meet you? Where? When?"

"This afternoon, at three. Toledo, at the Renaissance Hotel. You know where it is?"

"What? No..."

"It's next door to the Imagination Station science museum. North Summer Street. You got that?"

"Wait... I'm making a note. Aren't you going to tell me what this is about?"

"No. But tell Solomon something in Jackson stinks, and he'd better dispatch an independent team to Freedom, and especially the ranch. He needs to do that fast, and tell him they'd better be armed."

"Jesus..."

"And Cyndi? Bring a couple of bodyguards. You might need them."

I hung up. Then I called Avis at the Toledo Express Airport. It was on the I-80 just outside town. I prepaid for a Chevy Impala and arranged to pick it up at noon.

It was about four hundred and fifty miles to Toledo. As far as Chicago, I was able to give the Zombie its head, but after that, the traffic was heavier and I stuck to the speed limit. The last thing I needed was to be pulled over with an HK416 in the trunk and a chassis scarred by automatic rifle fire.

Even so, we reached the airport at ten minutes before noon. I left the Zombie in the airport parking lot and switched to the Impala. While I was there, I went to the airport store and bought a burner. Then we drove the rest of the way to the hotel, parked in the parking lot out front and went in to book a room. I paid with my AMEX, mentioned we'd arrived by taxi and had no vehicle and asked for somewhere nearby where we could have lunch. The receptionist recommended Giorgio's Café International.

At the restaurant, Grace had a salad, which she pushed around her plate, and I had a sirloin steak, which I ate hungrily. When I was halfway through it, I relaxed back in my chair and looked at her across the table. Her bruises were beginning to fade. When she glanced at me, there was a vitality and an intelligence in her blue eyes which was somehow enhanced by her copper hair. I said:

"This will be over today. Have you any idea what you want to do afterwards?"

Her eyes went wide. "Good Lord, Mr. Walker…"

"Lacklan."

"Very well, Lacklan, I have barely come to terms with the last few days…"

"I know. You'll need to take a rest. After that, you'll need a job, an income, a home. You'll need to rebuild your life."

"I'm aware. I don't intend to be a burden on you."

"Don't be stupid." She frowned and I smiled. "That's not what I meant. I didn't bust you out of Freedom to leave you high and dry out here. There's no pressure. I'm just curious. I also want you to realize that tomorrow will come, and Freeman won't be in it."

She poked a piece of feta cheese with her fork, skewered it and laid down her fork. Then she sighed, like the exercise had left her drained. "You're a strange man, aren't you?"

I shrugged. "I never met anyone like me."

"You see? Right there…" She trailed off, then started again. "I'm a teacher. I guess I'll go back to teaching."

"Are you qualified?"

She frowned again.

I raised a hand. "I know you're qualified, probably more than many. What I mean is, have you a recognized teaching qualification?"

Her eyebrows rose. "No…"

I smiled again and renewed my assault on my steak. "Out here, people don't matter. What matters out here is what officially recognized qualifications you have. You'll need to go to college."

She narrowed her blue eyes and shook her head. "We are being pursued by rogue federal agents, the Russian Mafia and Freeman, you have a clandestine meeting in a couple of hours with a senator and an FBI agent I am guessing you don't trust, our lives are almost certainly on the line, and yet..." She gestured at my plate. "Here you sit, eating steak and talking about my needing to go to college. Are you simply out of touch with reality, or...?"

Again she trailed off. I waited till she'd finished, then cut another chunk of meat and put it in my mouth.

"There are many secrets to survival. One of them is never to rest until the danger is over. Then rest completely. Another is to make long movies."

She smiled, then shook her head and began to laugh. "Make long movies?"

"Sure. We all make movies in our head, all the time, about the things we want to do and the things we intend to do. People who make bad choices usually make short movies that don't include all the consequences to the actions they take. Another drink, another cake, another snort of cocaine, I need to hit the sack with this woman or that man—they are all classic short movies. If those people made longer movies that included the hangover, the depression on looking at the scales, the morning after, they'd probably also make better choices."

"Huh..."

"At a more serious level, every war, every battle, every fight, must be fought in the light of what comes afterwards. Otherwise, what are you fighting for? This fight today only has meaning if you have a meaningful life afterwards. So I am making a long movie that includes your life when this is done. You should do the same."

She made a face and nodded. "Long movies, huh?" She smiled and studied my face for a moment. "You realize I have never been to the movies. I've read about them. Noah described them to me. But I have never been."

I smiled, then laughed. "OK, all right, Grace. Tomorrow, I will take you to your first movie. We will go to a classic black and white first." I waved my fork at her. "I know a few arty theatres in Boston where they may be showing the Maltese Falcon, or Casablanca. That's where we'll start. You have a treat in store for you."

She laughed. We were quiet, then, for a moment and the laughter faded from her face. "Supposing... I mean, how would I go about going to college? What would I need to do...?"

"Like I said, I didn't pull you out of Freedom to leave you high and dry. I have a big house. Stay with us for a time while you decide what you're going to do..."

"Us?"

"My..." I hesitated a moment, not sure what word I wanted to say. Finally, I said, "My wife."

"Oh..."

"She's ill."

"I'm sorry."

"She's in a coma. It's a long story. She has a nurse. A doctor comes in most days... But there is plenty of room. You'll be safe. When you decide what to do, we can get you an apartment..."

She stared at me for a long moment. "You're kind."

I looked at my watch. "We'd better get going. They'll be arriving soon." We held each other's eye for a second. "You ready?"

She nodded. "I'm ready."

By the time we got to the car, it was just after two. I'd positioned it so the sun was reflecting on the windshield and the inside would not be visible to anyone observing it from the parking lot. At two thirty, a dark Audi rolled into the lot. I said:

"Bingo."

The Audi parked. Ramirez and Calabrio climbed out and went into the hotel. Grace said, "How?"

"I don't know yet."

"What are you going to do?"

"I don't know that either."

Twenty minutes later, they came out again and stood looking around the lot. They exchanged a few words and climbed back into their Audi. I checked my watch. Grace said, "What time is it?"

"Ten to three."

"Your senator will be here in ten minutes."

"Yup."

"Do you trust her?"

"There isn't a human alive who is infallible, Grace. A wise man once said to me, trust no one absolutely. It isn't fair on them."

She was about to answer when a Dodge Charger rolled into the parking lot. It parked and Cyndi McFarlane climbed out of the back with a tall man in a dark blue suit and graying temples. Out of the two front seats emerged two men in gray suits with shades and lumps under their arms.

They looked around the lot in a way that only plainclothes law enforcement officers do, and Cyndi and the man I guessed was Solomon made their way toward the entrance steps.

That was when the doors of the Audi opened and Ramirez and Calabrio climbed out. They called to Solomon and McFarlane, who stopped, and the four of them spoke for a moment. Then they all went inside together.

Grace stared at me. "Now what?"

"We wait."

"What for?"

I sucked my teeth and shook my head.

She said, "You don't know yet."

I shrugged with my eyebrows. Five minutes later, a dark blue Jeep rolled in and parked near the exit. A minute later, another came in and parked by the steps. Nobody got out of either of them. Five minutes after that, a Mercedes Maybach S 650 pulled in. It parked and O'Brien climbed out of the driver's seat. He put on his hat, went around the back and opened the door for Freeman and Kuznetsov. The three of them made their way to the hotel, climbed the steps and went inside.

I looked at Grace and shrugged with my eyebrows again. "We could leave them to it and go to Boston."

She didn't look amused. She looked sick. "The only way Ramirez and Freeman could have known that we would be here is if your friends told them. Why would they do that?"

I pulled the burner I'd bought at the airport from my pocket and gave it to her. I called it and told her to answer. When she did, I put my own phone in my breast pocket.

"You keep listening, you understand? You hear me say 'freedom', you get the hell out of here."

"No!"

"I'm serious, Grace. You drive, and you do not stop until you get to Weston. It's just west of Boston, on the Boston Post Road."

"No, Lacklan! You're scaring me!"

"You ask anyone for Lacklan Walker's house, on Concord Road. Got that? Concord Road. When you get to my house, you tell Kenny what happened. He'll take care of you. You understand?"

"*No!*"

"Grace, look at me." She looked me in the eye. "I am going to come back and everything is going to be fine. But we need to make the long movie. So if things go wrong in there..."

"Why can't I come in with you?"

"Can you fire a gun?"

"No..."

"Are you an expert in martial arts?"

"Stop it..."

"Then instead of focusing on what I have to do, I'll be worrying about protecting you. So you stay here and wait. And if you hear me say 'freedom', you get the hell out of here and you drive to Weston, and tell Kenny what happened. He knows you might turn up."

She shook her head and tears welled in her eyes. "Don't you *do* this to me. You hear? You don't do this to me."

"Get in the driver's seat. I'll be back in ten minutes."

I kissed her head and climbed out, crossing the parking lot. I sprinted up the stairs and crossed the lobby to the reception desk. A pretty girl in a blue jacket smiled at me because she'd been trained to, but her eyes said she didn't like the look of me. So I didn't smile back.

"Senator McFarlane called and asked me to join her here. Did she take a room? She's with a party of federal agents..."

She pointed at the cocktail bar. "In there."

I went and stood in the doorway. They were sitting in the corner, gathered around a table: McFarlane, Solomon, Freeman, Kuznetsov, Ramirez and Calabrio. O'Brien was standing behind his master, staring at empty space a few inches in front of his nose. Ramirez and Calabrio had their backs to me. McFarlane and Solomon had their right side to me, partially obscured by a screen. Freeman and Kuznetsov were opposite them. I approached on silent feet and stood behind Ramirez.

"This is nice." I smiled and they all looked up. Ramirez went to stand, but I put my hand and my two hundred and twenty pounds on his shoulder and made him sit down again. Calabrio was less fortunate. He made it halfway to his feet, so I smashed the back of my fist into his jaw. His eyes rolled back in his head and he too sank back into a sitting position. The rest of them stared, like kids caught raiding the cookie jar after bedtime. I continued smiling, but not in what you could call a friendly way. "Cozy," I said, "Nice to see so many old friends." O'Brien was frowning at me, like he was wondering what I was doing there. I pointed across at Freeman, and Kuznetsov next to him.

"Freeman, you remember Vasiliev, Kuznetsov's friend? Did you manage to get your wall cleaned? I hear there's a lot of cleaning up going on at your ranch right now." I turned and looked at Solomon. I was aware of Cyndi staring at me, frowning. "Assistant Director Aaron Solomon, right?" He didn't answer. "Do I understand you're helping out with the cleaning at Mayor Freeman's ranch?" I shifted my eyes to Cyndi. "Or am I getting the wrong end of the stick here? Only it looks an awful lot like a big, happy family." I patted Ramirez on the shoulder. "Right, Ramirez?"

It was Cyndi who answered. "What the hell are you playing at, Lacklan?"

I smiled. "That's funny. Because I was about to ask you and AD Solomon that very same question."

Solomon said, "What are you talking about? You said you wanted to meet us here, and here we are. I'm assuming you asked all these other people too."

I nodded. "Yeah, here you are." Then I shook my head and pointed at the rest of the group. "But no, I didn't ask all these other people. Though I did kind of have a hunch they'd show up. So the question I am asking is, who *did* invite these guys?"

He didn't look amused. "Now you just hold your horses there, Walker. I don't know what you think you're doing, but what I am hearing is a very disturbing story from a federal agent who claims you have been making pretty wild accusations founded on nothing but your own word. More troubling still, he claims you may be guilty of several homicides, including a sheriff's deputy, and the abduction of a young woman. So before you start throwing around accusations and demanding explanations, perhaps you'd better start answering some questions yourself."

I glanced at Cyndi. She shook her head. "Lacklan, you need to explain what's going on here."

I turned back to Solomon. "Did you send men to Freedom, and Freeman's ranch, like I said?"

"Certainly not. In the first place, Jackson Field Office had charge of that operation and in the second place, you do not get to instruct the Federal Bureau of Investigation on where to deploy men. Now, Mr. Walker, I have been very patient with you, and I have to tell you that the only reason there is not a warrant out for your arrest right now is because Cyndi has prevailed upon me to..."

I was getting bored so I interrupted him. "Who told these men I would be here?"

He opened and shut his mouth, looking around.

I looked at Cyndi. "Did you?"

She shook her head. "No, I just contacted Aaron."

I looked at him. "Did you?"

"No, I..."

"I told one person, Cyndi. So I am asking, how did they know I was here?"

He was frowning hard, not sure whether to be mad or interested. Cyndi looked worried. I repeated the question, pointing at Freeman. "How did *they* know I was here?"

TWENTY

Ramirez was on his feet, pulling away from me and spinning to face me. Calabrio was stirring, groaning and holding his head. Solomon got to his feet too, and so did Cyndi. I didn't move. I glanced at Freeman. He was smiling.

Ramirez snarled. "I've had enough of this shit. You're under arrest, Walker!"

I said, "You going to start a shootout with a U.S. senator right here in our midst?"

Ramirez pulled his piece and trained it on me. Solomon held out a hand to him. "Wait! Hold it! He's right." He turned to McFarlane. "Cyndi, get out of here. Go wait in the car."

She ignored him and I pointed at Kuznetsov. I addressed the question to both of them: "Do you know who that man is?"

Solomon glanced at him, but otherwise ignored my question. "Just take it easy, Walker. Let's not escalate things. Just cooperate and don't do anything stupid. I have men outside. There is no way out of this for you." Again he looked at Cyndi. "Please, go wait in the car!"

I shook my head and gave a small laugh. "Open your eyes. I'm not the one holding a gun here, Solomon. I asked you a question. Answer it. Do you know who that man is?" He frowned, looking at him again. I spoke to Cyndi. "He's Peter Kuznetsov, of the Russian Mafia." To Solomon, I said, "Have your men check it out. Now answer my question, what's he doing here with Freeman?"

Cyndi was watching Solomon. "Aaron...?"

Solomon looked at Ramirez. "Agent Ramirez? Is this true?"

Before he could answer, I heard the tramp of running shoes behind me. The guys outside had been listening in and had obviously decided it was time to make their presence felt. I raised my voice.

"Hold your fire! I am unarmed and there is a U.S. Senator in this group. The only person present who is holding a gun is Special Agent Ramirez here. Now, I have asked the question repeatedly and so far nobody has answered me. So I am going to ask it again: Who informed these people that I was going to be here?" I looked at Solomon. "Am I getting through to you, Assistant Director Solomon? Right now, you are assisting a known member of the Russian Mafia in a kidnapping and several murders."

Cyndi stepped up to him and pulled his arm. "Aaron...!"

Ramirez was beginning to look distinctly uncomfortable.

I smiled. "I'll tell you what, Solomon. I'll let you take me into custody. I'll even give you my cell, where I have all the footage of Freeman's ranch, the cannabis plantations, the poppies and the lab, plus a recording of Freeman and Kuznetsov explaining their operation and offering me a part of it."

Everything went very still and very quiet. A second pulsed and felt like a full minute. I glanced at the four men who'd come in behind me in gray suits with wires in their ears. They weren't holding weapons. They were looking at Solomon, waiting for his lead.

Another second. I looked back at Ramirez and saw it in his eyes. In the same instant, I saw Kuznetsov and Freeman get to their feet. What happened next seemed to happen in slow motion. Ramirez swung to his right and fired almost point blank into Solomon's chest. Solomon was thrown back into his chair, which overturned under him. I bellowed at Cyndi to get down. O'Brien, Freeman and Kuznetsov were all pulling weapons from under their arms. I heard a voice behind me say, "Shit!"

Next thing, I was vaulting over the back of Ramirez's chair. I could hear the hiss and *phut!* of slugs passing my head. I crashed into Ramirez and dragged him to the ground with me, smashing my fist into his face three times in rapid succession till he lay still. Then I hurled myself at Cyndi and knocked her flying through two chairs and a table and dragged her screaming behind a pillar. I shouted at her, "*Stay down!*"

I stood. In a fraction of a second, I took in that the four feds were down and Freeman and Kuznetsov were running for the lobby, while all two hundred and fifty pounds of O'Brien was storming toward me. I pulled my Sig and put a round through his forehead. His eyes rolled up and he fell on his face. Then I was running toward the lobby, shouting, "*Freedom! Freedom! Get the hell out of here! Go! Go! Go!*"

I got to the lobby just as the Feds from the Jeep came storming in through the plate glass doors. They ran into a hail of bullets from Kuznetsov and Freeman. The receptionist screamed. I bellowed at her, "*Call nine one one!*" But she had ducked behind the desk, still screaming.

Freeman and Kuznetsov were out, stepping over the fallen agents, running into the parking lot. Freeman was hollering, "*She's here! She's here in the lot! I know she is! Find her!*"

My ears were straining to hear the roar of the Impala's engine. But there was nothing. I was shouting, "*For crying out loud, Grace! Go!*"

I heard a door slam. I heard myself whisper, "*No...*" Feet behind me. I ran down the steps, shouting, "*Grace, no! No!*"

She was standing beside the car, staring at Freeman. I heard her say, "You want me, take me. But let him go..."

They both raised their weapons at the same time, Freeman and Kuznetsov. My first shot hit Kuznetsov in the back of the neck. His weapon discharged and I saw the round shatter the windshield of the Impala. My second shot hit Freeman in the middle of his back. He had fired at the same time as I had and I saw Grace's knees buckle. I saw her hands clutch her belly and she slowly went down on her knees.

I ran to her, pulling my cell from my pocket. I tried dialing nine one one, but I was still connected to her burner. She was rocking gently, weeping. I dropped beside her, hung up and dialed again. My breathing was shaking and I was fighting to steady my hands.

"Why did you do that?" I said. "You should have gone like I told you."

She leaned against me. "It hurts, Lacklan."

"Nine one one, what is your emergency?"

"Renaissance Hotel, gunshots, several federal agents down, many injured, at least one critical. We urgently need police officers, ambulances."

"The incident has already been called in, caller. There are units on their way. What is your..."

I hung up and put my arms around Grace. "They're coming, kiddo. Hang in there."

"It really hurts. I feel so cold."

In the distance, I could hear the sirens wailing. I told myself I should not have brought her. I should have left her at the airport, at the restaurant, anywhere. Slowly, I became aware that she had stopped moving, that she had grown heavier. Maybe I wept. Who knew? Who cared?

Cyndi knelt in front of me, put her hand on mine. Beside her, Solomon was standing, looking down at me. Beyond them, fogged, distorted by tears, ambulances and patrol cars were streaming into the forecourt.

They took her away on a gurney, toward the black, gaping doors of an ambulance. There were cops everywhere. One in a suit was showing Solomon a badge. I heard Solomon say it was a Federal investigation, something about Senator Cyndi McFarlane and Captain Lacklan Walker, and we were with him.

I pushed past them and followed the gurney to the ambulance. The paramedics were closing the doors. I said, "Can I ride with her? I'm all the family she has."

The driver shook his head. "Sorry, pal, no can do. We're

going to the Toledo Hospital ER. Twenty-one forty-two Cove Boulevard. Ride with the cops."

They climbed in, slamming doors, and with the wailing of the sirens, they were gone.

I turned, scanned the forecourt, and made my way to where Solomon was still talking to Cyndi and the detective. I interrupted them. "Where is Freeman?"

The detective narrowed his eyes at me. "What?"

I pointed to where Freeman had gone down. "Six foot, silver hair and a beard, well dressed, in his sixties, gunshot wound to his back."

He pushed past me. "Hey! Smith! Tall guy, well dressed, in his sixties, silver hair and a beard. Gunshot to the back, lying there. Where'd he go?"

There was some laughter. Then several voices. "Nobody like that when we got here, Detective." The question did the rounds. Nobody had seen that body. I was staring at Solomon, his shirt scorched and torn where the slug had hit him, the Kevlar vest underneath.

"Son of a bitch." I wiped my eyes on my sleeve. "He was wearing body armor. He got away."

"What's this?"

It was the detective, looking at me and deciding he didn't like me. I pointed at Solomon. "He'll tell you. I have somewhere I have to be."

I climbed in the Impala, fired up the engine and made my way out of the hotel forecourt, with Cyndi, Solomon and the detective staring after me.

Grace was already in surgery when I got to the hospital. The information they had was minimal, basically what I knew already. The girl on the desk was sympathetic. I told her I was the closest thing Grace had to family and that I'd wait at the hospital. She told me she'd have the doctor let me know as soon as she was out of the operating theatre.

I sat on a blue and steel chair in a space where corridors met. There were two dispensers, one for snacks and the other for drinks. There was a desk-cum-counter in white melamine with a computer on it and a woman behind it who had seen it all before and had come to the conclusion that other people's tragedies were boring.

I sat there and remembered Marni, remembered sitting in an almost identical space in Oxford, for an almost identical reason. It could only be a coincidence, but every fiber of my being knew that it was too much of a coincidence.

I went over in my mind every step of the way from Jim's House in Malaga Cove, in Los Angeles, to our arrival at the Renaissance Hotel in Toledo. I went over every person I had spoken to, every call I had made, every place I had been. There was no way my stumbling into Freedom could have been predicted, far less arranged. And in any case, what possible purpose could it have served Omega? And who in Omega?

Was I imagining the parallels? Was I seeing a pattern where there wasn't one? I closed my eyes and was once again in Oxford. We were stepping out of the pub, into the warm evening and the bustle of the street. There were cars, buses, the eternal cyclists.

I had stood on the outside and she had clung to my arm with both of hers. We'd started to walk. The amber street-lamps washed the blacktop and the ancient sandstone buildings. She had started to talk about her father's research, how everybody had been searching for it. For a moment, I saw her bright eyes smiling, looking up at me in the evening light. "Omega were crazy to get their hands on it..."

I had told her I thought she and Gibbons had gotten hold of it when they'd arranged the conference at the UN.[1]

But she had laughed. I remembered her leaning against me, the weight of her warm body. I could hear the sigh of the cars as they passed, the slight chill in the air. There had been people on the sidewalk, crowds. We had dodged a couple of them. She had said, "Not exactly." Then she had told me, "All of his research was contained in the diary!"

I had found that hard to understand. I still did. Not only how he'd done it, but why, and why she had not accessed it. Why she and Gibbons had not accessed it. Why she had given it to me. What had she said? She had looked up at me. There had been something in her eyes, and expression, what? She'd said:

"It's crazy. I didn't realize it for a long time. He was a very clever man. *He wanted me to have it, and he didn't want anybody else to get their hands on it. So he put it in the diary.*"

As I recalled it, I knew with absolute certainty that I was holding the key—but to what? Questions crowded in on my mind. How had he hidden his research there? Why her? And why had she chosen me?

And why had she not used it?

I recalled he had left her a letter with his attorneys, to be posted to her on a particular date, telling her where and how to find the research. And then her smile had changed. She had looked down the street, ahead of her. I had followed her gaze. There had been a man, twelve or fifteen feet away,

---

1. See *The Hand of War*

walking toward us. His head had been down and he was walking quickly. He'd been on a collision course with us. I'd stepped aside and pulled Marni with me. By then, he was just a couple of strides away, but he'd changed course too, still looking down at his feet. I'd spoken to him. My blood went cold as I recalled it. I'd said, "Hey, pal, look where you're going..."

And in that moment, he'd looked up. For a fraction of a second, I had seen him, the same man I had seen in South Africa, by the river, floodlit from above by a bank of spotlights on the red Toyota truck, with the dark water lapping around my legs. Only then, I was in Oxford, with the traffic hissing slowly past in the amber streetlight. He had stared into my face, held my eyes with his. He had spoken softly. His accent had been strongly South African. He had said:

"You made a mistake, Mr. Walker."

And then he had shot her. I had heard the soft *phut* of the silencer, and he had shouldered past us. I could feel her still, heavy on my arm, sagging forward, her hands clutching her belly. She looked up into my face, searching mine with panicking eyes, asking me for a solution.

"Oh, God, Lacklan... I've been shot..."

"Mr. Walker?"

I opened my eyes. There was a woman looking down at me. She was wearing a white coat. She had dark skin, dark eyes and severe black hair pulled back.

"Yes."

"I am Doctor Patel. You are family of Grace O'Conor?"

I stood. "As good as. I'm all she's got. Is she OK?"

She shook her head. "It is too soon to tell. We'll have a

better idea in about twenty-four hours. She is in intensive care. We have done all we can for now."

I nodded. "How soon can I take her home?"

She frowned. "Not for at least a week." She gestured around her. "If there is an emergency, we need these facilities to hand."

I nodded again. "Thank you, Doctor."

I sat and watched her walk away. I could still see the guy in Oxford, the amber light washing his face, reflected in his eyes. I recognized him, and yet it couldn't be. I heard his voice, his hard, South African accent. "You made a mistake, Mr. Walker."

"You made a mistake..."

I had made more than one. I pulled my cell from my pocket and dialed a number. It rang a couple of times and I heard Bat Hays's familiar voice, with a small frown in it.

"Hello...?"

"Bat, it's Lacklan."

"Yeah, I thought so. What's up, sir?"

"A lot. I can't talk much on the phone. Everything OK with you?"

"Yeah, great."

"I'm glad to hear that. Listen, I want you to do something for me. You know any guys in the States?"

He hesitated a moment. "What... our lot?"

"Yeah."

"Well, there's me. What do you need, sir?"

"No, aside from you. There's something else you need to do."

"Yeah, there are a couple I know of. Mostly working for private security agencies. What's up?"

"I need you to do this real fast, Bat, you understand? I need you to get me two guys from the Regiment. I need them at the Toledo Hospital as of two hours ago. I'll pay them twice what they are making right now, plus bonuses."

"All right. I know who to call. Anything else?"

"Yeah, and don't argue with me on this one, Bat. Get Abi, get your kids, and go to my house in Weston. Do it right now, and get Kenny to explain the security system to you. I'll call him and let him know you're going."

There was no argument, no battle of egos. In the Regiment, you learned from the start that that kind of shit got people killed.

"All right. I'm on it."

He hung up. I called Kenny and told him what to expect, then went to the desk with the bored woman who'd seen it all before.

"Can you tell me where Grace O'Conor is? She's just come out of surgery for a gunshot wound. Dr. Patel told me she was in intensive care."

She regarded me with hooded eyes. "Then she's in intensive care."

"Where is intensive care?"

"You can't go in there. It's intensive care."

I leaned on the counter and looked down into her eyes. There was a look of pugnacious enjoyment about them. "Where is intensive care?"

"I just told you, you can't go in there. Do I need to call security?"

I shook my head. "Not unless you keep giving me the same answer. I don't want to go into intensive care. I just want to know where it is. That's why I keep asking you. Now, let's try again. Where is intensive care?"

She must have correctly read the expression in my eyes, because she sighed, averted her own and told me. On the way, I called Cyndi.

"Lacklan, where are you?"

"At the hospital. Grace is out of surgery. She's in intensive care. Where is Solomon?"

"On his way to Jackson, Ramirez and Calabrio are in custody and they're singing like canaries. It turns out they never alerted the Wyoming Highway Patrol. Aaron's taken a team with him, they're going to see how far the rot has spread. Another team has been dispatched to Freedom, with the WHP assisting this time."

"I spoke personally to a Detective Jim Hansen..."

"Yeah, Ramirez told him they were not needed, that you were some kind of nut..." I heard the smile in her voice. "I guess he at least got that much right."

"Yeah, I guess. Listen, Cyndi. We are very far from being out of the woods. There is a lot more to this than meets the eye. I've got some guys coming to keep an eye on Grace, but till they get here I need guards—and I mean real pros—watching her twenty-four seven. And you need to double your own security."

"Aren't you overreacting?"

"No."

"Is this because Freeman got away?"

"No."

"So?"

"It's because he knew I was going to be there. And something else I don't want to talk about on the phone. Just do it, will you?"

"OK..."

She sounded doubtful and I felt hot irritation in my belly. "Was I right about Freeman and what was going on at the ranch?"

She heard the anger in my voice. "Yes, Lacklan."

"Well, I'm right about this, too. If Grace had followed my instructions, she'd be alive now. Don't make the same mistake!"

"She is alive, Lacklan. Keep it together. I'll do it."

"Good."

I hung up and collared a nurse outside intensive care.

"Is this the only access to this unit?"

She gave me a nervous look. "Yes, sir."

I nodded, found a blue and steel chair and sat to wait.

EPILOGUE

DAN AND SCOTTY SHOWED UP THE NEXT MORNING. Dan was from Liverpool and Scotty was, as his name suggested, from Scotland. They were both of average build, wiry and dangerous. They sat on outside the intensive care unit and told me nobody would get close to Grace as long as they were there, and I felt about as safe as I was ever going to feel.

After forty-eight hours, she woke up. She was weak, but she was out of immediate danger. The day after that, they let her out of intensive care, and Dan and Scotty sat outside her room, pretending to read Marvel comics and being inconspicuous.

On the fifth day, Doctor Patel gave me the green light to take her to Weston. So, once again, I had the weird reenactment of what had happened in Oxford. I hired an air taxi, a private nurse and a doctor, and we flew her from Toledo to Boston, and then transferred her to the house in a small convoy of cars. Dan and Scotty came all the way, riding shotgun, and I set her up in the room next to Marni's.

Bat and Abi were already there, with the kids. The reunion was an awkward one. Abi was embarrassed and angry at me. She shook my hand in the entrance hall and didn't quite smile.

"Can't seem to get away from you, can I, Lacklan?"

"I'm sorry, Abi."

Primrose and Sean, her kids, were pleased to see me, and Bat and I embraced like old brothers.

On the steps of the house that evening, outside the front door, we shook hands with Scotty and Dan. I thanked them for their help and Scotty smiled with his eyes as he stroked his handlebar mustache.

"If ya need anythin' else, you know where ta find us."

I nodded. "I appreciate it. Same goes. You have my number. Take it easy."

Danny pointed his finger at us like a gun and winked. "Arright, lads. See ya 'round."

They climbed in their hire car and drove away, leaving me and Bat on the steps, standing in silence. When they had gone, Bat looked at me and said, "They ain't left, 'ave they?"

I shook my head. "No." I pulled a burner from my pocket and handed it to him. "If you need them, you can call them with this. In any case, they'll be watching the house."

"Good to know."

"Things are going to get ugly. I'm sorry about Abi. There was no way I could have known this was going to happen."

"Don't sweat it, sir. But you need to fill me in on what 'this' is. I need to know what we're up against."

I sighed. "I wish I knew, Bat. Right now, none of it makes any sense, and I just don't know who I can trust." He flashed a look at me. I smiled and slapped him on the slab of granite he called a shoulder. "I trust you, my friend, but there is something dark going on. Something I do not understand. Let's go inside."

We went into my study. I poured two tumblers of Bushmills, handed him one and we sat in the chesterfields in front of the fire.

"Cheers."

"Yeah, cheers."

For the next two hours, I filled him in on everything that had happened since that day, over two years earlier, when my father had sent Ben to get me from my place in Wyoming. How Marni had gone on the run, pursuing her father's research, trying to expose and bring down Omega. I told him how my father had been a leading member of that organization, how he had been forced to murder Marni's father. I told him how Marni had given me her diary, how she and I had become estranged, how I had set about destroying Omega in my own way, how I had discovered that Ben was not only Alpha, the head of Omega, but also my half brother, my father's son. I told him about Jim Redbeard and Njal, and how they had helped me. And finally, after I had refilled our glasses for the third time, I told him about the operation in Africa, where I had seen, or hallucinated, Ben.

We were silent for a long while, looking at the flames dancing in the grate. Finally, he shook his huge head and said, "That is a total mind fuck, sir."

I smiled. "It gets worse, Bat."

He frowned at me. "Worse? How?"

"The guy who shot Marni in Oxford, the same guy who was at the fusion reactor building site in South Africa..."

"The one who was trying to get you."

"Yeah, I realized in Toledo..." I paused and sighed.

He frowned. "What?"

"The eye color was different, the hair was different, the voice, the accent, he was South African, but, Bat, it was Ben."

He flopped back in his chair. "Come off it, sir! You told me you shot him in the heart, twice! They're fuckin' with your head. You can't let them get to you."

I smiled and raised an eyebrow at him. "You think I haven't been through that already in my own head?"

"I know, but..."

"I'm not saying it was Ben, Bat, but I am saying it could have been his twin brother."

"That's crazy."

"Yeah, but it gets crazier."

"More?"

"I have been over it a hundred times and there is no way that my winding up in Freedom could have had anything to do with Omega. I even mentioned Omega to Freeman to see if he would react. He didn't. Kuznetsov was sent to the States to capitalize on the fact that Omega had left a power vacuum at the heart of organized crime..."

"So...?"

"So when I realized that the guy who shot Marni was the spit of Ben, I realized something else."

"What?"

"Freeman looked just like both of them, only thirty-odd years older."

"Fuck off!"

"There is no way that Freedom was connected with Omega, but Bat, by the same damned token, there is no way that it wasn't. Which means one thing. The guy who shot Marni said to me that I had made a mistake. I thought at first he meant that I had made a mistake going up against them. But I realized what he really meant when I was sitting in the hospital, waiting for Grace to come out of surgery."

"What?"

"I thought I had been destroying Omega. I thought I'd brought them to their knees. I hadn't. Omega is alive and well. This whole damn thing has been smoke and mirrors, and all I have been doing is smashing mirrors."

Don't miss ENDGAME. The riveting sequel in the Omega Thriller series.

Scan the QR code below to purchase ENDGAME.

Or go to: righthouse.com/endgame

NOTE: flip to the very end to read an exclusive sneak peek...

DON'T MISS ANYTHING!

If you want to stay up to date on all new releases in this series, with this author, or with any of our new deals, you can do so by joining our newsletters below.

In addition, you will immediately gain access to our entire *Right House VIP Library,* which includes many riveting Mystery and Thriller novels for your enjoyment!

righthouse.com/email

(Easy to unsubscribe. No spam. Ever.)

ALSO BY BLAKE BANNER

Up to date books can be found at:
www.righthouse.com/blake-banner

ROGUE THRILLERS
Gates of Hell (Book 1)
Hell's Fury (Book 2)
Ice Burn (Book 3)
Judgement by Fire (Book 4)

ALEX MASON THRILLERS
Odin (Book 1)
Ice Cold Spy (Book 2)
Mason's Law (Book 3)
Assets and Liabilities (Book 4)
Russian Roulette (Book 5)
Executive Order (Book 6)
Dead Man Talking (Book 7)
All The King's Men (Book 8)
Flashpoint (Book 9)
Brotherhood of the Goat (Book 10)
Dead Hot (Book 11)
Blood on Megiddo (Book 12)
Son of Hell (Book 13)
Merchant of Death (Book 14)
Extinction C-14 (Book 15)

HARRY BAUER THRILLER SERIES

Dead of Night (Book 1)
Dying Breath (Book 2)
The Einstaat Brief (Book 3)
Quantum Kill (Book 4)
Immortal Hate (Book 5)
The Silent Blade (Book 6)
LA: Wild Justice (Book 7)
Breath of Hell (Book 8)
Invisible Evil (Book 9)
The Shadow of Ukupacha (Book 10)
Sweet Razor Cut (Book 11)
Blood of the Innocent (Book 12)
Blood on Balthazar (Book 13)
Simple Kill (Book 14)
Riding The Devil (Book 15)
The Unavenged (Book 16)
The Devil's Vengeance (Book 17)
Bloody Retribution (Book 18)
Rogue Kill (Book 19)
Blood for Blood (Book 20)
The Cell (Book 21)
Time to Die (Book 22)
The Reaper of Zion (Book 23)

DEAD COLD MYSTERY SERIES
An Ace and a Pair (Book 1)
Two Bare Arms (Book 2)
Garden of the Damned (Book 3)
Let Us Prey (Book 4)
The Sins of the Father (Book 5)
Strange and Sinister Path (Book 6)

The Heart to Kill (Book 7)
Unnatural Murder (Book 8)
Fire from Heaven (Book 9)
To Kill Upon A Kiss (Book 10)
Murder Most Scottish (Book 11)
The Butcher of Whitechapel (Book 12)
Little Dead Riding Hood (Book 13)
Trick or Treat (Book 14)
Blood Into Wine (Book 15)
Jack In The Box (Book 16)
The Fall Moon (Book 17)
Blood In Babylon (Book 18)
Death In Dexter (Book 19)
Mustang Sally (Book 20)
A Christmas Killing (Book 21)
Mommy's Little Killer (Book 22)
Bleed Out (Book 23)
Dead and Buried (Book 24)
In Hot Blood (Book 25)
Fallen Angels (Book 26)
Knife Edge (Book 27)
Along Came A Spider (Book 28)
Cold Blood (Book 29)
Curtain Call (Book 30)

THE OMEGA SERIES
Dawn of the Hunter (Book 1)
Double Edged Blade (Book 2)
The Storm (Book 3)
The Hand of War (Book 4)
A Harvest of Blood (Book 5)

ABOUT US

Right House is an independent publisher created by authors for readers. We specialize in Action, Thriller, Mystery, and Crime novels.

If you enjoyed this novel, then there is a good chance you will like what else we have to offer! Please stay up to date by using any of the links below.

Join our mailing lists to stay up to date -->
righthouse.com/email
Visit our website --> righthouse.com
Contact us --> contact@righthouse.com

facebook.com/righthousebooks
x.com/righthousebooks
instagram.com/righthousebooks

EXCLUSIVE SNEAK PEEK OF...

ENDGAME

CHAPTER 1

He looked at me with eyes that couldn't remember how to care. The muzzle of the Glock 19 he was pointing at my chest didn't waver. He was eight feet from me. He couldn't miss, and he was too far away for me to try anything. The only way out was the door that stood half-open behind him. I waited two seconds that felt like two weeks, but he didn't squeeze the trigger. He didn't say anything, either.

Cool as hell, I pulled a pack of Camels from my pocket. He could have shot me—he should have—but I figured he was going to do that anyway, so I had nothing to lose. I shook a cigarette free and glanced at him as I put it in my mouth straight from the pack. I spoke around the cigarette.

"You going to do something with that Glock, or do you just like the way it makes you feel?"

I rested my ass on the edge of the desk, flipped my Zippo and leaned into the flame. I took a long drag down into my lungs and dropped the old, brass lighter into my pocket again. I was expecting the hammer blow of the slug at any second, but I'd be in hell before I let him know I gave a damn.

He watched me do all that with a lack of interest.

"I have instructions to kill you, Captain Walker."

"So what are you waiting for?"

The muzzle of the Glock flicked down for a second to point at the beige carpet under my feet. I laughed out loud. "You don't want to stain the carpet?"

He gave a small shrug. There was no humor in his face. "It seems absurd to you, when compared to the importance you give your own life. But your life is nothing to my employer, and getting decent carpets out here is difficult. So they asked me to avoid ruining the carpet."

"Out here?"

"I won't be drawn into conversation, Captain Walker."

I frowned. "If they want me dead, why bring me all they way 'out here'? Why didn't she just kill me right there?"

"I don't work for Dr. Gilbert."

I smiled at him. So Marni wanted me here for something, and somebody else didn't. I studied him a moment. He had the eyes of a killer. He was dangerous.

"So how are you going to get me out of here?"

"That's not complicated. I'm going to offer you a choice. I shoot you in the stomach and then drag you out, trying to cause as little mess as possible." He gave a small shrug with his eyebrows. "It's inconvenient, but not the end of the world. In that scenario, Captain Walker, you die a slow and very painful death. The alternative is that you step out here into the corridor and I shoot you in the head. The floors are vinyl, so easily cleaned. I am pretty sure you'll take that option because you'll hope it will offer you a chance to disarm me and escape."

"That's some pretty cool calculating."

He stepped back and waved the weapon toward the doorway. "Let's go. I'll shoot on the count of three."

He counted one. I took a drag and pushed away from the desk, speaking as I released the smoke. "Take it easy, I'm moving. Just make it quick, will you?"

I moved toward the door and, casual as hell, I flicked the butt into his eyes. There are some things you just can't control, and autonomic responses are among those things. However good you are, if something strikes at your eyes, you will move to stop it. And that was what the killer did.

His head weaved, fast, and his gun hand moved to block the cigarette. It was a fraction of a second, but by the time he'd recovered, I was by his side with his wrist in my right hand and my palm slamming hard into his elbow. He should have doubled over and I should have broken his arm and dislocated his shoulder. Instead of that, he used my hand as leverage. He jumped and slammed his open left hand into my face, sending me reeling back a step.

Next, he was lashing back-handed at my face, with the Glock. I managed to block it and pounded his kidneys with my left fist, but before I could follow up, he was raining blows on my head, driving me back. I knew if I backed up too far, he'd be able to take a shot. The bastard was good, and I had to stay in close and finish this thing, fast.

I crouched, covering my head with my arms. The heel of his left hand struck my nose. The pain was intense and dulled my thinking. The butt of the Glock struck my temple and I knew I was going down. That made me scared and the adrenaline made the fire in my gut explode.

I roared and suddenly I couldn't feel the blows to my head and face. All I could feel was rage and madness. I drove the instep of my right foot into his balls. I clubbed his head with my right fist, closed in and smashed the heel of my left into his jaw. As he staggered back, I came in closer, dropped to the rider's stance and powered four punches to his floating ribs, then grabbed his head and yanked it savagely down onto my rising knee. His nose and mouth exploded into blood and gore.

I should have killed him. Instead, he swayed on his feet and leveled the Glock at my face.

If I had given in to astonishment, he would have blown my head off. But I'd seen what they could do to people with Freeman's drugs, and I was expecting this. In one fluid movement, I smashed his inside wrist with my right hand and grabbed the barrel of the pistol with my left, levering viciously inward, so the gun was pointing at his face. I pulled the trigger. A small, ugly, black-red hole appeared where his left eye should have been. An instant later, the back of his head exploded in spray. He did a little dance, like he didn't know what to do with his legs, and dropped awkwardly to the floor.

I smiled without feeling. "You've still got your mind on the carpet, pal."

I stepped out into the vinyl corridor and ran. I didn't know where I was running. I just knew I had to move, fast. I scanned the walls and ceilings as I went, searching for cameras. I didn't see any, but I knew that didn't mean much.

I came to an intersection. I could turn back, I could turn

left or I could turn right. There was nothing to choose. Each passage looked the same, and oddly familiar. I turned right and sprinted. At the end of the corridor, it turned right again, leading me back the way I'd come. But after fifteen feet, the passage opened up, with a bank of elevators on my right, and a flight of stairs leading down on my left.

I plunged down the stairs, taking them three at a time. I got to the bottom and found myself in a large, open plan area with maybe a dozen desks set in cubicles. Some of them were occupied, and the drones sitting at them stared at me a moment, then went on doing what they were doing. Behind me, another flight of stairs led farther down.

I swung over the banister and clattered down to the next floor. I was at the end of a long, broad corridor. To my right, a passage disappeared into darkness. Ahead of me, maybe thirty or forty yards away, the broad corridor opened into what looked like a large lobby. There, I could make out black plate glass, and beyond it the darkness of night.

I took half a second to think, but the sudden tramp of running boots echoing down the passages had me sprinting again, toward the lobby. I tried to get a fix on the direction the boots were coming from, but the acoustics were confusing, and it was impossible to pinpoint the source.

I skidded to a halt and froze. For a moment, it was like time and space had warped and I was back in the lobby of the Richard John Erickson Institute. Was I back in New York? I dismissed the thought and ran for the door. I could still hear the boots tramping, but I couldn't see anything.

I yanked at the door. It was locked. Outside, in the diffuse light filtering through the glass, I could see sand and rocks. Arizona? New Mexico?

I searched for the locks and shot at them. The glass was bullet proof. I fired at the middle of the glass, but only managed to cause a dangerous ricochet.

On my right, there was a long desk. I vaulted over it and searched for either keys or some electronic mechanism to open the door. I found nothing.

I stood, my heart pounding, listening. The boots seemed to fade. There were a couple of shouts, then nothing. I looked around. The damn place was identical to the Richard John Erickson Institute in New York State. I had not explored the whole building, but I had gotten as far as Dr. Ogden's suite, where he had lived on the premises, and I remembered there had been a small terrace: a terrace from which I could climb down—or fall and break my neck.

I shot out the lights, so that the place was in near absolute darkness. The cameras were probably infrared, but they might not be, and it was worth clawing back one small advantage.

With no light reflecting off the plate glass, I could now see the empty desert outside, an immense, translucent sky with trillions of shards of ice-cold light strewn across infinity. Only that invisible wall of glass stood between me and that emptiness. And freedom.

I went to the elevator and punched the call button. The doors slid open and I stepped inside. I pressed the button for the top floor, the doors closed and I began to rise. All the way up, I kept telling myself, it was over for them. So why were they toying with me? It had to be for a reason. It was too elaborate and too expensive for a game. What did they get from putting me in a rat's maze? How did that benefit them?

The doors slid open.

The landing was carpeted in beige, the walls and ceiling were cream and there were occasional steel-framed seats upholstered in blue. The layout was similar to the lower floors, except that, just as at the institute, the corridor ahead of me was shorter, and ended in a door. That door, in theory, should lead to the director's suite of rooms. The rest of it, as I recalled, had been for the scientists and students.

I stood for a moment, listening. There was absolute silence.

I took out all the lights, then approached the door and thought about the best way to breach it. I ran my hands over it. It felt like wood. I pulled the Glock from my waistband and blew out the lock. I stepped through and pushed the door to behind me.

I was in a broad corridor. It was dark, but ahead, I could see a faint filtering of starlight. As my eyes adjusted, I began to make out details.

It was more a passage than a corridor, broad and tiled in marble. It ran from left to right, and ahead of me was a third section that formed an inverted 'T'. In the angles of the 'T' I could now make out open patios with elaborate granite balustrades. The sound of lapping water made me peer over and I saw that I was on a second floor. Above me was the night sky, and below me were enclosed gardens with fountains, flower beds, palms and potted plants. I heard my own voice as a ghostly whisper.

"Where the hell am I?"

It looked like Mexico, Spain or Morocco, but something told me it wasn't. I followed the passage across the patios to a large, marble landing. In the filtered moonlight, I saw a vast, white marble staircase that curled down into a cavernous, shadowy hall. There, another fountain played among images of curly-headed titans and dolphins that shone with an eerie light in the darkness.

I moved down and around the fountain, and under the stairs I had just descended. I saw double doors, open onto a long dining room. The ceilings must have been twenty feet high, supported by carved wooden rafters. The far wall was open arches that showed a landscape of moonlit, rolling hills touched by the turquoise light of a full moon.

I crossed the dining room and passed through more tall, walnut doors into a small drawing room decorated in what looked like genuine rococo. It too was empty and dark. I climbed a further, smaller flight of marble steps, wondering where I was going and what I would find. They stopped at a small, polished granite landing where there was an arched, oak door. I pushed it open.

There was moonlight. First a dark antechamber, with a wicker table and several chairs with colored cushions. Then three arabesque arches separated the antechamber from a large, walled patio garden that was bathed in the wan light of the moon. Another fountain at the center of the patio played loud, wet music. It was shaped like a collection of sea shells, with the water, peppered with reflected gold, spilling from the center, where they met. At the corners of the patio, tall palms towered high, like black stencils against the night. There was an abundance of flowers, bushes and ferns, and the air was rich with orange blossom and jasmine.

I slipped the Glock into my belt behind my back and crossed the antechamber. Beside the fountain, there was a wrought iron table laid with a white, linen cloth. On it, there was a candelabra with seven candles burning. By their light, I could see a large glass jug of what looked like sangria, and a silver tray of glasses. A small group of people sat around the table, watching me, with the candlelight playing on their faces.

They were all there, every one of them, holding their blood-red glasses with small bits of fruit in them. Only one of them held no glass, and she had no expression on her face at all. The others all sipped from their glasses and smiled or smirked. At the center, presiding, he was there: the grand old man, the great master, the lord of all he surveyed.

He smiled at me, but it wasn't a real, warm smile. His voice was loud and startling when he spoke.

"Time to die, Lacklan. Time to die like a hero."

CHAPTER 2

ELEVEN DAYS EARLIER

THE FIREPLACE WAS THE SIZE OF A SMALL ROOM, and the logs that were burning in it were like small trees. The huge room where the fireplace was located was still and silent, apart from the occasional firecracker snap and shower of sparks that leapt from the burning logs onto the hearth.

The hearth was a slab of gray stone, and the floor around it was not so much wood as timber. By that, I mean that a wooden floor might be shiny parquet or highly polished inlay. But this floor was not that. Each plank of red cedar had been polished by time, not hand. They were smooth and shiny, but they were also notched, scarred and gouged by the passage of the years. They were strewn with rugs that Jim Redbeard had either bought or looted in his travels around the world. Though in front of the fire, there was a vast, black bearskin, and according to Jim, he had killed it with an arrow from a one hundred and fifty pound yew longbow.

There were other bearskins around the house, grizzly and black bear strewn on the floors, polar on the beds.

The room I was in was two stories high. The walls were paneled in yellow cedar and rose to a ceiling of bare, A-frame beams thirty feet above my head. Three of the walls were lined with books to a height of three or four feet, interspersed with a huge antique dresser, a long sideboard and an oaken chest. All of them looked like genuine medieval antiques from northern Europe. A wooden staircase climbed fifteen feet of the fourth wall to a galleried landing.

I sat in a huge, overstuffed leather armchair, sipped a large, Waterford tumbler of ten year old Bushmills, and gazed by turns at the dancing flames and the desolate Alaskan landscape outside the tall, arched windows.

There were three of them, like the invisible ghosts of Shakespeare's weird sisters, or the Norn that Jim was always talking about: what he called the Wyrd Sisters, Urd, Skuld and Verdandi—Fate, Being and Need. I stood and walked to the nearest of the tall, narrow windows. Dull, yellow-green grass fell away to the west where, three miles distant, you could just make out the glint and shimmer of the Bering Strait.

The tread of boots on wooden stairs made me turn. Jim was descending from the upper floor. He glanced at me like I was something he wasn't really sure about.

"How are you feeling?"

"I hadn't thought about it."

He grunted and smiled as he reached the last step. "Don't then. Hungry?"

"Yeah."

"Njal's in the dining hall. I want to go over all the details one last time before you sail."

I drained my glass and set it down on the windowsill. Jim was waiting by the door, watching me. I said: "How are they?"

"Stable."

"Any sign...?"

"Why don't you go and see? It might help her, to hear your voice."

I couldn't answer. I looked at the flames in the fire. Fate, Being and Need. For a moment I wondered if that was the sum total of human life: being, needing, and driven toward an inevitable fate. Jim's voice made me look.

"Njal has been talking to Grace.[1]" He smiled. "He is convinced that she is his destiny."

I gave a small snort that might have been humor. "His Urd? Maybe that's what he needs to believe."

Jim shrugged, then laughed out loud. "It is what it is. Come on, rise out of the gloom, Lacklan."

He held out an arm to me and I crossed the room. As I approached, he slapped me gently on the shoulder and pulled open the door.

"The monk warns us, 'Do not be flippant. Meditate and pray, for tomorrow you might be dead.' The warrior tells us, 'Sing, feast, drink and be merry, for tomorrow you might be dead!'"

"You have a philosophical quip for every situation?" I asked him as I stepped through into a broad hallway. Like the living room—what Jim called the Great Hall—it was

---

1. See *Death in Freedom*

strewn with bear skins and also had a fire burning. He followed me and chuckled a little complacently.

"Hey! I am obscenely rich, free and happy. I am also at peace with myself. Whatever I am doing seems to be working, right? Can you say the same?" He gave me a smile that advised me not to cross swords with him, stepped ahead and opened the dining room door. Njal was standing, warming his ass in front of another vast fire and jerked his head at me in greeting as I walked in.

The room was smaller than the Great Hall, but in a very similar style. The ceiling was high, supported by bare rafters, the walls were paneled in red cedar, and large windows looked out over rolling hills of yellow-green grass and, in the distance, dense forests.

A heavy wooden table ran down the center of the room. There were a couple of bottles of wine on it and a large earthenware dish containing several legs of roast lamb. There were other dishes too, of roast potatoes and roast vegetables. Three places were set, with Jim at the head, Njal on his right and me opposite Njal, on Jim's left. He sat and started pouring wine. We sat, too. A door opened in the far wall and three young women came in. They looked Inuit, or American Indian, with jet-black hair, high cheekbones and dark eyes. One carried a basket of hot bread, another a bowl of fruit and the third carried a large dish of dates, dried figs, nuts and a big wheel of cheese. They deposited the dishes on the table, smiled gracefully at us and left. Jim did not acknowledge them. When they had gone, he turned to Njal.

"How is Grace?"

Njal nodded and raised his glass. We toasted. "Old friends, well met."

We drank and as he set down his glass, he said, "Today she moved her eyelids when I said her name. I know when we return, she will be awake. She will know me. I have to thank you for this, Lacklan. You brought her to me."

"I just got her out of Freedom, Njal. But not far enough. I hope she comes 'round."

Jim reached over and helped himself to a leg of lamb, gesturing with his other hand that we should do the same. We did, spilling potatoes and roast vegetables onto our plates alongside the succulent meat. I said, "What about Freeman[2]?"

He started to carve into the flesh. It slid off the bone.

"You've asked me this every day for the last week since you've been here, Lacklan, and every day I give you the same answer. Freeman has disappeared. There is no trace of him. When he shows up, if he shows up, you and I will be the first people to know about it."

I grunted. "Yeah, I know. But there is nothing else I can do. What about his connection with Omega?"

He shook his head, glanced at me and shook it again. "What connection? *You* are sure there is a connection, but nothing has shown up—on the grape vine, the bush telegraph or talk on the street. He was a crazy, a Jim Jameson, a Bagwan, a charismatic nut who happened to be in the right place at the right time when you destroyed Omega, and the Russian mob moved in. Stop torturing yourself, Lacklan. Omega are fatally wounded, and now you are going to give them the *coup de grace*. Freeman was not Omega."

---

2. See *Death in Freedom*

I chewed on a hunk of meat, drained my glass and refilled it. Njal waved his fork at me.

"You should talk to Marni."

I didn't meet his eye. I concentrated on cutting into the lamb. "She's in a coma. She can't talk."

"But she can listen. She can hear your voice and you can help her to come out of the coma. It's working with Grace, it can work with Marni, too."

Jim eyed me a moment while we ate in silence. Finally, he said, "He is right, Lacklan. And you have nothing to lose, but everything to gain. You sail tomorrow. Talk to her before you go. It will be good for her, and good for you, too."

"Spare me the inspirational self-help, Facebook wisdom-bites."

Jim shrugged and shook his head. "I am not interested in your bitterness or your sarcastic insults, Lacklan. We have a lot to talk about besides how hard life is for you. But you would do us all a big favor if you stopped feeling sorry for yourself and actually did something about it. And when I say 'us' I include Marni, Njal and me." He held up a hand. "Please, don't answer. Let's move on to the plan."

I didn't answer. I hadn't intended to. I knew he was right and I knew Njal was right, too. But going into that room, where Marni was lying, dead in life, 'alive' in death, was more than I could deal with. The thought, the possibility, that she might not wake up, that she might not return from whatever dark place she was in, was something I could not face.

I chewed and looked at him, but offered him nothing in the way of an expression. He ignored me and kept talking.

"The *North Star* sails at eight tomorrow morning, from

the harbor at Teller. It's a crossing of about one hundred and thirty miles to Lavrentiya, across the Bering Strait, in Russia. At this time of year, the ice is at a minimum and the weather tends to be good. You should make it in no more than six hours, give or take twenty minutes. So you should be there for about two o'clock. The routine will be much like when you went to South Africa. You stay out of everybody's way and talk to nobody except Captain Johnson, and then only if he talks to you. You are ghosts. On the ship's records, you're a couple of deck hands: Bob Schell and Erik Jansen. I'll give you your papers before you embark."

He stuffed his mouth with lamb and potato and sat back in his chair, chewing. Njal said, "Weapons?"

Jim nodded, swallowed and drank, then smacked his lips and sighed. "You take with you one or two handguns. Njal, I assume you will take your Glock. Lacklan, I know you will take your two Sig Sauers. You can also take a knife." He nodded at me. "No doubt you will have your Fairbairn and Sykes in your boot. That will be it until you reach Vologda."

I frowned. "Vologda? This is new."

He nodded without expression. "A last minute change to the plan. You collect a plane at Lavrentiya and you fly to Magadan, on the Sea of Okhotsk."

I stuffed lamb in my mouth and spoke around it. "How far is that?"

"One thousand, two hundred miles. The exact coordinates of the landing field will be in a sealed envelope in the plane. You land. You hand over the bird and you leave. No questions, no answers."

"What about refueling?"

"It has modified tanks. It'll get you there, and farther."

I scowled. "It's modified for trafficking drugs?"

"I told you, no questions and no answers."

I glanced at Njal. He was watching me, sighing and shaking his head. I growled, "Fine," and drank.

Jim went on. "You'll find instructions on where to collect your car in the sealed envelope, with your flight plan."

"How many people know about this?"

"Me."

"What about the guys arranging the car? And the guys collecting the plane at the airfield?"

He shook his head. "The men at the airfield know a plane is arriving at a particular time. They don't know where it's coming from or who is on it. They are only interested in collecting the plane. As for the men arranging the car, pretty much the same deal. They know they have to deliver a car to a particular place at a particular time. They don't know who it's for or where it's going. Each little package of information is hermetically sealed, which is why you are finding out these details now."

I offered him the first smile I'd given him in a week. "So if they try to hit us, we'll know where to come."

He didn't return the smile. "I hope I wouldn't be that stupid, Lacklan. I hope I never decide to kill you, but if I do, you can be sure I'll be smart about it. Moving on, you then take the M56 and you drive another thousand miles, north and then west to Yakutsk. Don't worry about getting lost. It's the only road in Siberia. At Yakutsk, you abandon the car, it doesn't matter where, and you pick up a second car, which you will drive to Irkutsk. You'll receive the instructions on where to pick it up when you need them. At Irkutsk, you abandon the second car and you buy train tickets to Moscow, but you get off at Tyumen. There, you change and take a second train from Tyumen to Vologda. In Vologda, you will make contact with a man. He will hand you over a third car, and this one will be loaded with all the hardware you requested for the Ustinov hit. If you stick to the instructions I have given you, it should be impossible for Omega even to know you're there, let alone track your progress."

I wiped my mouth and drank. "Who is this guy? How much does he know?"

"This man will not know who you are, where you are coming from or why you are there. His instructions will be simply to hand you an envelope. Even if the envelope were to be intercepted, which is not feasible, the contents would mean nothing to anyone except you."

The food was good and we ate in silence for a while. When I'd finished the lamb, I sat back, drained my glass and refilled it.

"We ditch the IDs we've been traveling on. The new IDs will be in the car?"

He nodded. "I don't want you to get into the same trouble here as you found in Africa. You will be provided with backup IDs, and at each stage of the operation, the detailed instructions and papers you need for the next stage of the operation will be provided, too."

I went on, "We book into the Hilton, recon Phi's apartment, Gregor Ustinov, and then liaise with Phil, who will take care of all the messages..."

Jim nodded, wiping his plate with a hunk of bread. "Phil is set up in a secure location that not even I know. Tomorrow morning, when you board the ship, I will hand you a bag with a couple of unregistered burners each, to be used either in extreme emergencies or if it is vital to an operation. In Vologda, you will also collect an STD—a Scrambled Telecommunication Device. You can use this to communicate with Phil. In fact, it will be the only way anybody can communicate with him for the duration."

Njal pushed away his plate and pulled over the basket of cheese, dried fruit and nuts. He helped himself and passed it on, speaking as he did so.

"So Phil has already set up a correspondence between Ustinov and a supposed businessman from Texas. They arrange to meet and we intercept Ustinov on the way. We kill him, but before we kill him, we find out where Roth is."

I cut in, looking from Njal to Jim. "But to Ustinov's associates and family, he is going on a business trip for a few days."

Jim nodded and stood. "Bushmills for the dates and the cheese, I think." He went on, "The business trip will give you a window of opportunity to move to the next kill. The moment they are aware Ustinov is dead, even if it looks like an accident, they will go to lock down."

He brought the decanter over to the table and poured three generous measures. "We have to assume that Omega are on red alert, but as long as they think Ustinov is merely on a business trip, you have a clear shot at Psi: Liu Wang, and Chi: Haruto Kobayashi. But you will have to act fast."

I said: "OK, so we nail Ustinov and go straight to the airport, separately, and we fly to Tokyo..."

Njal interrupted, addressing Jim. "You gonna UPS us tickets and new IDs."

"As soon as you check in at the hotel. You use the hotel

telephone to call a number I will give you. The minute that call comes through, I will UPS you the travel documents and the IDs."

I continued, "Once we get to Tokyo, we go after Wang and Kobayashi, and we have to be damned quick. So Phil has to have prepared the groundwork and have set up a correspondence between the two of them to arrange a meeting in Japan. We do not want to go to China if we can help it."

Jim sat and crossed one huge leg over the other. "He is on it already. Before you kill Kobayashi or Wang, you need to get access to the Omega computer mainframe, so you can deploy Phil's neutron bomb[3]. I will get that to you when you board the ferry to Russia."

Njal sipped his whiskey and smacked his lips. "OK, so the point we have been avoiding. What about Omega, Abba Roth?"

Jim shrugged. "He is the unknown quantity in this. There is practically no information about him anywhere. A trained biologist, billionaire in the petrochemicals industry. He seems to have vanished without a trace. You will have to find out from Ustinov, Kobayashi or Wang where he is, then go after him. But with only one of them left, planting the neutron bomb is more important than finding Roth."

I said: "What about extraction?"

He nodded. "It won't be like Africa. You have a number of options. You have spare IDs and credit cards, so simply book flights back to the U.S.A. You also have the burners, so you can contact me if you need help. There are also friends

---

3. See *Kill: Two*

of mine on the ground in Tokyo that I can deploy to get you out."

I raised an eyebrow at him. "You have agents on the ground in Tokyo? How big is this non-organization of yours?"

He smiled and gave a small laugh. "I actually said friends, Lacklan, not agents. Point is, there are people in Tokyo who can help you." He unexpectedly threw his head back and laughed out loud. "One day, Lacklan, maybe you will learn to trust your friends."

The laughter drained from his face and was replaced with a frown. For some reason, I glanced at Njal. He had the same frown on his face as Jim. "We three have had each other's backs many times, Lacklan. Maybe it's time to trust, huh?"

I nodded. "Maybe," I said, and wondered whether I meant it. "Maybe."

CHAPTER 3

WE TALKED ON. AFTERNOON TURNED TO EVENING and then night. Jim's three girls, whom he referred to, rather unfairly, as Urd, Skuld and Verdandi, cleared away the dishes and, as darkness enfolded the world outside, lit lamps and candles, stoked the fire and provided us with more food and more wine. We covered more detail, in more detail, and went over the plan three or four more times, and on each review we refined it and polished it until we knew it inside out.

This—not the food and the wine, but the obsessive attention to detail—this was how I liked to prepare an operation. It was what they had taught us in the Regiment: meticulous, detailed preparation saves lives and allows you to improvise if and when you have to. Improvising, without prior preparation, leads quickly to failure and death.

Eventually, around midnight, the girls cleaned the table again and, when they had finished, Jim bid us goodnight and went upstairs with one of them. I don't know if it was Urd, Skuld or Verdandi, Fate, Being or Need, but she was tall and dark and beautiful. A moment later, Njal said, "I go up too," and he left the dining room with another of the girls.

As he opened the door, I said, "Njal, what about Grace?"

He gave me a curious smile and said, "Her eyelids flickered today, when I spoke to her," and he went out.

That left the third girl standing by the kitchen door, smiling at me. I shook my head. "I'm not comfortable with this."

"That's OK." She had a nice voice. It sounded Canadian. "What is it you're not comfortable with?"

I shook my head and shrugged. "He treats you like commodities. First you serve at table, and then we get to take you to bed? That's not how you treat human beings."

"Is it worse than how the army treated you?"

"That was different. We chose to be there."

"We choose to be here too." She threw her head back and laughed. "And I bet we get paid better than you did, too."

I shook my head. "Probably, but still, sex..." I trailed off.

"Not like killing people, huh?"

"No," I said. "Not like killing people..." I felt suddenly oddly ashamed, and asked, "What's your name?"

"Anne Marie."

I nodded and stood. "Good night, Anne Marie."

I climbed the heavy wooden stairs to the upper floor in the dark and made my way to my room. The only light in the corridor was from the moon outside, touching the low hills and the forests with limpid, turquoise light. My door was in shadow, but next to it, a distorted oblong of light lay across Marni's door.

I hesitated. In my mind I could see Anne Marie downstairs, smiling and saying, "Not like killing, huh?" If I had been killing, I would not hesitate, but giving life, giving love, that made me hesitate.

I opened her door, went in and closed it behind me. Her bed, a massive, absurd four-poster, was a black object on my left, touched on its corners by blue light from the open window. I moved around to the far side, where that light lay across her in the bed. She seemed peaceful. Her breathing was steady, slow and shallow. I pulled up a chair, sat beside her and took her hand in both of mine.

Three times I tried to speak. Three times I failed. I felt her fingers one by one, realizing absurdly that they were alive. I stroked her palm and her arm and felt the wet touch of salt at the corner of my mouth.

I wanted to tell her that I knew I had failed her, that I was crippled by shame, that all I knew how to do was kill and destroy and that she deserved somebody who could give her love and life, and make her whole.

But that was what I needed to say, not what she needed to hear. When my voice finally came, it sounded strange, disembodied, like somebody else's voice in the room.

"They tell me you can hear me." I hesitated again and then blurted on, "We're in Alaska. Jim has a house here." I laughed and wiped my eyes on my sleeve. "It's a crazy place right up by the Bering Strait. There's no phone, no signal, no electricity. It's about as remote and hidden as you can get. So you're safe here."

I sat in silence for a while, stroking her arm and her hand, not wanting to tell her what I needed to tell her.

"In the morning, Njal and I will be going away for a few

days. When we get back, I know you're going to be awake, because everything will be different then. I'm going to learn, Marni. You're going to teach me how to give life, instead of just taking it."

I kissed her and lay next to her on the bed, with her hand in mine, and slept peacefully.

————

TELLER IS LITTLE MORE than a fistful of clapboard houses perched on the edge of the Bering Strait, between the Chukchi Sea to the north and the Bering Sea to the south. It's not quite within the Arctic Circle, but it is less than a hundred miles from it. And everything, from the desolation of the landscape to the white mountain ranges across the water, and the creamy, silvery texture of the sea, speaks of the Arctic.

At seven AM, Jim parked his Land Rover on the quay, on Front Avenue. There was nobody about at that time. The sun was just rising and the wooden houses, with their gabled roofs, painted green and blue and yellow, were bisected with deep shadows at the bottom and golden sunlight above.

There was only one boat at the quay. It was an ugly, partially rusted, two hundred and forty foot hulk, painted black and dirty orange. The bridge, a tall, dirty, white tower, was set aft, with the rest of the ship devoted to cargo. I could see mainly crates, some Jack Daniels and Jim Beam, a couple of 4X4s and a bunch of goats. I wondered whether Russian and U.S. border control knew about the *North Star*'s trading trips. I kind of hoped not.

Breathing condensation like a human dragon, Jim

opened the back of the Land Rover and Njal and I pulled out our kit bags. As he slammed the back closed, we watched a man run down the gangway. Jim went to meet him. He was tall, with unkempt red hair and a thick beard. He and Jim embraced and Jim led him to where we were standing by the truck.

"Sean, these are my boys. They were never on your boat. Look after them for me, will you?" To us, he said, "This is Captain Sean Johnson. Stay out of his way, don't talk to him, and he'll take care of you."

They both laughed and we shook hands. When he spoke, his accent was Scottish.

"It's only six hours or so. I've made yiz comfortable in a nice cabin. Feel free to go on deck, but I'd appreciate it if yiz didnae talk to the crew. Tha's fair enough, hey?"

We said it was fine.

Jim handed me a sealed USB drive on a chain. "You know what to do with this when the time is right. Wear it around your neck."

I slipped it over my head, we shook hands with Jim and followed the skipper up the gangplank and aboard the *North Star*.

The journey across the top of the world was not a long one. September is the month when the Arctic ice sheet is at its lowest extent. Since 2007, it has become increasingly possible to navigate the Arctic from August to September, as year on year the sea ice, and the ice on Greenland, shrinks steadily.

The sea was flat and creamy, made dense by the cold. We spent most of the voyage on deck, watching the lazy icebergs drift by, and the occasional whale in the distance, rising like a mountain out of the ocean, then crashing down again in an eruption of foam.

Alaska had slipped below the horizon, and Njal, who had been cleaning and oiling his Glock in our cabin, stepped out into the September morning, peeling a pack of Lucky Strikes. He offered me one and we lit up. He exhaled smoke and the wind carried it overboard. He spoke above the rhythmic grinding of the engine, jerking his head north, toward the Arctic.

"That is what Omega is all about, up there."

I frowned. "Yeah? I thought they were all about mind control."

He leaned his elbows on the bulwark, cupping his cigarette between his hands to protect it from the wind, and shook his head. "No, controlling people's minds and emotions is just a strategy. It is not the big plan, or the big motivation. At the heart of what they are doing is the melting of the Arctic."

I sucked on my cigarette, took the smoke deep and thought about what he was saying. Before I had come to any conclusion, he went on.

"Macro politics, macro economics, whatever you want to call it, the destiny of our world is driven by two major factors, Lacklan, major catastrophes, and major scientific developments, especially in the field of war." He counted them out on his fingers. "Bronze, iron, the sword, the Viking long ship—transformed Europe—the English longbow, the cannon, the musket. The British empire was built with muskets and cannon."

"I get it."

"And the end of the Ice Age, the myth of the flood is all

about the end of the Ice Age, and nothing has affected the course of human history more than the end of the Ice Age."

"Really?"

"Really, whether you accept the myth of Atlantis or not, it was as the climate began to change in a big way, twelve, thirteen, fourteen thousand years ago, getting warmer all the time, that people started to move north, during the great floods. They built new cities, ships. Commerce began to happen, bronze replaced stone..."

"What has that to do with the Arctic?"

But even as I said it, I could see it.

"History repeating itself, Lacklan. But this time, it's gonna be a lot worse. Back then..."

"Back then, when?"

"Fifteen thousand years, man, at the end of the Ice Age. The population of the world was tiny compared with today, and they were all living around the belly of the planet, along the equator, where it was warm. A lot of what is ocean now was land back then, the Caribbean, the coast of India... And people like to live near water, you know? On rivers and on the coast. When the ice sheets began to melt..." He shook his head, sucking on his cigarette. "Man, millions must have died. This time, same thing is gonna happen, but not millions, this time billions are gonna die. And the melting ice will be just part of it. Mainly it's gonna be drought, famine, and a crazy, desperate fight for land." He squinted at me. "Land that isn't just sand and dust, land you can work to grow crops and feed animals. There won't be much of that. Not enough to feed eight or nine billion people."

I watched him as he took a last drag and flicked his butt

into the silver sea. "What are you saying? How is the Arctic relevant to that?"

"Professor Lovelock predicted that, when Gaia takes her revenge, humanity will be reduced to a few breeding pairs in the far north." He gestured over his shoulder with his thumb, toward the pole. "That ice sheet is a giant mirror, it reflects the heat of the sun back out into space, but it's shrinking steadily, year by year. In a few years, it will be gone, and the ice on Greenland will drain into the Atlantic, and then anything below parallel 52 is gonna be too hot to live there. And the Arctic Ocean is gonna become your new Mediterranean. Whoever controls Greenland, Iceland, the Russian steppes and Alaska will be lord of the world." He laughed. "Most politicians are arguing over shit, the WTO has lost its teeth, Brexit, trade wars with China... Bullshit! The visionaries are looking at the Arctic. Look at China."

"So this is what Omega is all about? The Arctic? How do you know that?"

He smiled at me. "Because I don't only go around fighting and killing people, Lacklan. I also listen. You should listen to Jim sometimes, instead of just fighting him all the time. He's an interesting guy, with an IQ of one seventy. Did you know that?"

"No."

"There are big, big changes coming to the world, Lacklan, bigger than the Industrial Revolution, bigger than the silicon chip. We have nothing in recorded history as big as what is coming. Last time there was a change this big, it became a myth. But there are people who know what is coming, and they are asking themselves the question, 'How do I come out on top when this shit goes down?' And the answer is, you have to control the far north. Makes sense, right?"

I nodded. "Yeah, it makes sense."

We were quiet then for a while. When I spoke, it was half to myself, thinking about Marni's diary, which was still sitting in my bedside table in Boston.

"So the major turning point will be when the Greenland ice sheet starts to collapse..."

He gave his head a jerk. "Man, that piece of information... If anybody had that piece of information, if anybody could predict that, they would own the game. That guy would own the game, man."

I felt myself go cold inside, my skin crawling and my hair prickling on my head. "We're like the Titanic, sailing through the blackness, headed irrevocably toward a vast iceberg. Everybody is singing and dancing, eating and drinking, and they are all going to die. But there is one, small group of passengers who knows it is going to happen, and instead of trying to stop it, they want to get the biggest and best lifeboat so they can rule whatever is left of humanity after the disaster. What is key to their success, what is crucial to them, is knowing exactly when the collision is going to take place."

He nodded. "That is pretty much it. But there is one thing missing from your simile, Lacklan."

"What?"

"There is not enough food and drink on the Titanic, or fuel, and if they don't die from the collision with the iceberg, they will die from starvation and overcrowding. Your group of well-informed passengers welcome the iceberg as a chance for a new start."

"Jesus…"

"The god of self-sacrifice? He ain't gonna help you much. Better invoke Indra, the god of weather. Or better still, Odin, the god of war."

"Isn't there a god of reason?"

He laughed loud, and a lot. "A god of reason? That is an oxymoron, my friend. Have you forgotten the Enlightenment? When men begin to reason, the gods die."

I studied him a while as he gazed out at the vast northern ocean, wondering at this side of him that I was so unfamiliar with. Perhaps he was right. Perhaps I needed to learn to listen more. After a moment, I went inside and tried to get some sleep.

Scan the QR code below to purchase ENDGAME.
Or go to: righthouse.com/endgame

Made in United States
Orlando, FL
02 January 2026

76166293R00159